D0615389

DO
UNTO
OTHERS

ALSO BY KRISTIN LATTANY

Kinfolks
God Bless the Child
Guests in the Promised Land
The Landlord
The Soul Brothers & Sister Lou

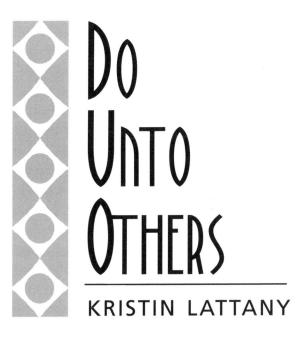

Do Unto Others

KRISTIN LATTANY

ONE WORLD

BALLANTINE BOOKS | NEW YORK

PS
3558
.U483
D62
2000

A One World Book
Published by The Ballantine Publishing Group

Copyright © 2000 by Palmetto Productions, Inc.

All rights reserved under International and Pan-American
Copyright Conventions. Published in the United States by
The Ballantine Publishing Group, a division of Random House,
Inc., New York, and simultaneously in Canada by Random
House of Canada Limited, Toronto.

One World and Ballantine are registered trademarks and the
One World colophon is a trademark of Random House, Inc.

http://www.randomhouse.com/BB/

Library of Congress Cataloging-in-Publication Data
Lattany, Kristin Hunter, 1931–
    Do unto others / Kristin Lattany.—1st ed.
      p. cm
    ISBN 0-345-40708-3 (alk. paper)
    1. Afro-Americans—Fiction.   I. Title.
    PS3558.U483 D62 2000
    813'.54—dc21   99-042406

Manufactured in the United States of America

First Edition: January 2000

10 9 8 7 6 5 4 3 2 1

42049265

For my real family—my brother-in-law, Emmett, his wife Gloria, their son Jusin; my cousins Francis Bagby, Constance Bridges and her two children, Donald and Pat Silvey and their three, Norma and Jimmy Claggett and their five, and Diane Bailey Alexander and her three. And, of course, my husband, John.

ONE

EVERYTHING IN AMERICA is arranged to make us feel ugly. Day and night, the machine cranks out propaganda about the glories of silky hair and milky skin.

I'm a beautician, and since women want above all to be beautiful, I really have my work cut out for me at my beauty shop, Zena's Curly Girl.

Zena is short for Zenobia. I asked my mother why she gave me such an ugly name instead of a soft, pretty one like Rose or Lily or Violet. She said, well, we were living in the projects at the time, and in our neighborhood it would be a definite disadvantage to be soft. Her strategy worked, too. I almost wore out a pair of fists making my classmates say my name right without snickering. Now I like my name, especially the short version I call myself, Zena. It's different. I own it. I like that.

Sometimes I think I have spent my whole entire life struggling against the notion that you have to look like Marilyn Monroe or Princess Di to be beautiful. None of the women who are being worked on this morning in Zena's Curly Girl looks like Marilyn or the princess, but when they walk out, each of them will feel beautiful. Each will feel that she looks better than Marilyn or Di, and it's a sure thing that she will. For one thing, my customers are all alive. Marilyn and Di, on the other hand, are probably not looking so good by now. I used to hear people say after funerals that So-and-so made a beautiful corpse, but I never agreed with them.

That advantage aside, the difference will be in the art and skill we use to bring out the best in each customer's looks. That, and the psychology I personally use to make each customer feel special. Every woman is an individual. You have to consider her face, her hair, and her personality.

For instance, when Ann Worthy, who is president of my club, the Downtown Divas, settles herself in my chair and says, "Give me something different, Zena," I know better than to do as she asks. The slightest deviation from her usual small overall curls, with a blue rinse to set off her gray, and she would have a nervous breakdown right there in front of my eyes.

Fanny Davenport, on the other hand, is in show business, and there is no style too wild for that child. Last month she wanted her hair sticking straight out, in stiff silver spikes. She got what she wanted, too. She walked out of here looking like the Statue of Liberty. Sometimes I wonder what she will think up next. When things get dull around here, we can always count on Fanny to liven them up.

The rest of my customers are somewhere in between Ann and Fanny—middle-of-the road, not too daring, not too conservative. Not too beautiful, either, but they all come in hoping for miracles, and we do our best to make them happen. I encourage my customers to be daring whenever I can. Right now I am encouraging them to be bolder in an Afrocentric way, with racks of colorful robes, displays of beautiful earrings, and pictures of Afrocentric hairstyles—braids, dreads, and twists. I am so crazy about African art these days, I even brought in my Ivory Coast masks and hung them in the waiting room, though they are not for sale.

The women are buying up the clothes and the jewelry, but very few of them are changing their hair. It's hard for black women to let their hair go all the way back to Africa, or even halfway to Jamaica. Vyester, who is my best friend and my best beauty operator, says I'm crazy to want them to change. We make our money creating artificial effects, not going back to Nature, she says. I suppose she is right.

It's a wonderful, bright, busy winter morning. Things are going just the way I like them in my shop: humming along briskly, with women chattering and background music playing and my elegant fountain tinkling. Two women are sitting under dryers, two more are waiting, and one is being shampooed by Florine, our shampoo girl, who is still in beauty school. I am paying her way, but I may stop if she doesn't change her attitude. She sulks too much.

Bonita, who is licensed but has to be supervised, is giving an older customer the old-fashioned tight curls she wants. It's Tuesday, but if I know this customer, who is one of the mothers of our church, she'll tie a black silk scarf on her head every night at bedtime, which for her is nine P.M., and she won't even comb her hair until it's time to go to church on Sunday. And then she'll hide it under a gigantic, ugly hat!

Vyester is working her scissors magic on a new customer's haircut, layering and feathering as she goes along. This young woman is a lawyer, and she can either send us lots of business or decide to sue us, so I would worry if she were being handled by anyone except Vyester.

Vy is the only woman I know who can cut hair. Before I found her, I had to send my patrons to male barbers. Cutting hair is only one of the things Vy can do better than I can, but I'd never admit that to anyone—least of all to her, though she probably knows it already. I don't mind. I'm the one who had the personality to attract a large following, and the smarts to save up my money and buy my shop.

I can't wait to tell Vy about the new development in my life— the new addition to my family. But she's got her back turned. She's busy gluing on a weave, so I have to wait till she has a free moment. Weaves can look beautiful, and we sure make a lot of money on them, but I wish women wouldn't make a habit of them. The receding hairlines you see on so many black women are due to the weight of all those extensions and weaves hanging off of their hair. Young people put a lot of weaves in their hair. The younger the women, the more obviously false are their wigs and weaves. As the kids say, what up with that?

I don't do weaves. I style wigs, though, and I have two of Monica Lewis's thirty wigs sitting on stands right now, waiting for me to style them. She is the one woman I know whose wigs I like working on better than I like working on her head. I would much rather have the wigs here than her, with her biggety airs and her malicious mouth.

Since my best talent is styling, I usually give instructions for the preliminaries to my other operators; then, after a woman has been shampooed, permed, and set, I apply the finishing touches. Right now I am combing out a short, boyish version of my Curly Girl (Pat. Pending) style. This customer, Gloria Watlington, is getting on, but she is slim and has young ideas, and she is going to love this style, as it makes her look fifteen years younger—not a day over fifty.

"Remember Audrey Hepburn in *Roman Holiday*?" I ask her.

"That was before my time, but I think I saw it once on the Classic Movies channel."

That movie was not before Gloria's time; she goes back to the silent film era, at least. I cough and hold up a mirror so she can inspect herself. You might say I shouldn't ask a black woman to compare herself to Audrey Hepburn, and you'd have a point, but at least Audrey wasn't a blonde. She was a stylish, skinny brunette, and some of us can approximate her look, though precious few of us are, or ever were, that skinny.

Gloria, however, is. She is one of those nervous women who burn up calories just by sitting still. While she studies herself, I reach for one of the Tootsie Pops (fifty calories) that I keep on hand to hold me till lunch. The lollipops prevent my sweet tooth from craving worse things between meals, like my favorite chocolate marshmallow ice cream or Black Forest chocolate cake. If I get another inch on my waist or my hips, I will not be able to wear any of my clothes, and I will have to buy new ones.

I hold my breath, because my customer is taking a long time

to make up her mind. "Aren't you glad I had Vyester cut it?" I venture.

"Ye-e-es," she says slowly. "I like it, Zena. I really do. But now my gray is showing, isn't it?"

I hastily dig in my bra and pull out the little reading glasses I have tucked there. My eye doctor prescribed bifocals for me last year, but I absolutely refuse to get them. If I did, I would have to tell my real age. These dear little gold glasses have a handy gold chain to hang them around my neck, and they are more of a fashion accessory than anything else, but I have been keeping them out of sight. I may have to change and keep them on when I am working, though.

Oh, dear, yes. The haircut has most definitely revealed Gloria's gray hairs. The sparkling little devils are everywhere.

"Are you in a hurry?" I inquire. "Because if you are, I can give you a quick cover-up, and do the permanent color later."

She looks at her watch, a mammoth, mannish one with a giant face and big numbers. Another useful fashion accessory. I must ask her where she got it.

"Yes," she says. "I have to show a house at one."

"No problem," I say, and get out my handy box of hair crayons. I perch my glasses on my nose and get to work coloring and rubbing like the artist I am, and soon every scrap of the hair I am working on is brown.

"Now," I say, and hand her the mirror again.

"Wonderful, Zena, you are a genius," she finally exclaims, and throws a tip in with her two twenties. I tell her she can come in any time for a complimentary color rinse, and I put the tip in the community jar for the other operators because, after all, I'm the owner and shouldn't accept tips—but I am never insulted by money. This woman, who is also a Diva, has plenty. She is a doctor's wife and has her own real estate business besides.

Her words, naturally, are music to my ears. So are the other shop sounds, except for the rap music Florine has going at her station, even though I have told her our customers do not like it. And the smells in here—a blend of perfume, bergamot, chemicals, and hair—are better to me than the most expensive perfume.

Vy looks like she's free for a moment, so I call her over to my booth for a quiet talk. "Girl, let me tell you my news. Lucius and I have a daughter!"

She looks at me like she thinks I have lost my mind. "You have a what?"

"Wait till you see her, Vy! She's beautiful." Ifa, my exotic child, is tall, graceful, and gorgeous.

All Vy does is roll her eyes.

"What's the matter?" I ask her.

She clears her throat like she is embarrassed. Then she says, "Excuse me, Miss Zena, but you know how this shop wears you out. Some nights you are so tired I have to help you to your car. Where are you going to get the strength to raise a child?"

"Did I say a child? I said a daughter! She's a big girl. She won't be any trouble." Someday I will eat those words.

"Where did you get her from? A relative? I never hear you talk about your relatives."

"That is because I only have one brother, and he and I are not close. No, she came to us from far away. From Africa. She's only been with us a little while, but she makes me very happy."

Vy is silent for a while, taking this in. I expected more of a reaction from her. I expected her to be as excited about my news as I am. But she isn't.

"Well, if you're happy, I'm happy for you," she says finally. But she doesn't seem too thrilled.

Just wait till she meets my wonderful Ifa. She will be. That girl could charm the sugar off of sugar cookies.

Vy goes back to gluing her weave, and I take a moment to look around. It took me years to afford this place. Years of working and saving and studying, and more years of working in other people's salons and saving after I finished beauty school. I love the way my shop is decorated, with a green-and-gold color scheme, and I love working with black hair, which is the most versatile hair in the world, and I love making women look good and feel good about themselves.

My reverie is rudely interrupted.

"God DAMN, this is hot!"

Ray Ray Richardson used to be a cheerleader, and she is loud. I run over quickly and switch her dryer from HIGH HEAT to COOL DOWN. But she isn't satisfied, she wants out of there, so I remove the dryer cap and let her out of prison.

"Feels like my head is on fire! God DAMN!" Ray Ray cries. Her head looks it, too. It is the brightest, most flaming shade of red I've ever seen. Her hair does not agree with her clothes. She is wearing ethnic bangle bracelets and an Afrocentric patchwork vest in a dozen gorgeous colors and patterns, with a black turtleneck sweater, black leather britches, and boots. I wish I could talk her into getting some braids. They would give her poor hair a rest.

"Owww! What are you bitches trying to do, kill me? Put some cold water on my head, then get me a mirror."

"Bonita," I say calmly, "come over here. What color is this supposed to be?"

Bonita looks scared. "Bright Gold blonde," she says. "But it looks like it interacted with the last dye job, or something. I told her, her hair can't take any more. But she insisted."

I am taking out the curlers and running cold water over Ray Ray's head while this is going on. She is panting and gasping for breath.

"If my hair is ruined," she threatens, "I'll sue you for so much money you'll have to close up. I will, believe me. All I have to do is pick up the phone."

Ray Ray is married to a basketball player, and can afford to change her clothes and her hairstyle three times a day if she wants. She pretty much does, too, and that is why we are having a little problem up in here. We won't let her change her hair color more than once a month, so she slips in and out of other salons between visits to us. I guess she does it out of boredom. She is a tall, beautiful girl with pretty black hair that she ought to leave alone. I shampoo her, but I conveniently forget about the mirror for a while.

"Relax, Ray Ray," I say soothingly. "You're going to like this when I'm done." I put on a mild dark auburn rinse, shampoo her and add a conditioner, then replace the curlers and dry her with a hand dryer on a lukewarm setting. I comb her hair into soft waves, holding my breath and praying none of it will fall out. My prayer is answered: it doesn't. At last, I hand her the mirror.

"I like it," she says finally. "This color is better on me than blonde."

You can hear me exhaling my relief all the way across town. Getting sued by Mrs. Tree Top Richardson, with all the negative publicity thrown in, is something I don't need. And I might lose, too, because her husband's team has as many lawyers as the park has pigeons.

"Then please, Ray Ray, if you like it this color, stay with it for a while. Give your hair a rest. Okay? And don't go to any other salons. Promise? If you do, we can't be responsible. I wish you'd try some braids."

She pretends not to hear my last sentence. "Promise," she says, for whatever that's worth, and leaves blowing kisses at me. I blow a few back. The beauty business isn't always easy. It requires quick thinking, talent, and diplomacy. And, of course, hard work.

I worked so hard to get where I am today, I never had time for friends. I was so busy, I almost missed getting married, and I never managed to have a baby.

But now I have Ifa, my lovely new daughter from Africa. My husband, Lucius, is bringing her to the shop today to have lunch with me and Vyester. I now have a husband, a good friend, a business of my own, and a daughter besides! Sometimes I feel so blessed, I get giddy.

Here come my biggest blessings now. My husband drives up in his shiny Mercedes-Benz, which I did *not* pay for. He bought it himself, because I do not believe in supporting a man. I will help out with joint projects, like our house, but my man has to pull his share of the weight. And Lucius does, bless him.

He does not come in. He says my shop is a round-the-clock

hen party, and roosters do not belong here. He is right. Sometimes the atmosphere in here gets so heavily female, the place is like a hothouse full of orchids and gardenias. If my husband or any other reasonably healthy man walked in here, these overheated hussies would steam it up so bad nobody could see or breathe. Some of the single women are desperate and shameless enough to do everything but undress in front of him—and me. There are some married ones, especially at church, that I wouldn't trust alone with him, either. So I am glad Lucius doesn't come inside the shop. He just eases up to the curb and leans over and opens the passenger door.

And my heart, my newly arrived African daughter, Ifa, steps out. She's twenty years old, as innocent as a baby, as graceful as a gazelle, and as sweet as sugar. And talk about gorgeous! She looks like a cover girl. She has a tan complexion, huge eyes, and a wide, generous mouth. She is tall, slim, long-legged, and soft-voiced, and she moves like a breeze going through a forest.

Ifa flashes her big, bright smile around the shop, and none of the women, not even mean old Lenore Wilkerson, can help smiling back. Then she heads straight for me and gives me a kiss on the cheek.

"Hello, Mum," she says, and drops into my customer chair. She smiles warmly up at me, and purrs, "I am sorry if I am late."

"You're right on time, honey," I say, and pull off my uniform coat. "Are you ready to go to lunch? I'm starved. How 'bout you, Vy?"

"Five more minutes," she sings out. I expected her to come around the partition right away and meet Ifa, but I guess she is still styling that customer's weave.

I haven't adopted Ifa yet, but I'm crazy enough about her to go to Attorney R. V. Evans and get the papers drawn up. I sure hope Vy will like her as much as I do. I will feel terrible if she doesn't.

If I love someone or something, it's important to me that Vyester loves them, too. She's my best friend, and what she thinks really matters to me.

TWO

WOMEN ARE A MESS! Why is it, when you have two female friends you hope will like each other, they refuse to get along? You expect that kind of thing from men. They start pawing the ground and measuring off turf and digging in their pockets for weapons right after they shake hands. But women are supposed to be the gentle, cooperative sex, or so I've heard.

Sibling rivalry, that's what it is. That's what I've got on my hands. The two girls I care for the most are fighting over me like I'm their mom and they are a couple of hateful sisters.

As soon as Ifa, our new daughter from Africa, arrived at our house, I wanted her to meet Vyester Sampson. Vyester is ten years younger than I am. I don't want Ifa's circle of acquaintances to be confined to my husband Lucius and me and the people she's liable to meet through us, a bunch of old heads who are already complaining about their aches and pains. I made the mistake of mentioning a pain in my leg at Maybelle and Jethro Wilson's house last week, and every leg in the room shot up in the air. Eight people were competing for the title of World's Worst Knee. Yes, Ifa definitely needs to meet younger people. That is why I planned this occasion for today.

Long ago, I made up my mind that I was not going to be one of those beauticians like Rose Lee Carrington, who never took time out for herself. I go out to lunch at least once a week, maybe more if I feel like it.

I planned today's outing to expand Ifa's social circle. I am treating her and Vyester to lunch at my favorite restaurant, the Mad Mango. Actually, Josephine's Soul Food is my favorite because of its coziness, but the Mad Mango is more of a fun place and has more atmosphere. It has a Bajan menu, tapes of reggae music playing, and murals of beach and market scenes. I don't know whether Ifa likes Bajan food or not—she seems to like all food; she's a human disposal, in fact—but Vyester is crazy about their flying fish and their fried plantains.

I leave Ifa and Vyester alone for a few minutes while I go back to the kitchen to greet the chef and owner, Desmond Jenkins. I make it a point to be friendly and sociable with all other black business owners. When I come back to our table, those two young women are staring cold steel daggers at each other.

I can't believe it. I expected better from Vyester. She is not just my best friend, she is the closest thing I had to a daughter, until Ifa arrived.

I've tried to be like a mother to Vyester in many ways, including offering financial and business advice. When I found out she was renting not just her apartment, but most of her furniture, I had a fit. I know I shouldn't have meddled, but I'm big on ownership. It's my personal belief that black people rent too many things. That's why we're losing Harlem—because we never owned property there, we just rented. You never get anywhere if you keep paying somebody over and over again for the same stuff. I'm proud to say that my husband Lucius and I own my shop and the building it's in, which has three apartments upstairs, plus our house, which we built only five years ago.

So I took Vyester that very day to a store I know that sells quality used furniture—no junk. For three of her monthly furniture-rental payments, she got a living room set, a bedroom set, and a dinette set that will be here when that furniture-rental man's sleazy stuff has turned to dust and ashes.

Vyester still gets a salary from me, but I'm working on her to become a partner. She stands to inherit the business from me, anyway, because she's always been like the daughter I never had. She's too old to be my daughter, of course. And if I'd raised her, she'd have more ambition. But she's sweet, and teachable, and she can do anything with a head of hair.

She's also supposed to be grown, so I don't expect her to be jealous of our visitor, who is young enough to be *her* daughter, plus is a stranger in our country—a poor, lost, confused child without a clue about what to do. I expect Vyester to embrace Ifa and take her under her wing like a big sister would.

Instead, she treats the poor child like she's a freak to be studied under a microscope—a carrier of TB, leprosy, and AIDS combined. She pulls back from the table and looks at her down her nose and sidewise. Refuses to address her directly and speaks only to me.

That's when I get the first clue that, for all our talk about the Motherland, a lot of African Americans don't really like or trust Africans.

Ifa reacts like a large parrot who is being stalked by a cat—her feathers stand up and she squawks and screeches a lot.

I'm halfway through a plate of jerked chicken with peas and rice, avocado salad, and fried plantains before it dawns on me that Vy is jealous of this girl I have begun to call my African daughter—that what I have here is a case of sibling rivalry.

See, Vyester has had a long time to get used to the idea that *she's* my daughter, even if I never went to Attorney R. V. Evans and adopted her legally. She should know where she stands with me—she's seen my will, after all. But I guess, since I'm forty-nine, she hasn't expected any competition.

Then here I come with this exotic upstart, who is looking pretty good since I set her hair and loaned her a red pantsuit and a pair of gold earrings. She had nothing suitable to wear, she said. Perhaps if I'd brought her to lunch all raggedy and straggle-haired like she was yesterday, Vy wouldn't be so jealous.

But what kind of mother—I mean, hostess—would I be if I let the girl come out all woolly-haired and raggedy and looking like a poster child for Third World relief?

Not to mention, what kind of businesswoman would I be? To be seen out in public with someone whose hair looks like a hurrah's nest would be the worst kind of advertising for my shop. My mama was always saying someone or something looked like a hurrah's nest. She died before I could ask her what a hurrah was, but I always pictured it as one of those colorful tropical birds with a wild crest—a cockatoo or a parrot. Ifa reminds me of those hurrah birds. Big, beautiful, and flamboyant, with large, bright, hard eyes. Also, like them, she is loud.

Last night, while I was putting a chemical relaxer on the edges of her hair and an herbal treatment on the rest, because Ifa has two textures of hair, she asked, "Mum, why don't you just take me to your beauty shop and let them do my hair there?"

"Because women simply do not show up at my beauty shop with their hair as wild as yours. My shop is the kind of place that women get dressed up for." The way she called me "Mum" sounded so sweet, I almost hugged her, but our acquaintance was too new for that, so I just patted her on the shoulder and said, "Your hair is done now. Good night."

I'm proud that the Curly Girl is a dress-up kind of place. I decorated it in my favorite colors, gold and green, with green marble sinks and counter tops and gold frames on the mirrors. In the lobby, I have a fountain with a cute Cupid statue peeing water that makes tinkling, soothing sounds. I play tapes of romantic music all day. I also hang pictures of beautiful women on the walls, and I use dimmer switches when customers are about to view themselves. I know that women have fantasies about the way they look, and my job is to keep those fantasies going.

Vy isn't big on promoting fantasy. I've tried to teach her, but she's too down-to-earth. What would life be without soft lights and veils and illusions? I ask her. Safer, she says. I tell her sometimes I need to wear rose-colored glasses. She says, "Take them off and smell the roses."

Vy's a very warm person, though. That's why I expect her to be sociable and not treat our visitor, who is barely more than a child, like a dangerous enemy. But Vy has her colors up so high she might as well be wearing a "Danger" sign.

I search for a neutral subject to ease the tension at our table. "How's the house?" I ask Vyester.

"It's coming," she says. "Fred painted the kitchen, but I don't like the color. It's gold, and I wanted a lemony yellow."

I am proud that I convinced Vy to stop renting and buy herself and her family a house. I know I sometimes have a tendency to butt into her business too much, but this is one time I was right. Home ownership has worked out well for her and Fred.

That child had all sorts of "yeah buts" when I talked about building equity and the pride you get from having your own place. Finally she admitted she was scared. Scared, she said, of being stuck forever in the same spot.

"How long you and Fred been in that apartment?"

"Thirteen years," she admitted.

"Seems like you two are already stuck." I meant to say "you three," because Vyester and Fred have a big old son who lives with them, but Vyester wasn't really listening anyway.

"I guess I'm scared of the responsibility," she finally admitted. "If we own our house, who fixes the plumbing when it breaks?"

"You do," I say. "Or you call a plumber. At least you'll be fixing something you own." Then she admitted that her landlord wasn't too prompt about fixing things anyway, and that she and Fred had done a lot of work on their apartment themselves.

Vyester is quick to learn, but slow to act. She looks at you solemnly with those big round eyes and nods yes, but if her jaw juts out at the same time and her bottom lip is pulled in, I know she is not going to do a thing I say. After we had this conversation, she and Fred painted all the rooms in their apartment. When the landlord saw how nice it looked, he raised their rent because, he said, the place was worth more.

She started house-hunting in earnest then, and found a place in about two weeks. Six rooms plus a finished basement, in one of the few neighborhoods in our city that hasn't begun to turn bad. She took me to see the house, which I liked because it had a nice front porch. I'm partial to porches. If you have a front porch, you can come out and sit down and survey your neighborhood whenever you want. You can be friendly and sociable with all of your neighbors without inviting anybody inside. I liked thinking of Vyester rocking comfortably on her front porch, and me sitting up there with her, but not rocking. I am not ready for a rocking chair yet. I am an older woman, but I am blessed with a youthful appearance, young friends, and young ideas.

Then Vyester came in to work one morning with her chin almost down to the floor. They didn't have enough money to buy the house, she said. She had known about down payments, but not about closing costs. When I saw the way her eyes were melting into puddles, I marched her straight to my bank, drew out a thousand dollars, and folded her hand around it. Oh, she protested about how she couldn't let me do that, but her face was shining so, I wanted to make her a present of the money. It would have been an easy thing to do, because she brings out my maternal instincts. Though she is well into her thirties, Vyester has kept her cute baby fat and that somebody-please-adopt-me look. She's adorable. Plus, she was already an orphan when I hired her straight out of beauty school. That was ten years ago, shortly after Lucius and I got married.

I didn't give Vy the money, though. I'm a businesswoman. I told her, "You'll just give me fifty a month or so till it's paid off."

Ifa opens her mouth too often and too decisively, but she can't help it, she's an Aries. "Why don't you paint your kitchen yourself?" she asks.

Vyester, who is a sensitive Cancer and doesn't want any interference in her home life, rolls her eyes. "I have a lot of other things to do. I have to scrub and wax the floors and the cabinets, and make curtains, and cut out a bathroom carpet. Plus, I have to work full-time for Miss Zena, here. Last week, it was more than full-time."

If you'd do like I ask, and go with me to Attorney R. V. Evans to draw up that partnership, you'd be working for yourself, I think. But, for once, I don't say it, even though I want to. I'm a Capricorn, which means I'm ambitious and good at business.

"Won't your family help you?" Ifa wants to know.

"No," says Vyester.

"That is strange. In my country, we live in family compounds. Mother, father, sisters, brothers, all in the same place, so there are always plenty of relatives around to help."

"All Fred's relatives would help with is drinking up our liquor. And all mine would help with is eating up our food," Vyester tells her.

"So your relatives all live in different places, and in separate houses?"

"Yes, thank God," says Vyester.

"That seems strange. It also seems very expensive. I think," says Ifa, "that I will have trouble getting used to this country."

"Then why don't you go home?" asks Vyester loudly. She is not smiling.

I drop my fork.

Ifa is too busy chomping on her jerked pork to reply, but I can see that she is upset. As soon as she swallows her food, she will begin screeching.

The horrible moment is dissipated by Waymon, the waiter, arriving with a ginger beer and gossip—the two items for which we are always thirsty. He bends low to fill my glass and whispers, "Did you see Miss Fanny Davenport come strutting in? What are those things on the poor child's head? It looks like she's growing tumors."

It is my turn to get huffy. "They're not tumors, they're amber beads," I say, "and I thought they looked good when I sewed them on her. It's an African hairstyle."

"Oh, my God, Zena, I'm sorry," says Waymon. "Forgive me, please. It's a new look, I'll need some time to appreciate it. How can I make it up to you? I know. Free dessert all around. I must say, you are all looking gorgeous. Who is this divine new friend of yours, Zena, and where is she from?"

"This is Ifa," I say. "She is from Olori."

"Olori-Buruku," she specifies. "I am from Buruku State, in the eastern part of Olori." As if anyone here knows where that is or what she is talking about.

"Well, child, if they grow them all like you over there, I am going into the export-import business. You are fabulous!"

I know Waymon is full of male bovine droppings, but Ifa says, "Thank you," and dimples.

"How long do you plan to stay in this country?"

"As long as possible," she replies. "now that I have found my family." I am watching Vyester, who is swelling up and looks about to burst. She reminds me of a frog I used to keep in my fountain, until it hopped away. Still, I am happy that Ifa considers us her family. She had a hard time knocking around other parts of the U.S. with her older sister before she landed with us.

"Lucky you," says Waymon. "You couldn't find better people than Zena and Lucius, and that's the truth. What will you have for dessert, darling?"

"I will try the mango sherbet."

We order the same.

"And now," Ifa announces in a ringing voice, "I must go to the bathroom." As if the world needs to know. I will have to speak to her about her announcements.

Vyester hardly waits for her to be gone. She leans close so I can hear her, not that she knows how to whisper. "Miss Zena, are you out of your mind?" she asks. "Everybody else I know is trying to get rid of trouble. Why'd you have to import some and move it into your house?"

"What do you mean? What sort of trouble?"

Vy hesitates. "Well . . . two women in one house—that's always a problem. "

A tiny worm of uneasiness wriggles in my mind, but I squash it. "She's only twenty," I say. "Just a child."

"Oh?" says Vy. "Look at that. Does a child walk like that?"

Swinging her hips, Ifa is making her way sinuously back to our table. But I am seeing not a hip-swinging hoochie, but a supermodel strutting on a runway. I had a model agency before I opened the Curly Girl, and I know good modeling material when I see it. It isn't simply beauty, though Ifa has big eyes, a flashing smile, and spectacular height. It's something you can't define that makes clothes look fabulous—flair, pizzazz, attitude.

Super confidence. The world is full of beautiful girls, but not many of them have that quality. Ifa does.

"That suit looks good on you," I say as she sits down.

"Thank you, Mum," she says sweetly, with lowered eyes.

"Yeah," says Vy. "I remember when you bought it, Zena, not so long ago. Macy's end-of-winter sale, wasn't it?"

Ifa eyes Vy's purple polyester outfit. "I have been taught that good used clothes are better than cheap new ones," she declares.

I am tired of sitting between this pair of hissing and spitting alley cats. I call Waymon over for the check, pull on my white gloves, and get up to leave. I don't care if they have been out of style for fifty years, I love my white gloves. Mama taught me about ladies always wearing white gloves, and since I married Lucius I want to project the image of a lady, so I always carry my white gloves when I go to lunch.

"Thank you for my lunch, Mum," says Ifa, looking up at me with adoring eyes. Her voice is so sweet, it sounds like church bells or an angelic choir. I can't bear to have Vy think bad things about this baby.

"Vy, I think you're jealous," I say. "You ought to be ashamed of yourself after all these years. You know where you stand with me."

"Yeah, I know, on the street corner. But I'll always be there for you when you need a shoulder to cry on," she says.

I don't think I'll ever have anything to cry about. My life is full to bursting with love and success and everything else a woman could need. My cup runneth over with so many blessings I can't drink them. I put a hand on Ifa's arm and steer her out. She thanks me again. She is ever so grateful for the things I do for her. Her gratitude causes so much love to well up in my chest, I think it will burst.

But as I am leaving, I see Vy take out a Kleenex and dab her eyes.

Lord, what do I do now?

 THREE

I LOVE MISS ZENA, but she makes me so mad sometimes, I just want to shake her. For a smart woman who's done a lot with her life, she sure can be dumb. I may not know much about business or real estate or investing, but I can spot trouble from a mile away. And that's what that gorgeous African girl is, trouble. She knows I know it, too. She can bat those long lashes at Miss Zena and call her Mum and coat it with sugar all she wants, but she can't fool Vyester Sampson.

Miss Zena knows a lot about being successful, but she's one of those people who don't always know the difference between glitter and real gold. She loves high-heeled shoes with ankle straps, even though her feet are too bad to wear them, and even though she will tell you she has toned down her style since she married Mr. Lucius, Miss Zena loves her some rhinestones and some sequins. And don't show her anything with animal spots on it! I don't think they make leopard-skin toilet seats yet, but if someone makes one, Miss Zena will buy it. She is a good person and she is very smart, but if something looks good, especially if it has movie-star glamour, she's liable to fall for it.

All that glitters is not always what it's cracked up to be. I had to point that out to her just the other day, when that junkie Butch Edwards came in the shop selling what he called Swiss watches. They looked good, but whoever heard of a Patek Phillippe for fifty dollars? Miss Zena would have bought a couple, too, if I hadn't shown her where the gold was already peeling off and the so-called diamonds were backed with tinfoil.

I think maybe Miss Zena is drawn to this African girl because Ifa's so exotic and glamorous, and also because she's a child who seems to need helping and mothering. Miss Zena's always trying to mother somebody—even me, and I haven't needed a mother in over twenty years. My *son* doesn't even need a mother anymore.

The girl acts nice, but I think it may be just that—an act.

I wasn't suspicious of her at first, but while Miss Zena was getting chatty with Mr. Jenkins and them other island folks back in the kitchen, I tried to make small talk with Ifa about the menu, explaining about plantains and banana bread and flying fish and monkey hips and so forth. I was just kidding about the monkey hips, but she didn't hear me. She wasn't interested in anything I had to say. You know how some people only waste their time on people they think can help them? Ifa is one of those. When I found that out, I got suspicious and asked her a couple of tough questions. She tried to get slick on me, and then she got nasty.

"How long are you going to stay with Miss Zena and Mister Lucius?" I ask.

"As long as they want me," is her reply. "I am very happy there." Well, at least she's honest about her intentions to freeload off my friends for as long as they will let her.

"Have you begun to look for a job?" I ask next.

"I am looking around, but I have to be careful until I get my green card."

"Well, what kind of work can you do?"

At first she laughs, which is what I have noticed all these Africans do when they don't want to answer a question. Then she turns nasty. "Why are you asking me so many things? Who are you to question me, anyway? Why do I have to tell you anything?"

Nobody, and you don't, I think, noticing how she got upset

and started shrieking at me. I'm a threat to her plans to get over on Miss Zena and Mr. Lucius, that's why.

Next, I come out with something I've been wondering about for a long time. "You know, a lot of my friends think we ought to help Africans, but I think you owe *us* something. Don't you think your folks ought to pay us back for selling us into slavery?"

Just like white folks, she says, "That was before my time. I had nothing to do with any of that."

I say, "Well, look here, you talk like you're educated, and you look like you're used to nice things. Don't you think your parents had a little extra something to give you because of the profits your people made from selling slaves?"

That's when she comes out with "I don't kno-ow," all sing-songy, like those slick Asian women in the stores where we got to go when we run out of hair for weaves. I ask them how come all of a sudden they got all the stores in our neighborhoods, and back comes "I don't kno-ow," sung by all of them in the same key, like they rehearsed it in the Sun Myung Moon Senior Choir. They do know, too. They know exactly how come they got the stores and where they got the money to buy them. From Reverend Moon and the American reverends who converted them, that's where. And from our government. They ripping us off with our own tax money! I told Miss Zena, please get an extra big order of weave hair next time, 'cause I hate to have to run out and go buy it at Kim's.

I don't much like eating at that monkey-chaser restaurant, either, but I don't tell Miss Zena, because she loves the exotic at-mo-sphere, and they make a big fuss over her, and she's paying. I think all these people from overseas got the attitude that they're better than we are. Last time we were at the Mad Mango, I overheard the owner say any black man could have a business like his, if American blacks were willing to work as hard as he did.

I'd rather go to Josephine's Soul Food and spend my money with another American-born sister, because she understands me and I understand her, even if her corn bread is too heavy and she don't change her fish grease often enough, and she ain't got no atmosphere except the smell of collard greens hanging in the air.

Now maybe that is ignorant of me, but if it is, I'm glad I'm ignorant. If you successful and high up in society, you got to do things that don't come naturally. You s'posed to love your brothers and sisters from overseas, even if they don't like you, and help them even if they disrespect you. I'm glad I ain't got to do all that. I ain't got money to be helping no strangers anyway. Everything I got is committed to the little stranger of my own that's on the way—to her and to Vyester Sampson, and to Fred Sampson Senior and Fred Sampson Junior.

It's a miracle. I had Fred Junior when I was twenty, and now, eighteen years later, all of a sudden, here comes this new one. Fred wanted to know how it happened and I told him, well, after nineteen, well, okay, fifteen, years of marriage, people get careless. So what if Sonny was three when we got married? He made a cute ring bearer.

My husband was upset at first when I told him, because it meant putting off buying a new car and driving our old Buick, Miss Thing, awhile longer, but now he's more excited than I am. I had to hide his charge cards to stop him from bringing home so many teddy bears.

I wanted to tell Miss Zena my news, but she was so thrilled by her foreign company I could see she was in no mood to listen. Ifa has been to college, she says. Ifa is going to be a model. Ifa is teaching Lucius about African religion. Ifa is teaching her to make jewelry. Well, shoot, how can I compete? I'd better sit quietly and see what Ifa can teach me.

I mean, all I'm doing is getting ready to have an ordinary little African American baby, and what's so exciting about that? I haven't been to the doctor yet, but I don't need to go. I can feel it moving already, just below my heart. Gentle, sweet little movements. I just know it's a girl.

Poor Miss Zena should have had her own baby long ago, and then she wouldn't fall so hard for this stranger. I do not mean to say that she's a fool, because she's real smart when it comes to things like business and finance and real estate. She has done me some wonderful favors, and has given me some very helpful advice, in a heavy-handed sort of way. But she should have had babies and grandbabies of her own. Without them, she's a sucker for any scheming young thing that comes along and shows her some affection. There were plenty of times I could have took advantage of her myself, because she treats me like her daughter, but I'm not the type to take advantage of people. Besides, I love her, and I don't want to see her hurt.

Maybe I'm too hard on that African girl, but we could afford this new baby a lot easier if Fred had been able to keep his second job at the parking garage downtown. That job didn't pay a whole lot, but the money made a big difference between bare-bones living and having a few extras. We had even begun to save a little something.

Then along came these Africans from Olori, the same place this girl Ifa is from, and took over all of the work at the garage, because they were willing to work for a dollar less an hour. Fred said they were lousy drivers, too, and they were nasty to him, just like that girl was to me. I think she sucks up to Miss Zena because she wants something from her, but she let her claws show with me, because I have nothing to offer her. Also, she thinks she's better than I am. All these foreigners do.

After he lost his job at the garage, Fred tried to get on doing valet parking at one of the hotels or driving a cab on weekends like he used to, but he soon found that the Oloris had those jobs all sewn up, too, even with their lousy driving and bad manners and not knowing our road rules. Management doesn't care if customers get scared to death or killed, as long as they can pay their drivers less.

Then Fred applied for the night shift at the hospital where he used to work as an orderly. Same thing. Everywhere he looked, there were Oloris in white uniforms, Oloris in green uniforms, even Oloris in gray uniforms, pushing brooms. After that, I had to wake him up twice in the middle of the night, when he was screaming, having nightmares about Oloris taking over. "They're everywhere, Vy," he cried. "Everywhere!"

Sometimes I think his nightmares were right on the money. I saw this woman from Olori who got pregnant with octuplets—with the help of some mad American scientists—on TV the other day. She looked a lot like Ifa, come to think of it—great big wide-set eyes and large white teeth with a liar's gap. She had eight babies at once, and I'll be lucky to have one!

Fred says these days, seems like every time a black person finds themselves a little hustle, here comes some foreigner who's willing to do it for less. Of course the man who owns the business is going to go for it—one, because he stands to make more profits and, two, because he would prefer to hire almost anybody rather than us. So here come all these foreigners. They move into our neighborhoods, because they have nowhere else to go. Next thing you know, they've taken our jobs, plus they have the nerve to discriminate against us. Not so long ago, they sold us into slavery. Now they come over here and try to take what little we have managed to get since. That's why I don't like them.

We'll manage, of course. Fred has seniority at the Post Office, and I bring home enough from Miss Zena's to put with his and keep us going, but we sure miss that extra money he used to bring home on weekends.

That young hussy wants something else from Miss Zena besides a free ride. I don't think she can do hair—at least, she didn't say anything about it—so I'm not too worried about my job. But Miss Zena better not ask me to teach her.

And she had better keep an eye on that girl, and lock up everything she owns—if she don't want to lose it all.

 **FOUR**

A DAUGHTER IS something I have always wanted, and, usually, I get what I want.

But I was thirty-nine when Lucius and I got married, and my hormone level was already dropping then. I have a habit of saying that I am thirty-nine now, but that is merely a distraction from the main point, which is that our insurance would not pay for fertility treatments, though it would pay for a sex change for anyone who wanted to reverse himself. This goes to show you that the Devil is very busy in this country I have learned to love in spite of its devilish ways, which include guns, tobacco, pointy-toe shoes, porn on TV, and prejudice.

I love America—especially now that I have learned so much about Africa—almost as much as I do Lucius, who was not in the least disturbed that I could not give him children. His first wife did that, he said, but he still couldn't stand to be with her. Whereas he wants to be with me all the time, and is upset if we are apart for more than ten hours. I love that, and I don't want anything to change it. No matter how busy things are at the shop, I am home for dinner, which I cook myself. And if Lucius is in the mood for fun and games afterward, I am available, no matter how many customers I have to keep waiting back at the shop. That doesn't happen as often as it used to, of course—we have been married for ten years, after all, and Lucius is fifty-eight—but, when it does, oh boy!

I also love waking up in the mornings with his arm or his leg flung over me and his warm breath on my shoulder. I even like the sound of his snoring, which is gentle and doesn't bother me at all. I spent almost forty years sleeping alone in a cold bed, so hearing Lucius snore is like being in heaven and hearing the angels sing.

I do not understand these women who are always complaining about their men. I have to listen to their complaints, though, because that is in the nature of my business. Once you put your hands in a woman's hair and she begins to relax, almost anything is liable to come out of her mouth. It's part of my job to listen, and not contradict my customers, and never, never repeat what they say.

I do not complain about Lucius when I get my own hair done, though, or at any other time. Before I met him, I was working so hard I had practically no social life, and when I did, I made do with pieces of men. You know—you meet a man, and his looks are fine, but he has turtle soup for brains. Or he has both looks and brains, but he's just a player who's running games on you. Or he looks good and can talk, but he gulps his drinks till he passes out—or his eyes look dead, like a pair of holes, and he comes around one day and steals your TV. Or he's smart and sober and good-looking, but he always needs a loan till payday, because he is supporting six kids. Or he has everything a woman could want, but he prefers boys.

I went through my twenties making do with these pieces of men, and not thinking too much about it, because I was busy planning my future and working. In my thirties I looked around, and I saw nothing but some more pieces and some good whole men who were already taken. I don't like stolen property. If you buy hot goods, the thieves you bought them from will come and steal them back from you. If you steal somebody's husband, he will let another woman steal him from you.

I went on making do with bits and pieces, some brains one week, some looks the next, some soul the week after that, for a few years, and was fairly content. The business part of my life was coming together, and I didn't have much time to think about my social life while I was building my businesses. All I had time for was work. But I remembered that my mother had a good man, so I knew that when I got around to looking, there would be one waiting for me.

Daddy died when I was small, but he called me his little princess, and treated me like one. He had rough hands and wore soft wool sweaters, and I always remember him as that combination of soft and strong. When I was bothered about something, he would put me on his lap and hug me against his chest, and soon I wasn't bothered anymore.

I would rather have a gay guy escort me to an affair than go out with a player and listen to lies like, "Baby, you so beautiful, if I can't get next to you I will die." Die, then, I would think, and do it quick, and don't expect me to come to your funeral. The players took themselves too seriously, and the pretty boys were too busy looking at themselves to look at me. I fell in love with a pretty boy once. Theodore had a rosebud mouth, long lashes, and a silky pompadour. He kissed me with that rosebud mouth when I went home with him, but when I messed up his pompadour, he slapped me. I was out of there in half a second.

Another guy I fell for was not pretty, but he had a way about him. Bernard knew how to talk the kind of trash women liked to hear. He had some poems he had memorized, and he knew all the words to a couple of romantic songs and had a good singing voice. That kind of stuff will take a man a long way with women. But when I found out he was singing and reciting the same poetry to other women I knew, I dropped him.

My gay friends were a lot of fun, good at gossip and laughter, and handy when I needed someone to take me to an affair, but of course they were more interested in the other men who were there than in me. I was going out with my own competition! I had just begun to panic when my thirty-ninth birthday arrived. I began praying in earnest for a husband, and when Lucius showed up, I threw up my hands and hollered, "Thank you, Jesus!"

Lucius is tall, tan, good-looking in a rough way—not pretty—and quite active for an older guy, in spite of the extra weight he wears around his waist. He definitely prefers women, and has no physical longings toward man or beast. When I met him, his first wife was long gone to a second husband in California, and both his kids were grown, so his money, though it was not very long, was all his own. He has no bad habits, really, except that he smokes those stinky cigars, and we have no problems except that he loves church more than I do. I try to put him first and other people lower on my list. I am determined that my big, fine husband will never have to go without loving and home cooking.

I am a soulful lover, and I am not a bad cook. I give Lucius his favorite, pork chops and gravy, only once a month, because he has pressure and has to watch his cholesterol. I have found fat-free pork gravy at the store, and I have developed about a hundred ways to make fish and poultry interesting. I put cornmeal on Lucius's fish when I fry it for him, but I don't fix it that way very often. Mostly, I grill it or bake it. My peppery baked whitings are famous, and so are my sweet-and-sour chicken and my garlic-marinated turkey cutlets. I am heavily into veggies these days, and I see to it that they are the biggest mound on his plate.

Some women don't like interference when they're cooking, but I love it when Lucius hangs around the kitchen and lifts pot lids and sniffs and asks silly questions. I especially love it when he also breathes on my neck. I know I caught something special when I caught Lucius Lawson, and it is my intention to hold on to him. I dress plainer on the outside these days, but you should see my collection of lingerie! Victoria's "Secret" is simple—she looked in my dresser drawers.

When I met Lucius, he had been divorced about a year. He had just put in for early retirement from the Post Office and was campaigning for a seat on our city council. I was active in politics in those days, so naturally I was invited to all of the dinners and fund-raisers and met all of the candidates.

People often ask me how I have the energy to do all the things

I do—business, beauty shows, politics, clubs, crafts—but I am just the type of personality who has to be doing something all the time. A doctor told me it's my high metabolism. All I know is, if I don't keep busy, I get nervous.

Lately, though, I have begun doing less. I have noticed that my energy drops in the afternoon and again after dinner, when I often need a nap. Sometimes I break out in a sudden sweat, and when that happens, I can't do anything but rest for a couple of hours. My doctor prescribed estrogen, but I told him nonsense, I'm too young for menopause to be happening! Besides, like most African Americans, I don't trust medicine. When I get those spells, I just make myself a cup of tea and put my feet up, and soon I'm fine. I may have to go on those little pills eventually, but not yet. I'm too young!

There are days when I feel my shop may be getting to be too much for me to handle. That's when I'm especially grateful to have Vy. I know I can always take off for an hour or two, and she will keep everything under control. I've done that quite a few times lately, and I hope she knows her Christmas bonus was a thank-you for covering for me. That's why it bothers me that she was upset by Ifa. I need her more than ever these days.

Sometimes a beauty shop can really get to be a mother, you know? There's the heat, and the standing, and the breathing in hair and smoke, plus putting up with the complaining customers, and the cheap ones who don't want to pay my prices, and the hardheaded ones who want what they shouldn't have, and the wishy-washy ones who don't know what they want, but are never satisfied. There are days when it seems those are the only types of customers who come in. Still, I wouldn't want to do anything else.

Owning my own beauty shop was always my big dream, even more than owning my own model agency, which I also did once.

My ambitions started, I guess, when I was about ten years old. Daddy died that year, and Mama had to go to work cleaning houses and scrubbing toilets in the subway stations. We had been poor before, but I found out about real poverty then. Where we used to have whole milk and some kind of meat every night, now she brought home government cheese and canned milk, which we drank and poured over our cereal. I liked the cheese, but I hated the canned milk, and there simply was no money for meat or new clothes. A big shopping splurge was when my mother took us—me and my older brother Daniel—to a thrift shop to buy almost-new outfits.

In between splurges, my mother sewed for me. When I got new clothes, it was because she had caught a sale on bargain remnants. I was never raggedy. What I was, was worse. I was a kid whose mom dressed her oddly.

Even though she was a scrubwoman, Mama had an artistic flair. She wore her thrift-store outfits in outrageous color combinations—orange with red, pink with purple, purple with green. And she used to wrap her hair in bright cloths, tied so that her head looked like a bird about to take off.

Mama had no sewing machine, and she couldn't sew anything but straight seams. So my dresses were all straight shifts made like pillowcases, with two holes in the sides for my arms and one at the top for my head. She made them roomy and extra long, so I wouldn't outgrow them too fast, and if there was any cloth left over she would use it to make a sash to belt my dress with and a wrap for my head.

Mama had gotten her idea of style from the fields of South Carolina, where women's heads were tied up for protection from the sun, and dresses were mainly print sacks sewn together at the shoulder seams. She made me a lot of those straight dresses out of remnants from the back bin at the Sewtorium. She made herself a few of these sad-sack numbers, too, and while I liked them on her, I hated them on me. They were colorful, and I was always clean, but they screamed "Homemade!" from a block away.

I wanted to die every time I got dressed. I mean, what other girl came to school in a long, straight cotton sack, red, with white flowers on it? I begged my mother to get me a dress from the store, or maybe some jeans. But I knew before I asked that she had no money for clothes.

Then, there was the hair problem. I liked Mama's flying bird wraps when she tied them on her head, but I hated it when she did the same thing to me. There was no use arguing with her that all the other girls had hard-pressed bangs and pageboys, and that no one else wore rags tied on her head. Mama didn't care what other people did.

She had no idea of how to deal with my hair, anyway. Mama had naturally straight hair with a loose wave in it, what we used to call washboard waves, part of her Lumbee Indian heritage from her mama's side of the family. But I came here with rough stuff like my daddy's. Thick, stubborn frizz that simply would not cooperate with her—hair that would jump up and slap her back every time she slapped some grease on it.

First, she would wash my hair and towel it dry. Then she would get me in a vise grip between her knees and part my hair with the tail end of a rat-tail comb and put grease in the parts like a professional. That felt good, because the grease would be cool, though her hands were warm. Then she would divide my hair into four or five sections, and tie them off in bunches as if she were going to make braids. So far, so good. But then she would start to pray, and I knew it was all over with.

"Oh, Lord," Mama would pray, "please help me to make this girl's hair look nice today," and she would slap on some more grease, and give out a lot of helpless little moans and sighs, and brush my hair, and moan and pray some more, and I knew I wasn't getting a hairstyle, I was getting my head wrapped again.

Once Mama started working, her lack of time put an end to even her feeble efforts to deal with my hair. Braids hadn't arrived on the scene yet, nor had naturals. So I would get up in the morning resigned to my fate, present myself to her, and bow my head to have it tied up. Then I would go to school with my fists balled and at the ready.

Little girls can be meaner than guys running prison camps.

They are merciless and creative. When my classmates yelled, "There goes Zena in the tablecloth, broke all the dishes when she snatched it off!" I tried to hold my head higher and walk tall, the way Mama had taught me. I even ignored the one who called, cackling, "You in some funny religion, girl? You sure don't look like no A-rab to me!" and the one who answered, "She ain't no A-rab, she's a African! That's Zena Green, the African Queen."

In those days, *African* was the worst insult you could throw at somebody. Worse, even, than *black*. They were fighting words then, proud words later, which is why I love the times I grew up into. But back then, when I heard them, I would sometimes fight, though usually I heard them and kept walking.

But when I heard, "There goes that country hag with her head tied up in a dirty rag!" *country* was too close to the truth to bear. My mother was puredee country, that's why she dressed me the way she did. They would be talking about her next. I turned and screamed, "It isn't dirty!"

Laughing, my tormentor snatched the cloth from my head. She was a pretty thing named Monica Pitts, with long eyelashes and long hair fixed in sausage curls. "Ooh, look at that woolly mess!" Monica yelled, and laughed. I knocked her down. Every time she tried to get up, I knocked her down again. I thought I had won. But then, because she was so quiet, I bent over her to check out her face. Her nose was bleeding. She looked up at me and yelled through her tears, "My nose will stop bleeding, but you'll still be ugly!"

If Monica Pitts hadn't been so pretty, her words wouldn't have hurt me so bad. I went home crying.

I only had one friend, a girl named Selena Johnson, who told me I was not ugly. She tried to show me I wasn't ugly by walking me partway home from school every day, even though she lived in the opposite direction. But I didn't believe her. I knew I was ugly, and countrified, and funny-looking, but I planned to change my looks, and grow up someday, and look fabulous, and get married, and have a daughter and name her Selena.

Selena had eight children before she was thirty, and died before she was forty, stabbed by a junkie who thought she had some money. They only found ten cents on her. Her mama is raising the children.

I went to a few other classmates' funerals besides Selena's. The ones who have survived are waitresses, barmaids, and mothers on welfare. I wasn't voted the most likely, but I was the one who succeeded.

Monica Pitts was one of the ones who made a beautiful corpse. But her insults live on. They still ring in my ears. It's true that words can break your bones. They can also make you ambitious.

After that girl insulted me, I vowed that I would become beautiful. Better than beautiful, fabulous. I started hanging around Madame Rose Lee Carrington's hair parlor on Saturdays and volunteering my services, sweeping the floor and shining up the mirrors and running to the store for sandwiches and pork yak for the hairdressers, who were always too busy to go out to lunch. In return they would tip me, but I wouldn't take tips until I got my hair done. After Madame Rose Lee treated me to a hard press and cut and curled my bangs, *then* I would take their nickels and dimes to save for an outfit. But only after, not before.

I would have hung around there for free, to get what I was learning. How to straighten hair with heat or perm it with herbs or chemicals. How to twirl hair into a curl, and how to set it on rollers. How to give a facial. How to make gray hair black or brown, and brown hair blonde or red. How to wax hair to make it shine. How to wax hair to get rid of it. How to pluck brows. How to do makeup. How to give a manicure. Oh, I learned enough to get a beautician's license before I ever went to beauty school. When the day got late and the hairdressers got pushed, they would let me do some of their work, and tip me some more. I was in heaven.

I saved my tips until I could afford a divine suit for the eighth-grade trip. There was not a laugh on the bus when I strolled up to the corner in my dark plum-colored jacket and skirt, with black stockings and heels, my hair and my hips both swinging. I still remember how that suit felt. I wasn't beautiful and never would be, but I was fabulous and knew it. I had my hair freshly done, and I had this plum print scarf flung carelessly around my neck, and when I got aboard the bus, a few of the fellows whistled. Good looks, I had learned early, were mainly about attitude. The girls rolled their eyes at me and stuck out their lips, except for Selena, who patted the seat she had saved me next to her. And I knew I had found my calling. Looking good, and getting paid for helping others look good, too. And never again being poor.

I never had time to have Selena's namesake, but I never forgot her, and I never had a friend that good again till I met Vy.

Back in the days when Lucius and I were courting, I didn't have my beauty shop yet, I had my modeling school, and the demand for models of color had fallen off, so I wasn't all that busy. How I met my husband was, I remember, one day I closed up early, dabbed on some perfume, put on one of my trademark green outfits—I was Zena Green, the Glamour Queen, then— and dropped by this Democratic fund-raiser.

I think what I had on was this kelly green suit with not too many buttons fastened and a little nothing lace tank top underneath. The idea was to look like your underwear was showing, yet not look like a hooker, of which there were quite a few at this party. There always are at political affairs. It's really a seedy scene.

But for a while politics can seem like a great, big, glamorous, swinging party, which is one of the reasons I was in it, and this party was really happening. The shrimp was good, the drinks were free, and the band wasn't bad, either. I knew most of the people and had spoken to all of them, when this big suave stranger asked me to dance.

That is, he looked suave. Come to find out, Lucius is anything but—he's pure country. Born and raised in the swampy part of Georgia, up here with cornmeal in his mouth and boiled peanuts in his pockets and a broad, genial smile, just as open and friendly and innocent as a baby. I'll never know how he survived so long in the big city, except maybe that everybody likes Lucius and you'd have to be really rotten to hurt him.

The country in Lucius is why he is so good at politics. City folk are mostly in a hurry, but Lucius really likes to take his time listening to people and their problems. Lucius is an Aquarian, which makes him love all of humanity and want to help everyone. That's fine, though I sometimes get aggrieved when he fails to show that he loves me more than the rest. He can play hardball if he has to, once he figures out that's the name of the game, but he's slow to pick up on the bad side of people, and it doesn't happen often, anyway. When you expect good you mostly get good—you know?

I decided then and there that this great big old country boy needed someone to look out for him, and that someone was going to be me. So I steered him past the hustlers and the hookers, who were trying to move in, and said no to the private party at an after-hours club to which he had been invited, and suggested dinner at my place instead.

It was a bold move, but a good one. I knew I had a bird stuffed and ready to go into the oven and some little red potatoes and apples to roast with it. My feet were killing me in those high-heeled shoes, which have ruined my feet for life, anyway, and I was dying to kick them off. All I needed to do was throw a caftan on over my clothes—no, I was not going to undress, not that first night—and pour some white wine and toss us a salad.

There were no leftovers. And that man did not want to go home. I had to shove him out my door. Right away, he started calling me every day and seeing me every night. Pretty soon he decided that he did not want to be away from me for more than a reasonably long working day.

We found a lot of ways to be together. One of them was the campaign. We went door to door together, or sometimes we would go separately and meet up for dinner afterward. Memorial Day and July Fourth we dressed up in red, white and blue—I bought the first of my little navy suits just for those occasions, I remember, and wore a red-and-white-striped blouse with it—and rode on floats in the American Legion and VFW parades. Lucius had a tie I had bought for him, with blue and white stars on a red ground. He loved it, and found some red-and-white-striped suspenders to match.

One way the country comes out in my husband is that he is not in the least bashful when it comes to his clothes, preferring wild plaid jackets to the navy blazers I buy him, and wearing cowboy clothes on weekends.

I hostessed a couple of coffee clutches for Lucius and one fifty-dollar cocktail party, and we put in appearances at a lot of affairs.

I remember one time, soon after we started seeing each other, when Lucius took me to his club dance. I wore a fabulous outfit—an emerald green strapless taffeta dress I'd had specially made, with a matching coat embroidered with big gold sunbursts. We got up to dance—it was a slow dance, it had to be, because my husband can't do anything else—and Lucius whispered to me, "Please put your coat back on. I don't like the way these m-fs are staring at you."

I did as he asked, and I think I stopped being Zena Green, the Glamour Queen, that night. The next day, I decided to lose the sequins and the flashy dresses and the crazy-colored wigs. I was getting tired of all that stuff, anyway. It was like putting on a Broadway production for me to just get dressed. So off came the long green fingernails and the false hair and the witchy makeup, and on went the clean face and the neat little suits and dresses. By that time, Lucius had decided he hardly wanted me out of his sight at all. We were too old for a long engagement, so we got married.

What a relief! I had thought I was going to be single for the rest of my life. I was so happy that, for once, I let Mama wear a green dress—apple green. It was made to fit her, too—cut with princess seams instead of hanging straight like an old pillow-case. I was wearing white, of course.

I think our marriage helped Lucius to get elected—I was well known and popular, and it looks better for a candidate to have a wife. People put more trust in a settled man.

First we bought the building where my shop is, and for a long time we lived in one of the apartments over it while I went to beauty school. After paying for all that, plus some of Lucius's campaign expenses, we didn't have twenty thousand dollars to pay for my hormone shots, and we had no immediate prospects of getting it because, even though he won the election, Lucius refused to steal the people's money.

I couldn't pay the doctors to help me get a daughter in the usual way, so I had to get one in an unusual way.

I looked at all the articles in the papers about children who needed homes, and even though they always featured "La Shauna, who has emotional problems" or "Andrea, who is mildly retarded," now and then I would show one to Lucius. But he would always say, "A child is formed by the time it's two, Zena. Take an older child, you take on other people's troubles."

"Maybe we could adopt a little baby, then," I would say.

And he would shake his head. "I'm too old, Peaches." (That's one of his names for me.) "Look at the mortality tables. It's not fair to take on a child if you aren't sure you will live till it's grown."

I did not point out to him that no one can be sure of that, or that if we'd had a child the regular way, we would still be the same ages. I did not like hearing his mortality statistics, not at all, so I dropped the subject.

Lucius thought we should be content to make a home and a life for just the two of us, but I had this urge to mother somebody or something. That big pile-up of congested feeling in my chest that had nowhere to go. You know?

Lucius had ruled out adoption. I wanted a daughter in the worst way, though, and I usually get what I want, especially when I pray for it. God sent me a husband when I asked for one, after all.

But I never expected Him to send me a daughter from way across the ocean in Africa.

FIVE

AFRICA, IT SEEMED, was in the air this year. I never wore as many Afrocentric clothes as I have this season, and I never got so many compliments, either. Vy says people who put on all that getup just don't want to be plain old American Negroes, and she may be right. I never liked the word *Negro* anyway. I thought *black* was better because it was equal to *white*, even down to having the exact same number of letters, but it is plain and not very interesting. *African American*, however, has lots of exciting possibilities, because, when you think about it, it covers a lot of territory. Jamaicans and Haitians are African Americans. So are Brazilians.

Of course not everyone loves Africa, or even wants to be African American. I would not be in business if women did not get upset when their hair goes back. Back to where? Back to Africa, of course, and the natural look that was worn there. The sixties was a time when we were proud of our naturally nappy hair. Now we're back to changing its texture and color with a vengeance. These days, as in the old days, if you wear your hair natural, some people will talk about you. They will get smart and mention beads, baked beans and jelly beans. As the kids say, what up with that?

Even though I wear my hair straight, I love Africa and its products. This winter I have bought myself piles of beads and earrings, and a scarf with black pond birds on white canvas, and a black coat with animal-print patches, and a mudcloth hat and vest—and those are just the pieces I remember! Black women can't wear all that gaudy stuff, but African American ones can. We can even wear it all at once if we want to! That is because "black" is ordinary, but "African American" is fabulous! I am older than when I was Zena Green, the Glamour Queen, and I am married now, but I still want to be fabulous.

Vy and I were discussing all this one day. "Miss Zena," she finally said, "when you wear all that African stuff, you think you might be pretending to be something you're not?"

"No," I told her. "I have always been fabulous, and I always will be!"

Vy may be right, though. Without Afrocentric clothes and accessories, I'm just plain old American me. But when I add some bangles, and a jacket with giraffes parading around it, and a pair of big copper earrings, I'm exotic. A head wrap would complete the look, but I still can't put on a head wrap, any more than I can put on an accent. But every chance I get, I wear other Afrocentric stuff. Now that I have my big, beautiful African daughter, the two of us together will knock people's eyes out.

Between Thanksgiving and Christmas, I went to three—count 'em—three African bazaars. I bought a spear and a shield for my husband to hang in his Back Room, and a wide cowrie-shell bracelet for Vyester, and some wrist bangles for myself.

I also got the names and phone numbers of the vendors whose wares I liked, and I called them later to arrange special bulk orders, because I'm a businesswoman. Three weeks before Christmas, we had racks of Afrocentric dresses, jewelry, and purses hanging in my beauty shop, Zena's Curly Girl.

Zena, as I may have mentioned, is short for Zenobia. Zenobia Green Lawson. Mrs. Lucius Lawson, to be proper and respectable about it. I am very happy to be Mrs. Lucius Lawson now. But I haven't forgotten that for years, in another chapter of my life, I was Zena Green, the Glamour Queen. I never wanted to be ordinary. I learned early that an ordinary black woman could only look forward to poverty, food stamps, and a lifetime of welfare or domestic work. I wanted more than that. I always wanted to be fabulous. If I could sing I'd have been a Supreme or a diva. I couldn't sing, so I became Zena Green, the Glamour Queen. And in my wigs and high heels and fake furs, my glued-on eyelashes and my sequin-trimmed blouses, I felt like a queen, too—just like I do today in my mudcloth scarves and copper earrings.

Looking glamorous was the least of what I did in the old days, though. I knew how to put on the drag and how to work it, but my main occupation was training young women to be models and booking them, when they had the right stuff, with designers, manufacturers, and magazines. On the side I also went to schools and Girl Scout troops free and taught the girls poise and confidence. See, I'm a businesswoman, but I know you have to give something away to get something.

But all that was a long time ago. I still visit schools when I can, but now I am Zena Lawson, happy wife and successful businesswoman. A youthful person who is in the prime of life and enjoying every minute of it!

Like I said, Africa has been in the air lately. That stuff I bought really moved, especially the purses, which were embossed with jungle animals in bright colors, and the jewelry. I grabbed the last necklace and took it home to see if I could make one myself. I bought big wooden beads and little bronze ones at Beadazzle, and I turned out a pretty good imitation. The half-dozen necklaces I made sold out the last week before Christmas.

My house is full of crafts. Mama used to say crafts were what women did instead of raising children. I would tell her to hush her signifying, and go right on embroidering my crewel pillows or painting my tole trays or decoupaging my kitchen chairs. Right now I'm into jewelry making in a big way. Lucius says he's glad I turned to jewelry, because it will go to my shop, and he won't have to worry about sitting on any more fresh-glued furniture or funny-shaped embroidered cushions. He hates it, though, when I drop beads on the floor and his foot slips on them. Can't say I blame the man.

At Christmas I sent out my usual Santa Clauses that said "Ho-Ho-Ho" to friends and wreaths that said "Season's Greetings" to acquaintances. Back came the biggest collection of African drummer boys, kente designs spelling out "Noel," Madonnas in boubous, black Wise Men kneeling at mangers, presents piled under baobab trees, and Kwanzaa candles I have ever received. I was out of step. Africa was in the air.

Christmas came and went, and the air was still throbbing with African rhythms. I turned on my favorite jazz station one night, and some guy with a heavy accent was playing something he called World Beat music. I almost turned it off in disgust, but then I found I liked it, especially a couple of African women singers, Sade and Angelique Kidjo. Actually, I had liked Sade for a long time, but I didn't know she was African. She doesn't look it. But then, Ifa doesn't, either, because her mother is part French.

Then *Ipi Ntombi*, an African dance special, came on public television, and it was so fabulous we pledged a hundred dollars to the station's membership drive just to get the video. It was the first time Lucius and I ever gave them any money, and probably the last time, too, because mostly they're into British comedies, which I do not find funny at all. If you want me to laugh, give me Chris Rock. But that African dancing was something! A chorus of beautiful women who did not mind shaking and showing their ample hips. Lucius christened the show "Hippy Ntombi." I rolled my eyes at him. I'm on the hippy side, myself, so I loved the video, even though I always cover my behind with long tunics or jackets. I have noticed that African styles are kind to all figures. Even Lenore Wilkerson, my uppity neighbor, could pack her two hundred pounds into a grand boubou and look terrific. Not that she would.

Africa in the air.

In January, *Essence* came out with a coal-black beauty on their cover, wearing bangles up to her armpits, huge gold hoops in her ears, and six rows of cowries wrapped around her throat. She was laughing big enough to show all thirty-two fabulous teeth, and was wrapped in yards of orange-and-gold kente. She was a model from Uganda. I couldn't pronounce her name, let alone remember it, but I framed her and hung her in the most prominent place in my shop—right over my front desk, where everybody would see her.

Yes, I've seen a lot of Africa lately—without ever leaving home. Not all of it has been beautiful, though. At the January cultural meeting of our club, the Downtown Divas, Ebony Morris showed videos of her trip to Senegal. When I looked at that slave pen on Gorée Island where they held our ancestors prisoner, I got so upset I threw up the crab salad Ann Worthy had served for lunch. I may be a businesswoman, but I'm also sensitive, and some things really hurt me. I am also allergic to seafood sometimes, but I don't think it was the crab.

I felt even worse looking at that video than I did the time I went on one of Rose Mary Jackson's black history tours and climbed down into a hole where people hid when they were fleeing on the Underground Railroad. It was so stifling down there I couldn't breathe. I could feel the ghosts of all the ancestors who were crowded into that hole, and their fear, too. It rose in my chest until I had a panic attack and had to yell for someone to put the ladder back and help me climb out right away.

At least the people who hid in that Underground Railroad hole had hope, though. The ones on Gorée Island had none.

And don't show me no models of those ships they used on the Middle Passage, either! You better not try to get me on one of those boats, or any boat, at any time. Don't even talk to me about a cruise.

Ebony promised our club an extra special surprise for Black History Month. She wouldn't tell us what, except to say that it, too, would be something about the Motherland. I like to look at the positive side of things, so I hoped it would be something more cheerful than her January presentation.

Then Fast Fanny Davenport came in with that bag full of amber beads she wanted sewn onto her braids. The Fulani women wear them that way in Mali, she said, and a friend had brought them back for her from there. I would have tried to talk most women out of an extreme look like that, but Fanny is show biz all the way. She is long and limber as a hoop snake, and she works at Klub Kit Kat, where she does the kind of dancing that Waymon, the waiter at the Mad Mango, calls "throwin' pussy." The beads were large and fat but surprisingly lightweight, and warm to the touch. They looked like a fabulous crown on Fanny's head, and made me want an amber necklace in the worst way. I will get one, too. I usually get what I want.

The same day, Laura Tyson, who has worn her hair in a dead-straight auburn pageboy for years, came in for her regular appointment with her gray showing and asked for twists. No color. Just twists, wrapped so they would stay in place. I couldn't believe I heard her right, so I made her repeat it.

"I want twists," she said. "I am going on safari in Kenya, and I don't want to miss anything, so I can't be bothered with setting my hair, or touching up the color, either." I did as she asked, and she looked great in the Curly Twist, which is one of the seven variations on my Curly Girl (Pat. Pending) hairstyle. There is a variation of the Curly Girl for every type of hair and every personality, from my permed, rolled, and blow-dried Soft Curly Girl to my short, sassy, and natural Career Curly Girl. How I achieve them is my trade secret.

Ebony Morris says the name of my shop is demeaning because it's rude to call grown women girls, but what does she know? I say most women like to be called girls, and most women want hair that is curly. That is why my Curly Girl (Pat. Pending) style and my shop, Zena's Curly Girl, are so successful.

Going on safari in Kenya to see the animals! Wow. I think Lucius and I would love a trip like that, but there's no way I can take that much time off. Besides, I won't go into debt for something like a trip, the way other people do—especially while we still have a car note and a few other bills.

We've had a few adventures, though. A honeymoon in Kingston, Jamaica, where we stayed at a hotel on Blue Mountain; an N double A convention in Los Angeles, California, where I took in a beauty show on the side; and a lot of trips south to visit his relatives.

One time, our rented van got stuck in the mud in the swamp down there and we had to wait until somebody came to pull us out. When help came, it was a poor cracker with a truck. I was scared, but he turned out to be one of the nicest people I ever met. Earl Graves was his name. He wouldn't take any money for helping us. I'll never forget him.

But the suspense until Earl Graves pulled us out and turned out to be a decent person, not a Ku Klucks, was something! Now, that's what I call an adventure.

Laura Tyson was my last appointment that day. Thinking about her fabulous new look, I left my shop singing "Let's Twist Again, Like We Did Last Summer." I'm not old, I just turned forty-something a short time ago, but I love the oldies, especially Aretha Franklin and Chubby Checker. My mother raised me on those sixties soul sounds.

My burgundy Dodge Intrepid, Duchess, was in the shop for her twenty-thousand-mile check-up, so I hailed a cab. It was driven by an Olori with a wide, sunny smile, named Joseph Okoye.

"Call me Magic," he said. "Where can I take you, beautiful lady?"

I was flattered, because this Magic man was much younger than I am—not more than thirty.

Next he said, "The girls call me Magic because I put a spell on them, you know. May I have your phone number?"

I explained that I am a married woman, and he said, "So? What's the problem? Tell you what. To make things easier, I'll give you my number, and you can call me."

And he flashed me another grin and tried to pass me a slip of paper.

I should have taken it, instead of refusing and sitting there all proper and righteous, because Magic got angry and began to drive like a maniac let out of the hospital on a weekend pass. He swerved in and out of traffic and flung me all over the backseat while I scrabbled in vain for a seat belt. Once or twice he even ran up on the sidewalk. Then he turned into my street on two wheels and roared up to my door with squealing tires and sat behind the wheel, so mad I could swear I saw smoke coming out of his ears.

Thank God Lucius wasn't home to see all this. He would have come running out and had a heart attack trying to drag that driver out of his cab and kill him. I was cool. I took my time. I counted out the exact fare, got out, and handed it to him through the window. No tip.

I have had the misfortune to hear a lot of bad language in my life, but that Olori called me some names and combinations of names that were entirely new to me. Then he sped off, leaving me with my heart pounding and my mind confused. Mainly, I was afraid. I never had a man react so angrily to a polite brush-off before. But then, I had only dealt with American men.

Like I said, Africa was in the air.

And my lovely African daughter was heading my way.

SIX

IFA CAME INTO my life because my club, the Downtown Divas, decided to add cultural programs to their meetings. We have about twenty-five members, and most of us were content to just get together every other weekend and play cards and run our mouths.

But Ann Worthy, our president, who is a cultural vulture, insisted that we ought to expose ourselves to the finer things of life. Ann is one of those high-minded board-sitting women. She is on the boards of Opera Ebony and three or four black colleges. She is also a subscriber to the symphony and she has an art collection. Not just pictures on her walls, a collection, as that museum curator explained to us a couple of months ago. I forget what the difference is.

Ann has a following, mostly women who want to be grand even though they wouldn't know culture if it slapped them 'cross the face with a wet towel, and that bunch supported her.

Then Ebony Morris, who is so militant you can't even style her hair—it just naturally locks—leaped into the discussion. We needed programs that would educate us about the struggle—programs about black history and politics, not just entertainment. Some of us groaned, but the guilty ones who felt they ought to be doing more for the struggle supported Ebony.

Then Ann helped the voting along by volunteering to have all of the cultural programs at her house, which meant that she would have to do the cooking, serving, and cleaning up. The lazy ones among us, who are a majority, quickly joined the others, and we voted to have a monthly cultural program.

The next vote was about the name change. We had been called the P.P.C.s —for pinochle, pokeno, and conversation—for years. The pokeno is for the women who like to liven up their card games with a little betting, the pinochle is for the rest, and the conversation is for everybody. If it had been left up to me and some of the others, we would still just play cards and talk. But the club's name had to be changed because "the Pinochle, Pokeno, Conversation, and Culture Club" is way too long a name for a bunch of women who just get together twice a month to kick back and catch up on gossip.

I suggested "the Three Cs," for culture, cards, and conversation—and I still think it was the best idea. But ignorance always shouts louder than good sense and drowns it out, and some of the others, especially Monica Lewis, who is running out of places to wear her gold jewelry and her mink accessories—I have a couple of suggestions for her, but she wouldn't like them—wanted to call themselves divas. So, even though most of us can't sing and none of us lives downtown in the business district, we became the Downtown Divas. Everyone liked the alliteration. I learned about alliteration from this serious lady poet who was one of our first cultural guests. I liked some of her poems and most of the things she had to say.

Oh, I complained bitterly about the change at first. I said I wasn't going to be forced to swallow culture on weekends when all I wanted to do was relax, and my husband Lucius said, "Well, Zena, nobody is making you go."

As it turned out, I liked most of the culture programs, especially this pair of poets who read their compositions with a drummer backing them up, and this young classical pianist Ann had been raving about. It helps that Ann has a grand piano in her house, when most of us don't even own a keyboard. The way his braids with their beads on the ends swung around and swirled and clicked when he got to the furious part of the concerto really knocked me out. So, while I had said I wasn't going to go to the cultural meetings, I began to look forward to them. I was in danger of becoming as much of a cultural vulture as Ann. I even began writing poetry myself and keeping a journal. I talked Vy into coming to some of the meetings, though she refuses to join. I think she feels some of the women are too uppity for her, though all she says is, it's hard for both of us to get away from the shop at the same time. I can't dispute her, because that is true.

At our February cultural program, this broad from Olori that Ebony had found came to tell us all about life in the land of our ancestors. She was some kind of history professor and was full of it, especially the part about how her ancestors were all royalty once upon a time—kings and dukes and queens. It's a tired old message and, as I told Vyester, that way-back-when royalty don't do nothing to help us here and now. I'd rather hear about people who are doing things in our time, like successful beauty shop owners. I always wonder—if all the way-back-when Africans were royalty, who did the work? I'd like to hear about those working Africans sometime.

Some of the highfalutin women in the Divas who teach school want me to go to college and become a professional like them, but I like what I'm doing, and I think I'm already a professional. Beauty culture *is* a profession, or it ought to be. You have to be an artist, a scientist, a psychologist, and the equivalent of an M.B.A. to do it right.

I'm proud to be a beauty shop owner and operator. I think it requires a lot of ability. Used to be, hairdressing was a simple occupation. Just wash, press, and curl; wash, press, and curl. Then for a while the business went down to nothing, because everybody was wearing their hair natural, until women found out that even naturals require care. Now, besides naturals, you got braids, weaves, wraps, twists, perms, dreads, extensions, sets, twelve different kinds of relaxers, and fifteen different kinds of color, plus frosting. Then there's nails. You got to know how to do all that, plus be a diplomat with women who want what won't look good on them, and a psychologist to them all.

Then, when you're the owner, there's the business part: keeping books and records, ordering supplies, paying salaries—and don't even mention taxes. If it weren't for Vyester I'd go nuts. She and Lucius keep me grounded.

In my mind, I go back often to that meeting. I am there, and I am thinking that this learned sister, Doctor Chiongo, could sure use a trip to my salon. Her hair looks like a bunch of her hometown monkeys have been hunting for lice in it, and have found some, too. She sure doesn't look like a queen, not with those run-over shoes and run-up stockings she has on, plus her raggedy clothes that look like they were rejected by the Salvation Army. I know I shouldn't be so critical of her looks, but I've spent my life helping women to look good, and here this sister is standing before an audience and not even trying to present a good appearance. Maybe traveling has worn out her wardrobe, but her hair is so raggedy too that I am thinking that she needs my help.

History professors always make things as boring as possible, but unlike most of the others in the group, I listen. I hear her say that her family was descended from royalty, but that none of us could be, because only common people were sold into slavery.

I am going to call Madame Doctor Cecelia Chiongo on that remark, because it is most definitely out of order even if it is true, but she is looking over our heads, with her nose pointed way up at the ceiling, and doesn't see my hand. It's a good thing, too, because Ann has volunteered me to take the royal visitors to my house afterward and feed them some of my sweet-and-sour chicken, and if I had read that woman out in the meeting or smacked her like I really wanted to do, dinner would be tense. Besides, just about all the members but me are asleep, and that would be what people call a rude awakening.

Right about then, just in the nick of time, when my ignored right hand is burning to slap an educated Olori, we have a change of pace.

"And now, Dr. Chiongo's sister, Ifa Olongo, will give us an African fashion show," Ann announces. She really knows how to plan these programs. At those two magic words, "fashion show," the women who have been snoring through all the history and the royalty jerk awake and focus on the front of the room.

I'll say this for Ifa—she was born to model. That girl has enough haughtiness and grace for three royal families. She is an African princess, sure enough, a BAP with the *A* standing for African instead of American, and when I first laid eyes on her, I immediately thought what a stunning model she would make, and how easily I could launch her career. I don't know how long she will be in this country, and I no longer have my model agency, but I am itching to dig out my old Rolodex and call up some people I know to get her started. She has the looks and grace of a big tan cat, including a cat face like the young Eartha Kitt's—big wide-set eyes, wide mouth, and all. She also has that insolence and that way of swaying from side to side while switching her little fanny that designers pay a fortune for. She is fabulous!

Ifa makes those African clothes look so good the women buy every single piece, right off her back. I'll bet her family could use the money, too, royalty or no, because Dr. Chiongo's book about Olori rulers that she brought to peddle isn't selling nearly as well as the fashions. Cultural and political consciousness takes time to develop, as Ann and Ebony are always pointing out. The Divas will need dozens of years to develop theirs.

Then, since Ann volunteered me, I load the royalty in my almost-new Dodge Intrepid and take them home.

"This is a nice car," remarks Dr. Chiongo. "I have a Mercedes at home."

"I have one in my garage," I inform her. My husband, Lucius, drives it most of the time, but I don't add that explanation, just let my statement stand.

"You have a lovely home here," she says when she gets inside our house. "My house is bigger, but yours is quite nice. Too bad you have no children."

I make no response to that. I never do. Whether my lack of

children is too bad or not is my business and Lucius's, and nobody else's.

Meanwhile, Ifa is looking around her with those big doe eyes, studying the setup, and she is not saying a word. Her silence automatically makes me like her better than her rude-mouthed sister. I almost wonder if Ifa is a deaf-mute, she is so quiet, but she is merely scared. Later, of course, she will more than make up for this hour or two of silence.

When I serve the salad, rice, field peas, seasoned string beans, sweet-and-sour chicken, rolls, butter, and tea, the Doctor's eyes grow wide with amazement. "How do you do all this without servants?"

"Oh, I manage," I say with a tiny bow, and pass the salad. "Please help yourselves."

"This place is very clean," she says, tearing her roll and dipping it in the salad, in the sweet and sour sauce, in the peas, in her tea, in everything.

What did she expect, a dirt floor? I have to grit my teeth to keep from uttering an angry reply to this woman, who is short and stocky, medium brownskin, and has none of her sister's grace or attractiveness. While Ifa has a broad, generous mouth and smiles often, showing about a hundred beautiful teeth, this one's mouth is thin and drawn in, as if she feels she has to be stingy with her smiles.

Looking at Ifa sitting beside her in a bright orange dress is like seeing the sun come from behind a cloud.

To make things even brighter, Ifa finally speaks up. Her voice is like low-pitched music played on a cello.

"I have been observing our hostess, Cecelia," she tells her sister. "She has a lot of energy. Perhaps that is why she can do so many things." She smiles, and the sun comes out a second time.

The older sister is like medicine that leaves a bad taste in your mouth, but the younger one is like the spoonful of sugar you take to get rid of it. Sweet and sour. It will be a long, long time before I wonder if this is an effect that they have worked on, like a stage routine.

"And you have a business to run, too, I am told," Doctor Chiongo says next.

"It's wonderful that she can do all that, and keep house, and cook such delicious meals, too," says her little sister.

I give a tiny bow to acknowledge the compliment.

My husband, Lucius, smiles and says, "Oh, I help out now and then. I'm pretty handy with a mop, and I know how to sweep the dirt under the rug. When I heard we were having guests this evening, I just put all the junk in the spare room and shut the door."

He's exaggerating and kidding, of course. Most of the housework I don't have time for gets done by a cleaning service. But he's a man with neat habits, and he does help.

"Really!" Cecelia says, amazed, and stares at him with something like pity and horror. "In my country, a man would never do housework. But then, men in your position usually have several wives to do it. My little sister is an excellent housekeeper, by the way." She pats the girl's hand. "Aren't you, Ifa?"

"Yes, Cecelia," the girl says adoringly, and smiles sweetly at her sister. "You know our mother trained me."

"Yes. Unfortunately, she didn't train you to do anything else, except look good. However—something will be found." She addresses my husband. "You are still a young man. Don't you find it boring, staying at home?"

Lucius explains that once he retired from civil service, he was free to go into his first love, politics. He served one term on our city council, but refused to run again, choosing instead to be our ward leader. We live in a big ward. Helping other candidates and their constituents is enough to keep him busy.

"The gods are favoring us, Ifa!" Dr. Chiongo exclaims. "This man is exactly the person we need to help us. I swear to you, Mister Lawson, I hoped to meet someone like you on this trip, but until this moment, it has not happened. All praises to God! You see, Ifa has only three weeks left on her visitor's visa. She wishes to stay in this country longer. Can you perhaps help her, Mr. Lawson?"

"Call me Lucius," says my husband, and leans back in his chair, and beams. He's a great politician because he loves to help people. Anybody can see that when they look at him. He doesn't mind getting up at one in the morning to get somebody out of jail, or visiting half a dozen offices to get a poor family food stamps. "Perhaps I can help."

Ifa claps her hands. Her eyes are shining. "Oh, that would be wonderful!"

I am so proud of my husband. It is wonderful, the way he always puts people at ease, promises them favors, and makes them happy.

"Tell me, how long would it take to extend her visa?" Dr. Cecelia asks. Four hopeful eyes are trained on my husband like searchlights.

Lucius wrinkles his big, handsome forehead, thinking. "I'm not sure. I have to call our office and find out who handles I.N.S. You say she has three weeks?"

"Yes."

"Well, then, we'll get it done in three weeks."

Ifa claps her hands and wriggles with so much excitement, she looks like a snake.

My husband is a big, generous, easygoing man. It's why I love him, and may be why these women felt free to approach him. Of course, as I have learned since, shyness and reserve are not Olori traits.

"You mentioned a spare room," Dr. Chiongo says next, and now all four eyes turn to me. "Could you possibly let my sister stay here while this business is being taken care of?"

I get that stiffness in my neck and that pain behind my eyes that always warn of a migraine coming on, or of trouble just ahead, or both. But it's only for a few days, I tell myself. At the most, three weeks.

"Of course, once she has her visa, she will stay with relatives or with other friends," Cecelia assures me. "I will give you their telephone numbers."

"Could you please let me stay here, Mum? I won't be any

trouble. I am a good housecleaner. I will try to be a help to you."
Those large, appealing eyes. That musical voice calling me Mum.
I do not even want to hear about these relatives and other friends.
I am hooked.

"Sure," I say. "Why not?"

"Then it is settled," Dr. Chiongo says. She smiles for the first
time, and now I understand her reluctance. She has two front
teeth missing. How I wish I could introduce her to my dentist.
Please, just don't get me started on the women I know who have
mink coats and diamond rings and missing front teeth. It makes
me crazy.

"Let me help you, Mum," says Ifa, and starts to clear the table.
"An old woman like you should not have to work so hard."

Old woman! Nobody has ever called me that before. Instant
rage rushes blood to my eyelids and makes me see red, but Ifa,
stacking plates, doesn't realize that she has made a mistake.

Her sister, however, is more observant. She will never see
forty again, either, or I am no judge of dark circles under eyes
and lines between nose and mouth—neither of which I have.

She says, "You must apologize to Mrs. Lawson, Ifa. What is
considered old in our country is still young here."

"I am so sorry, Mum," Ifa says in the sweetest of voices, eyes
lowered, long lashes sweeping her cheeks. "I hope you don't
mind if I call you Mum."

Mind? Do I mind it when Lucius calls me "Sweetheart"?

"Keep your mouth shut when you don't know what you are
talking about, Ifa," Cecelia says harshly. "That is most of the
time."

I want to smack her for being so rough on the poor child.

"Sorry, Cecelia," Ifa mumbles, and bows her head.

Sweet and sour.

"Please accept my apology, Mum."

Of course I do. Her eyes are downcast, her voice is soft and
sweet, and I am already halfway in love.

 # SEVEN

LATER THAT NIGHT, though, after Cecelia has left and Ifa has been settled in our guest room, I begin to have doubts. I lie awake wondering if we are doing the right thing. Ifa seems sweet and lovely, but what do we really know about her?

It is the middle of the night, when everything always seems worse than it really is, and I am getting cold feet, both ways. I am too sleepy to get up and turn on the electric blanket, so I press my feet against Lucius's warm legs. And I am worried, so I shake his shoulder to wake him up.

He begins making what I call his bear noises, grumblings and harrumphs and growls that mean, "Leave me alone."

I kiss his neck, then reach around and cup his privates gently in my hand. The noises become pleased sounds instead of grumpy ones.

" 'S late, Zena," he says. But he is growing hard against my hand.

He turns over like a mountain moving. "Lord, woman, do you know your feet are like ice cubes?" He slides his hands up under my gown and adds, "The rest of you is warm, though."

Lucius weighs well over two hundred pounds, which has made the bed sag down permanently on his side. This causes me to roll toward him every night, whether I am feeling affectionate or not. I can support his weight for a couple of minutes, but not for as long as he sometimes wants. Soon I am up on my hands and knees and grabbing him back there and guiding him in. Before he enters me, his hands tease my little man and make him stand up in his boat.

African women often have their little man cut out and thrown away. Maybe it was done to Ifa. That thought comes as Lucius does, banging against my butt, and makes me so sad I put aside my own pleasure. What makes matters worse is, I cough, and Lucius slips out. Love can fix everything. I really believe that. I put him back. But our rhythm has been interrupted. My excitement ebbs, and I am left feeling hungry and empty. This is not a good omen.

"Lucius," I say as we fall back on our pillows, "we don't know anything about this African girl. Are you sure we are doing the right thing, taking her in?" He seldom wants to cuddle afterward, but I tickle his chest hairs anyway.

He climbs out of bed and gets me a towel. "Of course we are, Zena," he says when he returns and hands it to me. "We're Christians."

Speak for yourself, Deacon, I think. Though I try to follow Jesus, I disagree with a lot of things about Christianity. The way it puts women down and won't let them preach. The way it goes on and on about the wages of sin. The way it was used to justify slavery and keep us down. Sons of Ham and daughters' drawers, cook and hew and obey your masters—all that stuff.

Thinking about church, going way back to Sunday school when I was a little girl, I remember all those missionary offerings on Sundays to help people in Africa. They usually came before the general offering, which meant the church got less than we had meant to give it—even though it had a leaky roof we were trying to repair. Either that, or some members of the congregation had to do without enough food on the table during the week.

I remember hearing all those sermons about helping the poor Africans and wondering how we could afford to, when some of the people in our own neighborhood were sick and hungry, and also wondering why we were supposed to help them, since they sold us to white folks. But I guess the sermons sank in. Even though I was full of doubts, I always figured that the preacher knew best. I gave what I could back then, and now I have agreed to take Ifa.

But the question keeps coming back. Why? I wonder, lying there discontented and irritable. "Why, Lucius? Why does the minister always tell us to help Africans, when we can barely help ourselves?"

"Because it's the Christian way," he says. "Do unto others as you would have them do unto you. We're supposed to help those less fortunate."

"How do we know that they are less fortunate? They may have more than we do."

He grumbles something I can't understand. If I didn't know better, I would swear that my husband was cursing. "If they are not saved," he intones, "they are less fortunate than we are, no matter how much they possess in the way of worldly goods."

My husband is a deacon at our church, Solid Rock Baptist, and he really does talk like that sometimes. Not all the time, thank goodness. "Besides," he continues, "you know Africans are poor. You've seen how they live in the movies."

I don't believe everything I see in the movies. I hope my husband doesn't. "Yes," I tell him, "I've seen those thatched huts and those skimpy outfits. But that doesn't mean those people are poor. You don't need central heating or sweaters near the Equator. Doesn't it say somewhere in the Bible that charity begins at home?"

"I don't think so," Lucius says.

Aha, I say to myself, I've got him. I just asked a Bible question he can't answer. In the dark, he can't see the smile on my face.

Lucius is really impatient now. "You know this home doesn't need any charity, Zena. The Word says to comfort the afflicted and afflict the comfortable. We are comfortable."

"I wasn't thinking of us, really, Lucius. I was thinking of places in this neighborhood that need help, like the emergency shelter and the soup kitchen, and the program for latch-key kids. And people with big families, like the Neils and the Emfingers." And why, I wonder, does my husband want us to be afflicted?

"She's only going to be here for three weeks, Zena. Surely you can put up with her for that long. Can we please stop this discussion now and go back to sleep?"

I was going to say something else—that Ifa gave me the impression of having been used to plenty of money—but my husband had that edge in his voice that told me it was really time to back off.

I knew what the problem was, besides sleepiness. My husband is a man who just has to give. When he has promised someone a favor, nothing had better come between him and the object of his generosity. I believe he would run over somebody if they tried to get in the way of his giving.

I lay awake for a long time, wondering about this new person who had come into our house, and feeling tense about her presence. Something else was keeping me awake, too. I was stirred up down there, swollen and aching from lack of completion.

I don't like doing it, but I had to bring about my own satisfaction before I could fall asleep.

 # EIGHT

"MISS IFA OLONGO," Lucius rumbles in his deepest baritone, which reminds me of Paul Robeson singing "Old Man River." "Well, well, well." It is Sunday morning; Ifa's first day with us. He rears back in his chair and studies her from head to toe. "Why do you want to stay in our country, anyway, Miss Ifa Olongo?"

I have been wondering that myself. Why are all these foreign people suddenly coming here? Everywhere I look, I see Indians, Africans, Chinese, other foreigners, shopping in stores, driving cabs, working in shops, crowding the sidewalks. I hear some of the Chinese ones pay as much as five thousand dollars to get here illegally. Last week, a whole boatload of them got caught and locked up. And they say the Indian ones are giving up high-paid jobs as professors and doctors to come here and work in gas stations. It doesn't make sense to me. Why?

The girl looks scared to death. She hesitates and licks her lips, trying to find the right answer to Lucius's question, as if she's taking an exam and her life depends on giving the right answer. He sounds loud and scary, that's why. I know that he is kind-hearted and basically harmless, but she doesn't.

"Well, Dod, I, I, I want—" When she is upset, I notice, she stutters.

"Come on, come on," Lucius booms. "You've come all this way, you must have a good reason."

"Lucius, you're scaring the child," I tell him.

"I am less afraid here than I am at home," she shoots back. "At home, the police and the army are everywhere, and the government keeps changing. One minute it is stable, and the next minute"—she throws her hands in the air—"everything has blown up. Poof!

"Here," she continues, "it is safer. It is more settled. Also, there are greater opportunities for women. At home, I was expected to be married by now. Since I am not, I am, I am—"

"Criticized?" I suggest.

"Shunned?" says Lucius.

"Yes, yes, all of that, and worse. Because I have not yet married, I am not considered a proper member of our society. And there are other things they do not like about me."

"Such as?"

She lowers her eyes. "I, I, I—I do not want to say. But my father was a rich and powerful man, a chief, and he was able to protect me. No one dared to hurt me while he was alive. Now that he has died, I am in serious danger at home. Certain people do not like me, and they feel they can do anything they want to me now that my father is gone."

Lucius reaches out and pats her hand. "Well, you can relax here. No one's going to hurt you while you're with us."

He already has his shirt and tie on. Now he shrugs into the jacket of his shiny gray herringbone suit. "Anyone for church?"

I shake my head. "Not me." Lucius tries, but he can't make me get up and go to church most Sundays. Sunday is supposed to be a day of rest, and damn if I think listening to a shouting preacher and a bellowing choir is restful.

Lucius is a more regular churchgoer than I am. He is already a deacon, and sometimes he threatens to go to Bible college and get himself ordained as a minister. I hope that doesn't happen, because then I'd have to be in church every Sunday, and I'd have to wear big, hideous hats and ugly dresses with high collars. What a horrible thought. And I'd have to keep digging in my purse for money to give to the missionary offering, the general offering, the sick and shut-ins, and the building fund.

"I would love to go, Dod, but I have nothing to wear," Ifa says. She is dressed in a simple length of fabric that winds around her body, and her feet are bare. "I will stay here and help Mum prepare dinner."

"Let's eat early, Zena," Lucius says. "I want to get to the park for some riding this afternoon. You and Ifa come, too. The fresh air will do you good."

I will not ride today. I refuse. I will go, and I will wear the big white hat and the boots and the brown suede fringed jacket. I will even wear the riding britches—with the long jacket, they make a good-looking outfit—but I will not climb up on a horse. I do not want to start the week off with a sore behind like the last time Lucius made me get on Snipes, his black stallion.

Lucius goes horseback riding in the park on weekends with his club, the Urban Cowboys. I said they ought to call themselves the Black Cowboys, but he said that would be saying the same thing twice, because almost all of the original cowboys were black. The proof, he says, is that they were called cow*boys*, not cow*men*. So Gene Autry and Roy Rogers and John Wayne were fakes. Herb Jeffries is the real thing, though. Randolph Scott was, too. He was just passing for white, as so many of us had to do to get work in those days. He disappeared from movies in the sixties because he got his consciousness raised by all the marching and protesting that was going on back then, and told his studio that he was black. They told him, "Good-bye, then." He left without looking back, because he had plenty of retirement money. And that is the real answer to the question in the song "Whatever Happened to Randolph Scott?"

The Urban Cowboys keep their horses in the park, where the city rents them stable space. Lucius's first horse was Pickett, a big brown stallion as gentle as his owner. Pickett was named not for the Reb general but for the black movie and rodeo star. I was scared to ride, but when I got up on Pickett and he started to walk, it was as easy as sitting in a rocking chair.

Lucius doesn't ride so much anymore, but on weekends he and the other older Cowboys teach kids to ride and to take care of horses. He still wears fringed shirts and ten-gallon hats and kerchiefs around his neck when he rides, though, and every other chance he gets.

Pickett went to horse heaven a few years ago. Lucius has a new stallion now, a black one named Snipes, after the movie star. Snipes used to be a circus horse and can do lots of tricks, which is why I am afraid to get up on him. I am afraid he will try a trick or two while I am on his back.

Lucius turns back just before he leaves for church. "Oh, and Zena, the Cowboys are having their dance next month, don't forget. The thirteenth. We have two fiddlers and an out-of-town caller."

Oh, Lord. I don't know how I managed to find a country-and-western-type man in a black urban environment, but that's what I've got. Lucius can't dance, except for slow dancing, but he tries. What he does when the music gets fast is country shit-kicking. Left boot forward, kick; right boot forward and kick. If you're his partner you have to holler "Yeehoo!" every now and then, and watch your shins. It cracks me up.

For all their disagreements, southern black folks and southern whites sure have a lot in common. I don't like country music un-less Ray Charles sings it, but Lucius can get down with a whole lot of blue-eyed singers, though they mostly sound like whiny would-be suicides to me. He says country music is just our mu-sic sung by white folks. He might be right. I would never admit it to him, but sometimes I think Willie Nelson has a lot of blue-eyed soul.

I thought I had months to go, but it looks like the time for the Cowboys dance has almost rolled around again. I groan. This means I must put on a corny Western outfit and join in the shit-kicking and the promenading. I have tried to tell Lucius that this isn't his culture, that his thing is the Funky Chicken and the Electric Slide. But again he says, "What you mean, woman? This is our country. It's all our culture!"

He's right, I guess. At least the Cowboys' corny dance is being held to raise money for a good cause—a new horse to replace our friend Duncan's horse, Do-right, who is retiring to a pasture, and a week at a dude ranch for some city boys who are considered underprivileged and at risk. Yeehoo! Oh, my poor shins.

Ifa is still hanging around half naked in that wrap thing she wears in the house. After I make some chicken à la king with red bell peppers, snow pea pods, and evaporated skim milk and put it in the oven, I tell her, "It's time to get dressed now, Ifa. Dod— I mean Dad—wants us to go with him to watch the horseback riding."

"But, Mum, I have nothing to wear," she says.

"This is not a dressy occasion," I tell her. "We will be out in the park, walking on bridle paths and trying not to step in horse droppings. You can wear anything."

She lowers her eyes in embarrassment. "I did not mean I have no dress-up clothes, Mum. I meant I have nothing at all to wear. I did not understand about winter. I did not bring anything for your cold weathers."

Unwilling to believe this news, I ask, "What is in that heavy suitcase you dragged in?"

"Art for me to sell. Let me show you, Mum." She rushes enthusiastically out of the room, brings the suitcase back, and opens it. It is stuffed to overflowing with serious Ugly—wooden masks, statues, and other carved horrors. Some of her statues have penises that dangle to the floor, others have breasts like nose cones, and all have faces like gargoyles. She also has some very scary masks with eyes that seem alive.

A shiver starts way inside my chest and spreads to my fingers and toes. "Close the suitcase, please, Ifa."

She does so, but reluctantly. "I was hoping you could sell these for me at your shop, Mum."

I shake my head. "I don't think so."

"Mum, there is a type of woman in Africa who is very successful in business. She takes her wares to market, and she always comes back with an empty basket and plenty of money. You are that type, Mum. You would do very well in my country. I am sure you could sell my art. You could sell anything."

"I said no," I tell her. I know my customers, and they are not ready to move too far away from European notions of style and beauty. Ifa's carvings may have artistic and religious value, but they are plumb ugly, with wild raffia hair and buck teeth, wide nostrils and spooky eyes. Let's get real. My shop is a beauty shop. We're not selling ugliness there.

Nor are we selling sex. They do that down the street. So I do not want my salon to feature a display of pornographic statues with big butts and prominent tits and enormous penises. I mean, most of my customers like penises, and most of them have big butts and tits, but the image of themselves that they carry in their heads is more Tyra Banks than Nell Carter. I wish to do nothing to break that illusion. My job is to bolster it.

"But, Mum—"

"I said, no," I repeat. "Ifa, I can't believe you have nothing at all to wear. What about the things you modeled at the meeting?"

"Your club members bought them all, Mum."

Did I mention that it is still February? A cold February, with quite a few below-freezing days. I am ashamed of picking on the poor girl.

"Come with me," I say.

I have been thinking. Ifa is about four inches taller than I am, but otherwise, she and I are about the same size. Maybe there are a few things in my closet that I can let her have. But first, she will have to do something about her horrible armpits, as I explain. I hand her some of Lucius's super-strong deodorant, because the way she reeks, mine won't do.

She is insulted. "What do you mean, Mum, by saying I am smelling? I only smell the way healthy people are supposed to smell!"

"Maybe so, but we are crowded in this house, and your smell overpowers everybody else." I am still holding out Lucius's container of deodorant.

"I don't want that stuff. It is unnatural," she tells me.

"So are indoor plumbing and electricity, and I wouldn't want to live without them. Take this."

"To me, you and Dod are the ones who smell funny," she

counters. "All sweet and perfumed and disinfected. You smell like a pair of big Air-Wicks."

"Take it."

She does, but reluctantly. "We do not use such things in our village."

"You are not," I say, shoving her toward the shower, "in your village anymore." I am thinking that this will probably become my refrain.

When she comes out, things are much improved in the aroma department. Tomorrow I will talk to her about shaving those beards under her arms.

I sit her on my chaise lounge and hand her things I seldom wear: an old pair of black slacks, some bright green ones, a black leather skirt, a white shirt, a couple of cotton turtlenecks, a checkered sweater, a short red coat. To these I add a couple of sweat suits and some heavy socks for around the house.

As if she were shopping with a platinum credit card, she hands the sweat suits back to me. "I do not wear this sort of thing, Mum," she informs me.

I refuse to take them back. "Wait till the temperature drops at night. You will," I tell her.

My closet is overstuffed with my mistakes. I do not mind passing some of them along to her. I am just put off a little by her choosiness. I am also infuriated by the nerve of her sister, who left her on my hands with nothing to wear but her birthday suit.

"These should hold you till we can go shopping," I tell her. "We'll go next week, maybe even tomorrow. You do have the money the women paid you for those outfits, don't you?" The way the Divas bought and bought, I figure she must have cleared at least a couple thousand dollars.

"Oh, no, Mum. Cecelia kept the money, because she is traveling and needs it."

"You have other money that you brought with you, I hope."

Usually she shouts, but now her voice is so low I can barely hear her. "No, Mum. I am sorry, but we are not allowed to take money out of the country. I hope Cecelia calls me tonight."

"I hope so, too. If she does, please let me talk to her." I want to know what the great Doctor Chiongo means by leaving this girl with us with no clothes and no money. "Now that you've had your bath, you can try the things on."

I don't know whether she has used the deodorant. I will know, of course, before long.

Before I finish dressing, Lucius is back from church and is in the kitchen hollering, with fake bossiness, "Where are my ranch hands? Where is my grub? I need to eat hearty. I have lots of riding to do on the range."

Ifa appears, looking much too good in my castoffs. She also looks scared, because my husband is so loud, and she is not used to him.

"Come and eat," I tell her. "Dad wants to take us out to see the horses and the Cowboys." My checkered sweater, a fad of three seasons ago, looks so fabulous on her skinny figure I feel like asking for it back.

It is sunny in the park, but it is February, after all, and there is not much warmth even in the thin sunshine. Ifa shivers as she is introduced to the other Cowboys and to their trainees, a dozen teenage boys.

"The first thing they learn is to walk a horse," says Lucius's old friend Charlie Matthews, holding the reins of his big gray mare, Beulah. "Stay by your horse's side, make no sudden movements, and never get so far behind your horse he can't see you." He holds the reins out to Ifa. "Want to try it?"

During the week Charlie is an undertaker, with all the seriousness that goes along with it, including a black suit, but on weekends he blossoms and becomes a total cowboy, with a red neckerchief, big white felt hat, chaps, boots, and spurs. Sometimes I think the main reason these guys go in for riding is the chance to wear the getup.

"No, thank you," Ifa says through chattering teeth. "I am too cold. I will watch."

Lucius says riding would warm us up, and I know he is right, but Ifa is scared, and I am wary myself of horses that I don't know very well.

"I wish I could get under one of those blankets," Ifa says, eyeing the horses' heavy plaid covers with envy. We settle for cups of hot chocolate from a vendor. It helps.

There are about ten boys who have turned out for riding lessons, plus six horses and six aging Cowboys in colorful outfits. The boys will spend half of the day caring for the horses, grooming them, cleaning their hooves, and combing their manes. Only after all that work do they get to ride. We watch them parade past us, and it is a beautiful sight, brighter than the park's display of leaves last fall. "Beautiful, aren't they?" I say to Ifa.

"Yes, Mum, but I do not understand. These are black men. Why do they dress up in costumes from Wild West movies?"

"They are not costumes from movies, they are their heritage."

She snorts as if she does not believe me. "Mum, how can that be? I have seen many movies of the Wild West, and the cowboys in them are always white."

I do not feel up to arguing with Hollywood's lies today. Live here a while longer, and you will understand, I think. "I will get Lucius to explain it to you," I say.

One by one, the Cowboys are mounting their steeds to show their pupils what their horses can do. The boys look excited. Ifa looks bored.

Lucius gets up on Snipes last, and puts him through his paces—left turn, right turn, circle left and right, up on his hind legs, a low, kneeling bow. Then he gallops away on Snipes as fast as they can go. As they tear by us, horse and rider seem like one beast, muscles rippling, thighs gripping. I am so excited I forget to breathe. Then I looked at Ifa. She is breathless, too, and has a glazed look on her face.

I am glad when Lucius dismounts and puts one of the teenagers, Wayne, up on Snipes instead.

"That was very exciting, Dod," she says, clinging to my husband's arm. The whole idea of a two-thousand-pound beast moving between my legs is more scary than exciting to me, but I understand why it turns some females on.

"Do you want to try it?" he offers.

"Oh, no. I would rather watch you," Ifa says.

On the way home she squeezes between us to get warm, which makes shifting gears difficult for Lucius. As she huddles down between us, I think that, for all her size, she often reminds me of a little girl.

"Dod," she says, "I like your secret society. They seem to have more fun than Mum's."

"What is Mum's secret society?" asks Lucius, and swears under his breath when the car stalls a second time. "Move your knee, Ifa, so I can shift gears."

"That ladies' club where I modeled African clothes."

"And what is my secret society?" he asks her.

"Oh, Dod, don't tease me. You know who they are. Those men who ride horses, Mister Charlie and the rest. I saw your gods all over the park today."

"Gods? What gods?"

"Those statues of spirits on horseback. Those gods of war."

I start to laugh. There are so many statues of generals on horseback in our park that nobody notices them. Except, I guess, foreigners like Ifa.

She rebukes me. "You should not laugh at the war gods, Mum. They can be very vengeful. Those boys I saw today, Dod, when will you initiate them into your secret society? What is the ceremony like?"

Lucius who looked very serious at the mention of gods, has begun laughing, too. "I can't tell you, Ifa. Like you said, we are a secret society. We have our secrets."

NINE

ONE OF THE JOYS of having a daughter, I always imagined, would be buying her pretty things. When my friends had baby girls, I would go on shopping sprees in the infant wear departments, marveling at the details of rosebuds hand-embroidered on collars, of denim made into little rompers and bloomers, of little checkered shoes cut out of the same fabric as little checkered dresses. I would also marvel at the prices, as high as for adult clothes, but I had so much fun I never minded paying. Later, I would enjoy myself just as much in the toddlers' and girls' departments.

All the fun of shopping for my friends' daughters always stopped when they hit their teens and insisted on doing their own clothes shopping. Writing checks and inserting them in birthday cards is okay, it's a given duty, but it's hardly fun.

On the morning after our excursion in the park, Ifa wakes me first thing, because she has decided to clean out my closet. I have forgotten that I agreed to let her do this. She pulls out piles of things I had forgotten: a vest with peasant embroidery, a black catsuit, a bright orange tunic, a long, ugly brown dress covered with dust balls.

"Do you want thees, Mum? How about thees? It looks like it has never been worn."

Peasant embroidery is for peasants. Catsuits are for cats—

skinny ones. Orange is a color that looks best on oranges. And the one time I wore that long brown dress, Lucius was startled. He said he thought at first that I was naked, because no matter where he looked, he saw the same color.

"No, no, no," I tell her. "Toss them all out, unless you can use them." When I come out of the shower, the heap of discards has become a mountain. Ifa is queen of the mountain. She stands atop it holding a navy blue jumper up to herself, considering its possibilities.

"It's yours," I tell her. "Help yourself to anything in that pile you want. No, wait a minute." I can hardly see in the morning before my coffee, but I have just noticed my favorite wool blazers, a gold crepe one and a long red one with a black velvet collar, sticking out of the pile. I rush to retrieve them.

"Don't toss out any more of my clothes unless you ask me first, Ifa."

"But, Mum," she reproves me, "you must clear out the old stuff, or you will never get new. Old stagnant stuff clogs the pipeline from the gods."

I give her a thoughtful look. Ifa seems ignorant, but apparently she is wise, too.

"Well," I say, "help yourself, if you can use anything in that pile. We might find you some better things later on, though. After I get some coffee in me, we might go shopping."

Ifa discards the jumper like a piece of distasteful garbage. She cheers and yells, jumping up and down on the pile of clothes that will probably go to Goodwill. I am happy, too. As a child I only had one doll, but my biggest joy was dressing her up in the scraps left from the clothes Mama made for me.

And now I have a great big doll to dress! I am so excited as I take Ifa to our mall, I assume that she is, too. But when I steer her toward the discount houses where I get most of my clothes, she balks. "I do not think I will find anything there," she says.

"Why not?" I ask.

"Mum, I am looking for quality."

We pause at the window of the International Bazaar, where I

look longingly at some ivory bangles, a matching necklace hung with elephants, and an assortment of long, lovely swooping clothes in exotic fabrics that need Ifa's height to show them off.

"You would look marvelous in that," I say, pointing to a three-piece outfit in orange stuff that includes a knee-length kente vest. "Or that and that," I add, indicating a black tunic bordered with a row of parading market women. The tunic next to it is white, and adorned with a row of giraffes.

She snorts. "And where would I wear those things, Mum? To a costume party?"

I was thinking of dressing her up for the next Divas meeting. I say so.

"Mum, am I not exotic enough for those women as it is?"

Chastised and guilty, I trot behind my tall visitor like a faithful sheepdog as she charges through the mall with her long-legged strides. Finally she stops at a boutique—one of those places where prices are never displayed, and languid saleswomen study their fingernails in the shadows. I have always avoided stores like this on principle.

I catch up. I am short of breath, and my toes and calves are hurting. My lower back will act up next. "Where do you think you will find this quality you want, Ifa?"

"Here," she says decisively.

I have told Ifa in advance that our total budget is $350.00. We have agreed that our first purchase will be an all-purpose, all-season coat, something that repels rain and has a removable lining. I had in mind a little number I'd seen at the Fashion Wearhouse for $79.95, your basic trench with a zip-out acrylic lining. A neutral-colored coat like that, as I explained to Ifa, showing her my black one, would take her through all three coat seasons.

Apparently she listened to part of what I said, the part about style, because a trench with a removable lining is what she comes out of the dressing room wearing. But she did not hear the part about price. This item has about as much in common with my coat as a champion poodle has with a short-haired mutt from the junkyard. Both come under the general heading of "dog," but that is about all.

This coat is black, generously cut, and belted, with a fake caracul collar and lining, and yards of beautiful braid embroidery on its shoulders and lapels. Its price tag, of course, gobbles up our entire budget in one bite. But it is well made and beautiful, and it looks fabulous on her.

"You see, Mum, this fabric will last," she says. "It is real quality. Feel."

I take it between my thumb and forefinger. I never thought gabardine could feel like silk. "Ask the saleslady to hold it for you, Ifa," I say. "Tell her we will be back in a little while."

That haughty person has mysteriously appeared. "You will never find a better coat for your daughter, madam. That coat looks as if it were made for her."

I melt when she calls Ifa my daughter. I suppose I will get used to it someday. But this is all so new. Like a new romance. A honeymoon.

Asking the saleslady to hold the coat for us is a mistake.

"As you wish, madam," she says, and takes it from us. I do not mean that offending her was a mistake. I mean that putting off the purchase was not so smart. We end up going back for the coat, and before we do, we have spent all of the money I have allotted. We look at sweaters, and I discover that Ifa has a taste only for cashmere, and that nothing else, not even the finest wool, will do. We look at slacks, skirts, and jackets, all with designer labels. Ifa will not even look at the no-frills clothes I usually buy, or enter the bare-bones discount stores where I buy them.

Finally I give in and pay for the three pieces she wants most— a pair of slacks, a matching sweater, and a skirt, each with a famous label. We have already blown our budget, and Ifa still does not have a coat.

I steer her toward an outlet store where I have sometimes found amazing bargains—an Ultrasuede skirt set, for instance, for twenty dollars each piece. But she is not interested in the coats this little place called the Treasure Chest has for sale. None of them fit her, anyway.

"That coat I tried on is the only coat I want," she declares.

"But Ifa, I have bills to pay." There is the huge water bill at the shop, for instance, and the electric bill there. There are also the shop insurance and my life insurance, and the extra groceries I must buy, now that there are three adults in the house.

"It is okay, Mum," Ifa says. "I will just wear the coat you gave me." Maybe I am imagining the hint of martyrdom in her voice and the resignation in her expression. But I know that if I have to see her in that short flame-red jacket every day for even a week, I will go blind. I can't imagine what made me buy a coat in such a blazing tomato red.

"Come on," I say. I pull out my Visa card, which is supposed to be only for emergencies, and head back to the boutique.

"I will wear it," she tells the saleslady, with a haughty attitude that humbles that grand person a little, and puts the flaming shorty jacket in one of her shopping bags. The new black coat is a vast improvement, I must admit. She looks like a queen in it.

Like her faithful old lady-in-waiting, I tote some of the bags and follow her to the car.

"I love you, Mum," Ifa says with a big smile that would melt a glacier, and plants a kiss on my cheek. "Thank you very much." To hell with the bill. It is worth it just to see her smile like that.

Before I catch myself, I am on the verge of asking if there is anything else she wants.

TEN

VYESTER NEVER CALLS ME on the phone unless something urgent has come up. She's not the type to just gab and dish on the telephone. Lucius is the same way. They act like they're afraid a telephone is a live animal that might get irritated and turn on them and bite them if they talk too long. Country people who aren't used to telephones and poor people who can't afford them are like that.

So I am prepared for a serious crisis when the phone rings early on Saturday morning and I pick it up and hear Vy's voice. But she works her way around to the crisis gradually, as usual.

"How you doin', Miss Zena?"

"Fine, thank you."

"Are you having a nice weekend so far?"

"Yes, we really are. Last night was quiet, but nice. We just stayed home and talked for awhile after we watched that new show on UPN—you know, the one about the black family who are trying to get used to the suburbs. Did you see it?"

"No." Something more urgent than TV is on Vy's mind. "Miss Zena, you remember you heard me speak of my sister, Magdalene?"

"Of course." Vy's younger sister has done her best to live up, or down, to her name. She had four children before she was twenty-one, and had a total of eight the last time anybody bothered to count. Her trials and tribulations with men, children, landlords and the law would keep a soap opera going for at least five years.

"Actually, I think I met her once." Maggie is ten years younger than Vy, but that day when she stumbled into Vy's kitchen, she looked twice her age. Haggard, bedraggled, and hung over.

"That's right. You came over one time when she dropped by for a little visit. Well, she's in a bad situation."

When was she not? I am wondering, while I wait for Vy to fill me in.

"She's three months behind on her rent, and if she don't pay at least two months of it now, the landlord is going to put her out."

"That's a shame, Vy, but I don't see why it's your responsibility." Vy and I have had many talks about the burdens imposed on black people by their families. I feel that's why most of us never get anywhere. Soon as we get two slices of bread together and start to think about making a sandwich, here comes a relative to claim one slice. I maintain that Vy has had too much family in her life. She says that I haven't had enough. Maybe we are both right.

"Miss Zena, if I don't help her out, she'll have to move in with me. Me and Fred, we can't stand to have her and her bad kids here. We got enough on us now."

"I understand." Maybe we just think we've moved far away from Africa. When it comes to dependent relatives, we're in the same place. The only difference between Africa and America is, Vy doesn't have a compound where she could build her sister a house.

"You know, Miss Zena, Maggie's had a hard life. She was only nine when our mother died, and she got passed around to our different relatives. She lived three or four different places before she was eighteen. I couldn't take her, I was just getting on my feet, so she got the notion nobody really wanted her. I think that accounts for her changing mens so often and getting herself so many bad habits. Now she just cleaned up her act and got her kids back and found this place for them, and they took away her Section Eight. It doesn't seem fair."

"No, it doesn't, does it?"

Of course I am going to help Vy to help her sister, and she knows it. I would do anything for her. But I don't think Maggie is a good risk.

"But, Vy, if you lend her that much money, how are you going to get it back?"

"She has a job now, Miss Zena. A good job downtown— short-order cook in a busy restaurant. Plus, she helps out a caterer on weekends. You know Maggie always could cook. But she just started working, so she won't get paid for a couple of weeks, and her landlord won't wait that long."

"How much does she owe her landlord?"

"Twelve hundred. See, she lost her Section Eight when they caught her son using drugs, so now she has to pay all her rent herself. But she only got to pay eight hundred right now."

I sigh at the misery that seems to get handed down the generations. Maggie on drugs, and now her son.

"Can it wait till Tuesday?"

"Yes, ma'am."

"Don't call me that." I don't want any more titles from Vy. It's bad enough, after all these years of friendship and working side by side every day, that she keeps sticking "Miss" in front of my name.

"Okay, Miss Zena. I'll pay you back two hundred a month, if that's all right."

"Fine, but a hundred a month would do." I can imagine the strain paying two hundred a month would put on Vy and Fred.

"So, how's Mister Lucius?"

"He's fine."

"How's your bush baby?"

"My what?" I can't believe Vyester just said that to me. Of course, we are on the phone. Bold and bigmouthed though she is, she would never have the nerve to say that to my face.

"Vyester, what are you talking about?"

"That big old African girl, Ifa. She's from the bush, ain't she?"

"Well, yes." Ifa has begun to tell me about her village home, how it's way out in the country near a big river, and how her relatives all live in a cluster of houses with a courtyard in the middle. They have money, though, so the houses are not all round, thatched homemade jobs. Some of them, like her mother's, have regular walls, floors, windows, screens, even electricity and running water. Her mother has the biggest house, the village spiritual leader has the next biggest one, and the poor relations who depend on her family have the smallest ones.

"She's from the bush, and she's your baby. So, she's your bush baby," says my sassy friend.

Black people are usually very sensitive about being compared to animals. If Vyester were in the room with me, and no one else was around, I might really jump on her case. I might do it even if our husbands were present, though not in front of customers. But over the phone, she knows she's at a safe distance.

"Why are you so hard on Ifa, Vy?" I ask her. "Do you have something against Africans?"

"I just don't want you to get hurt, Miss Zena. I can tell you care a lot for that girl."

"There's more to it than that," I say suspiciously.

"No, that's it. I can't really explain why I'm worried. It's just a feeling I have. I enjoyed my lunch on Wednesday, but she gave me a funny feeling. Something about her just ain't right."

"I think you just don't like Africans."

"That's not true. Africans are okay with me." She is silent for a minute. "Although they have cost us a lot of money."

"How have they done that?"

She explains to me about Fred's second job, how it was taken away by Oloris, and how they seem to have all the other part-time hustles in town sewn up tight. Sometimes I forget how life must be for a hardworking couple like her and Fred, how people like them have to squeeze every nickel and always be on the lookout for ways to make extra money. I don't know how I could have forgotten. It wasn't so long ago that it was the same way for us. Of course, if they made that lazy son of theirs get a job, it would take a big load off of them. Sonny's eighteen, and unoccupied except for lawbreaking.

I decide to show her how it feels to have a family member compared to a beast. "How's your big grown house ape?"

"My what?"

"Your son."

"I guess I deserve that, Miss Zena. Sonny's not doing so good. In fact, that's another reason why I called. I have to take some time off next week to go see about him."

Sonny just turned eighteen, but his rap sheet is as long as a medium-sized telephone book. "What did he do now?"

"Got caught robbing a sporting-goods store, and why he needed any more sneakers is beyond me. We bought him four pairs last year. Two pairs at Christmas."

I do not say what I think, which is that Sonny has graduated from wanting sneakers to wanting money for other things. "Did he take any sneakers?"

"Well, no, he didn't. He didn't have time. He and his friends set off the alarm, and the cops got there before they could leave. The worst thing is, one of his friends shot the store owner. That makes it felonious assault, not just burglary. And if the man dies, it's felony murder. One year to life."

Thanks to her son, Vy has acquired quite a vocabulary about crime and punishment, one I do not enjoy hearing. Once, recently, she spent a half hour regaling the women in the shop with the differences among Murder One, Murder Two, and manslaughter. I have to keep a very watchful eye on what goes on in my shop, to keep it tasteful and pleasant for my customers. I finally pulled my dear friend aside and explained to her that a fascinated audience does not always mean people think well of the speaker. They might be enjoying the same thrill of disgust some people feel when they watch a snake handler.

"Let's hope the man recovers, then."

"I'm praying for him, Miss Zena. Will you and Mr. Lucius pray, too?"

"Absolutely."

"I'd ask Ifa to pray, but she might not believe in the same God we do. I wouldn't want her foreign prayers to clash with ours and cancel them out."

I sigh. "She told me she is a Christian, Vyester."

"Yeah, well, they all say that. In private they pray to snakes and alligators. What happens next week is a preliminary hearing, and we have to be there to show support for him. I'll let you know which day."

Crisis after crisis after crisis. Sonny's arrest, Maggie's eviction, Lord knows what next. This just in: Today's emergency will be followed by tomorrow's disaster, and the next day's catastrophe. That's Vyester's life. That's probably the average black woman's life. At least, every day, I make a few of them feel better. At least for a few hours.

"Well, I gotta go. Thanks a lot, Miss Zena."

She hangs up before I can say, "You're welcome."

Bush baby. What a horrible thing to call that lovely girl who makes me feel like she has spent her entire life with me. Who calls me Mum. Who is so thoughtful and so full of affection, and is always all smiles and helpfulness. Yesterday, for instance, she cut some ivy from the front yard and put it on the table in a water glass, to add some life to the place. She made a pot of tea and brought it to me. She boiled some leaves in a pan and made a potion for Lucius to use as an aftershave, and rubbed it on his face to show him how. He loved it. Then she sorted and shined up all my jewelry.

She is country, there's no denying that, but since my mama was puredee country, too, I love that about her. Mama never wore shoes indoors if she could help it, and neither does Ifa. All day long her big bare feet pad back and forth in the house, and she'd rather squat on the floor than sit down. I love her for being so country, just as I love the country in Lucius.

Last night the two of them had what Lucius called "an old-fashioned back-porch lying contest." They sat around the living room telling tall stories, while I listened. They swapped stories of ghosts and magic, giant yams and cornstalks, brooms that could fly and turtles that could talk, and they kept topping each other till I couldn't tell who had won. I got sleepy around midnight and went to bed and left them still talking.

I think Ifa is good company for Lucius. He isn't as busy as I am. He needs an outlet besides politics.

I hope Vy doesn't force me to choose between her and my new baby, because the way I feel now, I know which one of them will have to go—and it isn't Ifa.

 **ELEVEN**

"ZENA, DID YOU PAY the taxes on this house?"

Lucius is sitting at his desk in the Back Room, surrounded by bills, checkbooks, and ledgers. He is holding up our joint savings passbook.

"Of course not, Lucius, you know you always do that."

"Then what was this eight-hundred-dollar withdrawal on Saturday for?"

It's my money, too. Why do I suddenly feel so guilty?

"I had to loan Vy some money to keep her sister from being homeless," I explain. "She will pay us back. A hundred dollars a month."

His voice is mild and gentle, not disapproving at all, and I am grateful. "Well, when she does, make sure you put it back in this account. Little sums like that have a way of disappearing."

"I know." And when, I am wondering, did a hundred dollars become a little sum to us? We used to get excited when ten dollars was left over at the end of the month.

"You took out another three hundred and fifty dollars last Monday. Mind telling me what for?" He asks this mildly, too, so I don't mind answering.

"Clothes for Ifa," I tell him. "She didn't have a stitch to wear."

My Lucius is a patient man, and his blood pressure has been under control so far. But now he is beginning to go ballistic on me. "Good God, Zena," he says, "are we supposed to take care of the entire world?"

"You're the one who's always lecturing me about being Christians and helping the less fortunate."

"Christians, yes. Crazy, no." He looks up at me over his reading glasses. He looks old. With a pang, I see how his hair has receded in high Vs on either side of his forehead, leaving only a widow's peak and gray tufts in the center. But the tufts are long. He needs a haircut. Are we that poor?

"Dammit, Zena, the real estate taxes are six months delinquent. But if I pay them I'll have to borrow money for gas and newspapers."

"Borrow enough for a haircut while you're at it," I say. "How much do you need?" I am a little short now, after helping out my friend and clothing my daughter, but I can always make the electric company wait.

"I charged a coat for Ifa. Another three-fifty," I admit next. I might as well tell him. He will find out anyway. When I get too busy, he pays all of our bills. Some of them are mine, but I just let him do a total and tell me what it is, then write one big check.

Our friends never talk about money, but I think every married couple has a different way of handling it. We tried a joint checking account, but it didn't work out for us. One of us was always forgetting to write something down or to mention it to the other one. Now we have joint savings and separate checking, and have agreed to discuss all items over a hundred dollars. Usually Lucius takes care of the cars and the house, except for groceries. I take care of food and the shop, and we pool the rest of our money.

"Three Hundred and Fifty Dollars!" he exclaims in capital letters, the way Langston Hughes used to write it. I can hear his high blood pressure kicking in now. "Dammit, Zena, when have *you* had a coat that cost that much?"

"Not in a long time," I admit. "If ever." Back in my Glamour Queen days, I had a few spectacular custom-mades, but the seamstresses I knew were so glad to get the work, I don't think any of them ever charged me that much. Even my favorite, that wine-colored velvet evening coat with the collar that stood up in back like Queen Elizabeth's ruff, was only two hundred.

"But, Lucius, the coat is well made, and it looks great on her. Children are expensive. When they need things, they really need them."

"Ifa is not a child!" he explodes. "She is a needy person, yes, but you do not have to indulge her every whim. If she needed a coat, you should have taken her to Goodwill, not a designer boutique."

"But she's used to the best!" I exclaim. "I told you she wasn't poor. Her family was rich." Besides, I think, Goodwill would not have been fun. Shopping for Ifa was the best fun I'd had in years.

"She'll have to get used to what we can afford," he grumbles. Self-pity creeps into his voice. "I need a coat, too, but I'll have to wait. The sewer tax is due. So is the house insurance."

"Then pay them," I say.

"We owe the dentist four hundred. What are we going to do about the real estate taxes?"

"Pay half."

That's something I learned from an article in one of those supermarket magazines. When you have a big bill, pay half. When you get a big windfall, save half. Never lay out all of your money.

"When will we pay the other half?"

"The next time we get a large sum of money."

"And when will that be?" he demands. "Zena, what's wrong with you? Next you'll be talking about what we'll do when we hit the number." That hurts. Both of us despise the government's numbers racket and pity the people who fall for it.

"And whatever happened to our agreement to discuss all items over a hundred dollars? You've broken it twice! No, three times."

I lower my voice. I learned long ago that this is an effective way to counter his shouting. "I know, Lucius. I'm sorry. But they were emergencies."

"Seven hundred dollars' worth of clothes for Ifa was an emergency? Zena, I don't know what's happened to you. You've been throwing money around like a drunken woman, buying frills for a girl we never saw until a few days ago. What are we getting into here, Zena? Is this your adoption fantasy again? Or have you just gone out of your mind?"

I don't deny either. My husband knows me all too well.

"Well," he mutters, more to himself and his ledger than to me, "I know what I can do about this. Put pressure on them to speed up her visa. Then we can send her on her merry way."

This sends a cold chill down through my chest to the bottom of my stomach. Yes, I think, I am crazy. But I won't admit it.

Last night Ifa said "I love you, Mum" again before she went to bed, and added, "I am so hoppy here with you!"

Well, maybe I'm crazy, and maybe we are going broke, but I am hoppy, too.

 TWELVE

SHE IS A MARVEL. She is a miracle. She is an angel from heaven come straight down to earth.

This has been a very hard day, and when I get in, I expect to have to do some more work around the house. Though I have spent ten hours styling hair in a steaming shop, I expect, like most women, to at least have to pick up a couple of rooms before I start cooking dinner.

Instead, my house is shining. My living room is so neat and clean, I have an impulse to go outside and check, see did I walk in the wrong house. But my key opened the door, after all, and that's my same zebra-striped rug, and my same red couch and black chairs. The framed picture of me and Lucius with his horse Pickett hanging over the fireplace convinces me I'm in the right place. But it isn't the same place I left this morning. There are no magazines and newspapers tossed around. No half-empty coffee cups, snack plates, or glasses. No cigar ashes, which Lucius is liable to leave in all the rooms when I'm not home.

I go in the kitchen and am almost blinded by the glare of light reflecting off a freshly waxed floor, a polished stove top, and shiny pots and pans. I breathe deeply. The room has a lovely lemon smell instead of the stink of the fish I baked last night.

"Anybody home?" I call out.

Ifa steps from behind the door. "How do you like your kitchen, Mum?"

"It's beautiful," I say honestly. "I don't think it's been this clean since it was new."

"As long as I am with you, it will look like this," she promises. "I am sorry I only did these two rooms, but I had to stop." She holds up her hand. There is a rag wrapped around it.

"What happened?"

"Oh, it is nothing. Just a little burn. Don't even think about it."

Of course, I unwrap it in half a second. The side of her hand is red and blistered and looks angry. "What happened, Ifa?"

"I was shining your stove, and I must have touched one of the burner buttons, Mum. The burner lit, and the rag caught on fire, and before I could do anything, the fire touched my hand." She shrugs prettily. "It could have been much worse."

I want to kiss it and make it well. Instead, I direct her to hold her hand under cold water, to cool the burn, and then pour peroxide on it to prevent infection. Finally, I squeeze on some aloe vera gel. No bandage, because burns need air. Then I make her sit down.

"I am so sorry this happened to you, Ifa."

"It is my fault. I did not feed the fire gods. Usually I throw an offering of salt in the flame to them. But I thought I could skip that, since I was not planning to cook." Before I can react to this, she asks, "How was your day, Mum?"

"Typical," I say. "Six women who were happy with my work, and one who complained."

"That one who complained did not know what she was talking about. She was very lucky to have her hair fixed by you."

"Thank you."

"It is only the truth. You are very talented. I know I am a very lucky person to be living in your house. You and Dod are special, wonderful people. If God is kind, I will get my wish to repay you someday."

I mumble something about no repayment being necessary. I mean it. These days, I feel complete, as if the third person who was missing in my life has been supplied. In the mornings I wake up bright and cheerful, looking forward to a happy day. Normally I am very sensitive to weather. Two cloudy days in a row used to depress me, but not anymore. Now, it is as if the spirit of sunshine has come to live with us. She glows, she is so warm and beautiful. Sun child; daughter of Africa. And she calls me Mum. How could anyone not love her?

I want to smack Vyester for being so cruel and rude to Ifa the day I took them to lunch, but she is still my best friend, and I know she means well. Since that lunch date, though, we have not had as much to say to each other as we once did. We are not cool to each other; we just find plenty of reasons at work to be too busy for talking.

"I wanted to do some laundry for you, too, Mum," Ifa says, smiling shyly, "but I did not know how to operate your machine."

I pinch myself to see whether I have died and gone to heaven.

"I would have had your bath ready," the angelic creature continues, "but I did not know what time to expect you. I will run it now."

I know I ought to stop her, but I don't. She assures me that she only needs to use her good hand to run my tub. My evening slump has set in, the way it always does an hour after I get home. I kick off my shoes and let the sound of rushing water and the fragrance of honeysuckle bath salts seep into my pores, driving away the smells of chemicals and scorched hair that cling to me.

"Would you like a massage, Mum?" Ifa asks when I finally come out of the bathroom

"Why not?" I say, momentarily forgetting her injured hand.

But with the fingers of only her good one, she is able to press out all the knots and kinks of my day from their hiding places in my neck and shoulders. When she is done, I feel rested and pampered, like a queen.

"How does your hand feel now, Ifa?"

"I forgot all about it. It is nothing, Mum. There is pain that is merely annoyance and inconvenience, like this burn on my hand, and then there is real pain. Have you ever heard of female circumcision?"

"Dear God. Did they do that to you?"

"No. I escaped. But they did it to my sister Cecelia. My father paid the priests and the women who do it to leave me alone. I had a fake operation, where they held me down and told me to scream, but that was all. But later the people found out that my surgery was faked. They are angry because I have cheated them and the gods. Now that my father is dead, and I no longer have his protection, to be at home in our village is dangerous for me."

Her recital makes me shiver in my most private places. Later, puttering in the kitchen, I ponder the goodness of God, who brought me Ifa, and wonder what He wants me to do for her. She is too beautiful and too fine to spend the rest of her days doing housework. So was my mother, of course, but that was a different time. In those days, there was nothing else for an uneducated black woman to do.

I think some more as I mold a turkey meat loaf and pop it into the oven with some red potatoes, then thin-slice some carrots to stir-fry with Italian green beans. She has no skills, that is the problem. I have seen her diploma from a place called, I think, the University of Calabash. It is decorated with so many fruits and vegetables it looks like an ad for a produce store. But I have yet to find out what they taught her. Also, she has no green card, but maybe she will get one.

When Lucius finally comes in, he has that look on his face I hate to see on any of our men, the look of failure. An expression that is droopy and apologetic. Feet that are dragging. Head and shoulders that are bowed. I hate to think that our foreign visitor has caused him to look this way.

Ifa doesn't seem to notice. She runs to him and pulls on his arm, crying, "What news, Dod? Tell me what has happened. Did you go back to that office today? Did they extend my visa?"

"No," he says, and flops into a chair. "It will take longer than I thought. It's not so easy anymore."

"Senator Russo's people were not happy with her," I translate.

"Well, they were not exactly full of enthusiasm. Besides, there is a quota for legal African immigrants."

Lucius and I exchange glances. We know why there is a quota. It is one reason we have been helping Ifa.

"In the meantime," he goes on, "the best thing she can get is a student visa."

"But I have finished school," Ifa declares.

"Don't tell anybody," I warn her.

"They probably wouldn't respect her degree, anyway," Lucius says. "You know, when I came north, I had to repeat high school, because the colleges would not accept my Georgia high school diploma. Unless she wants to go back to Olori, she had better get a student visa and take some night courses."

"That will not put any money in my pocket," Ifa complains.

Lucius shrugs. "It's the best I can do right now. Here." He lays some community college and adult night school brochures on the table. "Find something that interests you, a course that you can't get at home, something that will train you for work that is needed there."

After dinner, she begins reading the brochures. "China painting? Ceramics? Tai chi? What is Tai chi?"

"No," I say. "You need something that might lead to a job."

"Something," Lucius adds, "that you can take home and use to serve your people. That is what our government seems to want you to do. What do they need in Olori?"

"What is a stationary engineer?"

"Someone who takes care of heating systems," Lucius explains.

"Oh. We do not need heat in Olori." She studies some more. "Ah. Refrigeration and air conditioning. Good. There are not enough facilities at home for keeping things cold."

Lucius nods. "Good idea. But you would need a lot of math and physics in that course. Are you good at math?"

"No. But it does not matter. I will soon have a job."

"What did you major in at school, Ifa?" I ask her suddenly.

"Drama," she tells me. I should have known. "I had starring

roles at school in everything from Shakespeare to Soyinka. I am going to be a great star someday." She adds, "But do not worry, Mum. I know I have to work. Before I finish that course, I will have my green card and a job."

My confident daughter. My discouraged husband. How sorry I feel for them both.

 THIRTEEN

IFA OFTEN HAS the phone tied up all day. Like any teenager, she has a serious phone jones. I can almost always find her by following the telephone cord. Once I get to it, there she is, jabbering into the receiver. She has only been in this country a short while, so who, I wonder, can she find to talk to?

When our phone bill comes in, we find out. I also find out that she has some extremely strange ideas about America and Americans, as well as some very annoying ideas about what she calls "block people," meaning African Americans.

Block people, she says, do not realize how fortunate they are to live here in America, where everything is easy. They do not have to struggle the way their counterparts do in the rest of the world. If they do not succeed, it is because they are lazy. Most of them are also stupid, immoral, dirty, and inclined to criminal behavior.

I catch on to her attitudes when we go for a ride and she has much to say about the sloppiness of those "block people" who have so much trash in their streets. I inform her that the trash collectors have been on strike. I also say that I have heard that open sewers are common in the capital of her country, and that friends who have visited there say that the bathrooms were in poor working order, if they worked at all, and were seldom clean. This shuts her up—for a while.

Later, while standing in the checkout line at the supermarket, I hear a delighted yell behind me. Ifa has dipped both hands into one of the bulk-food barrels and filled them with peanuts.

"Groundnuts!" she exclaims, stuffing her face with roasted peanuts. "I just love groundnuts!" A shining smile stretches across her face as she dips into the barrel again. And, before I can stop her, again.

I whisper to her to put the nuts back. "Next time," I say, "do not announce to the world that you are stealing food."

"I was not stealing, Mum," she says, drawing herself up haughtily. "At home we always help ourselves to foods in the market."

I wonder how the poor vendors earn a living. This is a problem that does not concern Ifa.

"They seem to sell everything in this store, Mum," she says next. "Why do they not sell blood?"

At first I think I have not heard her right. "What did you say?"

"I said 'blood.' Blood from cows, sheeps, and chickens. There must be a lot of blood when those animals are killed."

"Ifa," I say, "here we do not drink blood."

"Well, at home we do. I miss it. It is very nourishing and gives lots of energy."

For my own peace of mind, I decide to forget about this conversation. We run around the corner to the fish market for some catfish fillets, and next door for some bread crumbs and eggs to coat them with for baking, because I have forgotten those items. We are waited on in both stores by Koreans. Leaving, Ifa declares that "block people" do not own the stores in their own neighborhoods because they are too lazy to run businesses.

In the evening, on TV, we watch the nightly crime reports. "Look at that," she says. "It is always block people who break the law."

I remind her that most of the police, as well as the owners of all the TV stations, not to mention their advertisers, are white, and that is what they want their audiences to think.

I also remind myself that she is still a child in many ways. She forgets when making these loud pronouncements that her adopted parents are also "block."

But it is when I look at our phone bill that I realize she also thinks all Americans are rich.

Eighteen calls to Olori; the longest, a hundred and twelve minutes. Our phone bill is upwards of fifteen hundred dollars.

"I am sorry, Mum," she says, sincerely. "But I was homesick for my family. A telephone bill—what is that to rich people like you and Dod?"

"What makes you think we are rich?"

"Of course you are rich. Look at your cars and your clothes. Look at your house. Everyone knows that all Americans are rich. That is why everybody wants to come to America. Once a person is here, it is easy to succeed."

It must be the fault of our State Department, Lucius decides later, after we have been to the telephone company and made arrangements to pay off our bill in six months. Who else has spread all these lies around the world about the wealth of all Americans and the ease of success here? It has to come from official sources.

But I want to know why. Why do they excite everyone's imagination with dreams of wealth and easy success? Why do they make America so attractive everybody in the world wants to come here—and half of them do?

I put it down to the natural human tendency to brag. Our leaders and our spokespeople just have to mouth off about how great their country is. It is also human nature to exaggerate when blowing one's own horn.

Lucius sees a more sinister purpose. White people are angry with us because we rioted and demonstrated in the sixties and got some civil rights. They want, he says, to flood the country with other minorities so that these new people can take our place and take away what small gains we have made. Whether that's the plan or not, it certainly seems to be the result. And we dumb blacks are so generous and hospitable—with nothing— that we are assisting in the takeover.

Include Lucius and Zena Lawson in the dumb, generous, and

hospitable category, even though we are not in the lazy, immoral, dirty, or criminal bunch, and certainly not in the rich group to which our visitor thinks we belong.

When we get back from the phone company, I really let her have it.

"What kind of fools do you think we are, Ifa? What do you think gives you the right to call overseas on our phone? Girl, I am not rich. I slaved like a dog to get to the place where I could even think about being comfortable. I scrubbed floors and toilets to pay for beauty school. Lucius did farm labor before he came north, and afterward, too. There are no easy roads for any of us black folks in this country. Where did you get such ideas?"

"I don't know, Mum. Everyone in Olori thinks you are all rich."

"Well, we're not. Paying off this bill is going to be a real hardship for me and Dod, I mean Dad."

"Mum, I am sorry. When I get some money, I will repay you."

"I certainly hope so," I say, my anger running out of steam.

Later that evening, I go to the Back Room, which I regard as Lucius's and my sanctuary, almost as private as our bedroom. I am aggrieved to find her there before me. She has brought her treasure chest and opened it for Lucius, who is thoughtfully studying a small mahogany idol with enormous genital equipment.

She turns to me and says, "Mum, this is real art, the very best, not the commercial stuff you have now. It has been used in ceremonies. It has the true African spirit."

Now, Lucius and I were always very Afrocentric, in a conservative sort of way. We didn't demonstrate against apartheid or run around shouting "Free Mandela!" but we wouldn't invest in South Africa or in any companies that did, and we gave money for Rwandan relief. Lucius contributed to Africare and Transafrica, until he decided that some of the people who staffed those organizations were in it for the money. It was the same discovery that stopped him from holding office. He went into politics because he thought it was a way of helping his people. He gave up holding an elected office when he learned that most of the politicians were making false promises and selling us out.

We began going to Kwanzaa when they first started having it at our community center. I even took African dance lessons at the center, and scandalized our refined neighbors with my dancing.

One night last summer, the Nairobi African Drum Ensemble was performing half a block down from my house. Actually, they're just a bunch of neighborhood kids who perform in parades and who get together with some congas, djembes, shekeres, and a bata to practice. Usually I don't say anything when they play, because I hate to discourage young people who are doing something creative instead of breaking the law, but it was after ten-thirty, and we do have a noise ordinance around here.

I came outside to complain, and there was Lenore Wilkerson on her steps with her nose wrinkled up as if she was smelling garbage. "Disgraceful!" she complained. "How is a person supposed to get any sleep with that horrible noise going on?"

I mumbled something that was supposed to sound like agreement, though, actually, the boys sounded pretty good. They had a little Latin hiccup mixed in with the jungle sound that made me want to dance.

"If I wanted to hear noise like that, I'd move to the Congo," she continued. "And I am definitely not going to do that, because the Doctor and I are not African."

"Oh?" I asked, because no one could mistake her for white.

"No," she said. "His people are from Bermuda, and mine are from Barbados."

"I see," I said. I had a hard time keeping myself from laughing, and an equally hard time restraining myself from asking that fool where their ancestors came from before they got to those islands, and how they got there, and for what purpose.

"Well, Zena," she demanded, "are you going to call the police, or am I?"

I believe the Devil must get into us now and then. Otherwise there is no explaining why I began doing some movements I had just learned, down my steps and up the street toward those kids and their irresistible drumming.

"I'll do it, I promise," I said with my hips churning and my arms waving, "as soon as I get this African thing out of my system."

She shook her head in disgust and stomped back into her house. And I did the samba on down the street to tell the kids to cool it, because the cops might be on the way.

We had some even better tapes of drumming which I used to practice for class, and kente place mats on our table long before they were fashionable, along with a Kwanzaa candlestick and a replica of "Reflections of Love," that famous wooden African mother and child statue, in our living room. We had a pair of ebony masks in the Back Room, plus the shield and spear I got Lucius for Christmas. I have a large collection of Afrocentric jewelry, and I gave Lucius a kente tie and cummerbund to wear with his tuxedo.

But all of the decorations we placed around our house were what I would call civilized. We had nothing that had to be hidden when people brought their children around.

Whereas the things Ifa brought with her are, to my American eyes, obscene.

Lucius puts the grotesque little statue down and picks up a thing that looks like a hollowed-out honeydew melon. On top of it are some small black iron prongs that look like nails. "What is this?" he asks.

"That is an African piano, Dod," she informs him. She takes it from him and plays some notes. The sounds are pleasant, like pattering raindrops.

Behind her back, I nod. This is something I wouldn't mind displaying in my home. I might even start a collection of African musical instruments like Ebony Morris has. A xylophone, a flute, a couple of drums . . .

"How much are you asking for this, Ifa? Fifty cents?" he asks in a teasing tone, with a smile playing around his lips. I know he doesn't expect her to name a price.

Deadly serious, she says, "I was going to ask five hundred dollars for that piano. But for you, Dod, the price is only three hundred."

I have to sit down suddenly on the sofa, to keep from falling flat on the floor. "You mean you would charge us for that?"

She turns and says to me, just as seriously, "I have to, Mum. I have no money."

"Put your stuff away, Ifa," I tell her. "Dad is not buying anything."

 # FOURTEEN

IFA WILL HAVE to go to work. I can't afford to support her anymore. And I have thought of a wonderful career for her. Actually, I thought of it the moment I laid eyes on her, but I know more about the business than I used to, and I was inclined to be protective of my lovely new daughter.

Ifa will be safe, though. She will not be out there alone. I will go with her to every assignment—and there will be plenty, because I never saw a girl with as much modeling potential as Ifa, not in my entire seven years of running the Nubian Queen Charm School and Modeling Agency. You can tell by the name that I was very Afrocentric even back then. I trained every girl who came and had the money to attend my classes, as well as some who didn't have the money. I always explained to them that, while I expected all of them to be successful people, very, very few of them, if any, would become successful models.

None of my pupils were ever booked steadily by my modeling agency. What I had, instead of graduates from my classes, were Emfingers.

Claudia Emfinger, my mother's dear friend from Alabama, had given birth to thirteen children. Like her, all of them were six feet or over. All of the six boys were good workers, and I always had a male Emfinger around the business to provide muscle—to sweep the rooms, carry out trash, and discourage burglars with his towering presence. The trouble was, as soon as I came to depend on an Emfinger, he would go to jail. Another Emfinger brother always turned up to replace the incarcerated one, though.

The male Emfingers were all gigantic, gentle, soft-voiced men who were all polite and willing to work hard, but they were all sneaky, subversive criminals. Not that I was ever one of their victims. No, around me they were uniformly helpful, honest, and polite. I would get along fine with each of them, until he gave in to the inevitable impulse to steal somebody's car or lift his wallet, and then I would have to take on a new one.

Claudia's seven daughters were unbelievably, identically gorgeous. At fifteen or so, they all had willowy figures, graceful movements, and exquisite faces with smooth, perfect cocoa skin. One by one, I taught them to walk like models, and, since I couldn't improve the way they talked, made them keep their mouths closed after I took out the chewing gum. One by one, I found them steady work in downtown stores and with local advertising agencies. And one by one, around the time I finished training each one and built her up to steady bookings, she became pregnant. It was like clockwork: the first inquiry from a top designer would arrive, or the first call from an upscale store, and my current Emfinger star would develop morning sickness.

After having a baby, the Emfinger women tended to put on weight, so modeling was out of the question for them. Like their inexhaustible supply of brothers, though, there was always another, younger Emfinger girl available. My clients couldn't tell one from another, but each one required exhausting boot-camp training before I could send her out on a job. I was sick of the whole pointless cycle by the time Claudia brought her oldest granddaughter around. Essence Emfinger was, if anything, taller and more beautiful than her predecessors, but she cracked her gum, said "peoples" and "He do," and would probably get pregnant sooner than her aunts, who usually had their first child at about eighteen.

I grow nostalgic even now when I think of Essence's youngest aunt, Estelle Emfinger, who waited to have a baby until she was practically elderly—twenty-one. Estelle had been ready to move on to the big time when she turned up with that telltale bulge. And no wonder. I recall the time Miss Claudia introduced me to her offspring, starting with the oldest and ending with her youngest, unmarried daughter, and saying, "And this is Estelle. I don't know what's the matter with her. She doesn't have any children yet." I knew my luck with models had run out when Estelle, too, became pregnant.

But Ifa is twenty, she does not know any men, and her stomach is still as flat as an ironing board. I am excited. Through her, I can feel young and beautiful again. I can experience the joy of being applauded and admired, and still be safe. We will both be safe, because I will be watching over her proudly and protectively.

When I had my school, none of my students had the promise of an Emfinger, let alone Ifa's poise and magnetism. I am honest. I wasn't ripping off those young women or their parents. I told them what the deal was with modeling—the limited opportunities for black models, the shortness of even the most successful career—but I also said I could help them, because I truly believe that poise and style are helpful to everyone.

My classes were limited to twenty students, and ran ten weeks that were devoted to makeup, carriage, movement, posing, hair styling, social graces, and wardrobe. When I was finished with them, the students all knew how to dress well, walk gracefully, make introductions, modulate their voices, set a table, and pour tea, which was all that I had promised. Maybe one pupil in every class would have modeling potential, and of those, only one in three would find work. Of those, none earned enough to support herself.

But then, none of them was Ifa.

She has the height, the bold look, the flirtatious walk. She knows how to show off an outfit—how to pose, how to smile, when to turn. At our club meeting, I saw that she has a gift for flirting with an audience, and that she instinctively plays with a hat or flips her collar or grabs her lapels to make a point. And, boy, can she swivel her hips and shake that booty! All she needs is a little more polish, some contacts, and a portfolio. I can give her all three.

I call Raymond and Roland. They are a pair of Geminis, life partners who are excellent photographers, and who have been together so long they seem like the two halves of one person. Raymond and Roland are so excited at hearing from me, they bubble all over each other like warm, freshly opened soda pop, and I can't understand half of what they are saying. But I get the point. They are glad I called. It's been too long.

"Come on over for dinner, child," says Raymond. "I have a new recipe for asparagus quiche I want to try out on you."

"Sorry, but I have to be home to cook dinner. Didn't I tell you I'm a married woman now?"

"Well, married doesn't have to mean buried, does it?" asks Roland, the more sarcastic of the two.

When I was younger, the three of us used to hang out a lot together—go to dinner, go to shows. It was like having a pair of perky girlfriends I could always count on to cheer me up. But those days are behind me now.

"No, and I'm very much alive," I tell him. "I have a wonderful new modeling prospect, and I want you to do her portfolio."

"Modeling is something that is really dead, dear," says Roland. "At least, it's dead for black models. Haven't you heard? If your name isn't Tyra or Naomi, forget it. If it weren't for weddings and graduations, Raymond and I would be on the street. Be glad you're in the hair trade."

"I know the modeling business has fallen off for us, but this girl is something special," I insist.

"She'd better be, to be worth a portfolio. We have to charge more than we used to, you know. Does she have any money?" Raymond wants to know.

"Don't I get a special rate?"

"I guess. Just for you, Zena." We exchange telephone kisses, and I hang up with an appointment for Ifa in the morning.

 FIFTEEN

THERE IS A weekly half-hour fashion show on TV that I just have to watch. Lucius calls it "watching the hos." I got furiously angry with him the first couple of times he said it. Then I stepped back and took another look, and, by God, he was right. It wasn't just the flimsy tops some of the models had on, or the obvious lack of bras beneath them. It wasn't the provocative way some of them walked, swiveling their hips practically a hundred and eighty degrees. Nor was it their sly smiles and bedroom glances, the way they looked at people sidewise from under half-closed lids. It was all of these things.

And I remembered some events in the past that I had forgotten—deliberately, I think.

Black models were just beginning to break into the big time in the early seventies, and I thought I could, too. I think I tried so hard to succeed at modeling because so many black women are in occupations that are dirty or disrespected. Houseworkers. Cooks. Practical nurses. I wanted to be special, not ordinary. Admired, not despised. So I worked for stores when I could, and for black social affairs like cabaret parties and luncheons on weekends, and I paid the bills by working for Mr. Barab of Top Notch Creations.

Mr. Barab was a manufacturer who sold to a few individual customers out of his showroom, but did most of his business with stores. Mainly, I was a fitting model for his seamstresses, but I would also show off his clothes to private customers. My boss would often say, "Now, Zena, there is a very special customer out there, Mr. So-and-so. I want you to be extra nice to him." It was usually women who selected the clothes, but he never said to be extra nice to them. It was the men who paid, and they were the ones who required extra niceness. Mr. Barab never explained what "extra nice" meant. I guess he thought he didn't have to.

One time, I remember, a woman was interested in a dress I had shown, and she asked that I put it on again. I'll never forget that dress. It was a hideous thing, light blue moiré taffeta, with ruffles across its shoulders and down one side, and I couldn't imagine why anyone would want it, but I put it on a second time and walked out there.

"Come closer, dear," said the woman, a hard-looking blonde.

Her man said, "Yes, we want to feel the goods," and actually crooked his finger at me.

When I got close to where they were sitting, he stuck his hand out and rubbed the taffeta skirt between his fingers. Then he reached up under it. *I* was the goods he wanted to feel!

I pulled back, but that horny old devil had a grip on the dress, and wouldn't let go. I had to scratch his hand with my fingernail to get free. I always kept one fingernail extra long and sharp as an emergency weapon, and this was one of the times it came in handy.

But when I got back to the dressing room, Mr. Barab was furious. He had tried to apologize to the customers, but they had stalked out.

"Who do you think you are, insulting those people? They do fifty thousand dollars' worth of business with me every season! Listen, Zena, I happen to know you are no Mary Magdalene." He had it wrong, of course, he meant to say I was no Virgin Mary, but I didn't correct him. "If a man wants to touch you, let him touch you. Where is the harm? Take off my dress."

I obeyed. I was glad to get out of the ugly thing.

"Now take off the slip."

"Mr. Barab," I said, "that ugly blue thing is your dress, but this is my slip, and while you are in this dressing room, I am keeping it on."

"This is my dressing room," he said, "and I can be in it as long as I want, and do anything in it I feel like doing. Take the slip off. While you're at it, take off your underpants, too."

While we were talking, he had moved closer and backed me up against the wall. I looked with horror and saw that his pants were open.

"I am going to show you what I mean when I say, be extra nice to my customers," he said, and pushed himself up against me. "Relax. You are going to like this."

I said, "Mr. Barab, there is only one thing uglier in this room than that dress, and that is you." And that was the truth, because he had a pot belly, and a red face, and hairy warts, plus one normal eye and one walleye. And then I surprised him by raking his face and his one good eye with my trusty fingernail. While he was holding his eye and yelling in pain, I got out of there without my clothes, only my raincoat pulled tight around me. Of course, that was the end of the job. The end of my modeling career, such as it was. I went downtown and rented the rooms for my modeling school the next day.

Now, every time I watch that show, much as I enjoy the fashions, I wonder what else those poor girls have to do. Plenty, I guess, judging from the way they swivel and shimmy.

Now we both call my habit "watching the hos," and laugh about it. I feel sorry for those poor girls. I'm sure some of them may be strong, but if they are out there alone without backup, they will probably cave in sooner or later.

Knowing what I know, I probably shouldn't push this idea on Ifa. Nothing like that would happen to her, of course, because I would go with her on every assignment, and I would have the job of fighting off the men. And the money is good, and where else could she earn it?

That night, I pack up a few accessories for the shoot—a crushable hat, some jewelry, a boa, some extra hair. In the morning, Ifa buckles her new black coat over her only dress, the orange one she wore the first time we met, and off we go.

"Put that tacky stuff away, Zena," Roland says when he sees my collection of accessories. "It's useless."

"And, Zena, you are really dating yourself with that patent leather hatbox," Raymond informs me.

I know it. Models carried their accessories in leather hatboxes back in the fifties, a habit that stuck for a decade or so, but hatboxes are history now. "I couldn't find anything else at the last minute," I explain.

"We understand, dear, but it's backpacks now, or nothing. We don't need it anyway. The mood of today is stark. Simple. Stripped down to almost nothing." Raymond is waving his hands around to make his point.

I am dubious. "Are you sure?"

"Absolutely. All they want to see is this beautiful child in invisible makeup and the simplest possible black dress. And she is beautiful, you were right about that."

"Oh, my, yes," agrees Roland. "She is something special. She doesn't look very multicultural, though. The new look is multicultural."

"I am multicultural," Ifa declares in a huff. "My mother's father was French."

I haven't heard the word *multicultural* used a lot, but I thought it meant life was going to be a big party where we would all get to eat chop suey, play African drums, wear feathers, and dance the cha-cha. This is the first hint I have had that it is just a new way of keeping us black folks out of jobs.

"I'm sure he was, dear," says Raymond. "I said you don't look multicultural, at least not to Americans. In Africa, I am sure you do."

"In a way, it's a shame she doesn't look more purely African," says Roland. "Did you see the videos of What's-his-name's latest show? He had ten models. Nine blondes and that little Ebonic thing, What's-her-name from Uganda, Miss Unpronounceable, in shiny red dresses and boots. What a shocker it was when she came out! She got all the attention."

"Using a black person to shock an audience sounds like another kind of racism to me," says Ifa. She is right, I think, though I sometimes wish she would tone her pronouncements down a little.

"I am sorry I am neither black enough nor white enough for you," she adds.

"Dear, you are fine for us. We are not talking about us. We are talking about them. The people who pay money."

"Well, this is the only dress I have," Ifa says. She is still wearing the bright orange number she had on last weekend. It is wrinkled and stained, and, frankly, when I get close to her, I notice that it is more than a little bit pungent. I wish I had checked her out more carefully before we left the house. I could have loaned her a dress and made her smear on some deodorant.

"It'll have to do, then," says Roland. "Unless—are you wearing a slip?"

"Of course."

"Then let's see you in that."

Anger blazes up in Ifa's eyes. "Mum—do I have to?" she asks.

"Not unless you want to be a model," I say, wondering if I am pushing her too far. She has great modeling potential, but she is also a child who has come under my care. "It's up to you, Ifa. Do you want to do this, or not?"

With some difficulty she unzips her dress, steps out of it, and crosses her arms over her chest. Her slip is black, fortunately, and clings nowhere, not even to her bony hips.

"Perfect," says Raymond. He is right. "Now, relax, sweetie. Come over here and let me get you in my viewfinder."

"I do not like undressing in front of strange men," she says.

"Then you need to become a secretary," Raymond says. "Listen, darling, the last time I did a shoot, there were about four models running around stark naked all day, and nobody paid them the slightest attention. Roland ran a feather over their nipples to make them stand up, but the way he did it was about as sexy as arranging flowers in a vase."

"I do not think I like this story. What is the point of it?" Ifa asks.

"Nobody was interested in those models as women, do you understand me, dear? The people were only interested in shooting their catalog without going over budget. You would have to get rid of your modesty pretty quickly in this business. Now come on over here and make pretty for the camera."

What he says is the truth. I had forgotten how callous the employers and photographers were when I was modeling. To most of them, the girls were things, not people. I would protect Ifa from the bad things that happen to most models—the drugs, the men, the meanness. But most girls are out there alone, and not every girl has the spirit and spunk to fight back. No one has the strength to refuse all the time. Sometimes, I guess, the girls just go along—just give in because they are tired of fighting.

Still, Ifa has to do something, and she's not qualified for much of anything else.

She obeys Raymond, standing in front of the white backdrop sheet he and Roland have set up, but her poses are uninspired, and she does not have her usual luster. They coax and cajole as they point and click away, but for all their little cries of "Great!" and "Wonderful!" and "Beautiful!" I don't think they are getting anything worthwhile. I don't know what it is that makes Ifa glow, but today it is missing. I hand her the hat, and she plays with its brim creatively, but her inner light does not come on. She is unhappy, I guess, and her unhappiness has clouded it over.

"What's wrong, Ifa?" I ask her.

"I did not want to come here this morning, Mum. I wanted to go with Dod to arrange my visa."

It takes all my patience to keep my mouth shut. I know that if I open it I will turn into a screaming maniac. This session is costing me two hundred bucks an hour.

"I am sorry, Mum," Ifa goes on, "but I do not think I want to be a model. I do not like strange men looking at me without my clothes on."

I make a decision. You can lead a horse to water, but you can't make it swim. "Well, come on, then, put on your dress and let's go home. Sorry, guys. Send me the bill."

"We'll hold off until you bring her back to finish the session, Zena."

"You heard what she said, didn't you? She doesn't want to be a model."

"We're betting that she'll change her mind, once she sees what the job situation is like out here. It's rough."

"Thanks, Raymond."

They will probably not bill me at all, bless their kind hearts. Those two men are among the funniest, liveliest people I know, but Ifa's gloom is so heavy, she has given them the blues. She probably broke their cameras, too. She flounces her way to the car. Once in it, she sits as far away from me as possible, her back turned, staring out the window. A moody adolescent, that's what I am dealing with, I think. She reminds me of my friends' teenage children.

"That session will cost me at least two hundred dollars," I say, weaving my way through noontime traffic. It has also made me late for work, so I may have lost some more money, but I don't mention that.

"I am sorry, Mum." Her voice is barely audible. "I don't want to be a model."

"You should have told me so," I say, and lapse into a silence as sullen as hers for six or eight blocks. Finally I say, "Those men weren't interested in your body, you know."

"I know. They love each other. I do not approve."

"It is not up to you to approve or disapprove," I reply.

"I don't think I liked those men. They talked about me as if I were not there."

Ah, that is her real problem. Someone who is used to being the center of attention misses it when she doesn't get it.

At the next traffic light I ask, "Suppose Lucius does get you a visa, what are you going to do with it? You have to find some kind of work."

"I am a college graduate," she says haughtily. "I can do more with my life than stand around and pose all day."

"Well, according to your sister, you have no skills except

looking beautiful. If you don't model, what will you do for a living?"

"I am going to be a movie star," she says.

I make no comment because, for once, I am speechless.

Lucius is just arriving home from his morning rounds when we reach our front door. She gets over her slump in an instant. She jumps out of the car, runs up to him, and flings her arms around his neck.

"Dod! What news do you have for me?"

Bringing up the rear, I think that she is still behaving like an adolescent daughter. Moody and impulsive, like all teenagers.

When I catch up with them, Lucius, with a slightly amazed look on his face, is gently removing her hands from his shoulders. "Let's talk about it inside," he says. Over her head, he rolls his eyes at me and meaningfully nods his head to the right, toward the house next door. He is thinking, as I am, about our neighbors, the Wilkersons. They disapprove of us and consider us working-class riff-raff, so we try to avoid bringing our business to their attention. Lenore Wilkerson is the kind of woman who wears pink all the time, carries perfumed lace handkerchiefs, and calls her husband *Doctor* Wilkerson, even though he is only a dental mechanic who makes false teeth. I almost refused to join the Divas when I found out she was a member.

"Tell me, Dod, tell me, tell me what you have found out," she says when he has dropped into a chair. Her words are all running together like alphabet soup. "What have your people decided about me?" She is breathless. She looks at him adoringly. The glow has returned to her face.

"Well, I saw my friend who handles I.N.S.—"

She claps her hands with excitement. "Yes, yes, please go on, tell me."

"—but the guy he needs to talk to is out of town. He will be back next week."

Her face drops instantly into a mask of tragedy. "Oh, dear, what shall I do? I only have a short time left."

"It will be enough. Didn't I promise you that?" he reminds her.

"Yes, Dod, of course you did. I am sorry. I must have more faith."

"Yes, have a little faith. And sign up for night school, just in case." Lucius detaches her arms from his neck once more. "Pretty cold downtown. Those new office towers create wind tunnels. Brrr. I think I want a fire." He goes over to the fireplace, rubbing his hands. "I could use something hot to drink, too. Any coffee left, Zena?"

"I think there's some," I tell him, and start for the kitchen.

But Ifa is faster. "I will get it for him, Mum," she says. She is younger, after all, so when she races me she wins. When she comes back with the coffee, she flashes me her brightest smile. "You should not have to do everything, Mum," she says.

I know. I am an old woman.

As she hands him the cup, I feel like an interloper in my own house.

I do not like this new feeling, not at all.

 SIXTEEN

"DAMN, MISS ZENA!" Vyester says when I pick up the phone, "Who is that you got answering the phone at your house? Sounds like the FBI done moved in."

"Something like that," I say, and lower my voice. Ain't that a bitch? Here I am, lowering my voice in my own house because I don't want to be overheard, something I've never done before in my life. "What did she say when she answered the phone?"

"Is it a 'she'? The voice was so deep, I couldn't tell. It said, 'Who ees on the line? Who ees spikking? *Who* ees on the line?' It scared me so bad, I hung up."

Vyester doesn't scare easily. All her life, she has been standing up to drug dealers, pit bulls, bill collectors, armed burglars, a husband with high blood pressure and a raging temper, and a trifling teenaged son.

Now I understand why nobody has been calling us. Ifa has scared all of our friends away. She has nothing else to do but talk on the phone, and when it rings, her hand reaches out for it like a shot.

When I complained that she was monopolizing the telephone, she pouted and said "But, Mum, that is my only fon!" Yeah, well, I wish I had as much time for "fon" as she does.

"And the rest of the time," Vyester goes on, "your line is busy. It's been busy all weekend. I wouldn't have tried anymore after that spooky accent answered, but I need to ask you a favor. I'm glad you finally picked up. I prayed for you to pick up, and the Lord must have heard me. Listen, you got anybody who can cover for me on Thursday?"

Vyester doesn't ask for favors often, so this has to be something serious. But no one can cover for her. Nobody can take a challenging head and turn it into a thing of beauty like Vyester. Except, of course, yours truly.

"How many appointments do you have on Thursday?" I ask. I know what I am going to do. I am just stalling.

"Just four, and one of them is Miss Doreena James, she only gets a wash and a set. Then there's old Mrs. Wilson, the deacon's wife, she gets an old-fashioned hard press and tight curls, doesn't even want a comb-out. And little Latasha Morris has to get a style for Sunday—her hair is thick, but it's soft—and Phlora Wilson just wants some color in hers. Oh, and Tanya DeLoach is coming in for a finger wave, because she's in a wedding this weekend."

Vyester's appointments all sound easy, but her customers are used to her expertise, so it's best not to turn them over to an amateur. I try to think. I don't have my appointment book at home.

"Sometimes you just have to step out on faith," my mother used to say.

I step out. "I'll take your appointments," I say.

"Girl, thanks," she says. "I didn't know what I'd do if you said no. They postponed Sonny's hearing. His new court date is Thursday."

I don't try to talk her out of going to court and doing whatever is necessary to get him off. Fred Junior is of legal age, but his parents still provide him with everything he needs and plenty of extras, so he had no excuse for ripping off a sporting goods store with his no-good pals, but he's her child. Her only child. I don't have to go through such things because God never gave me children, and I guess I ought to thank Him—but I wouldn't mean it, and it's never a good idea to lie to God.

Fred Junior, who might grow up if his parents stopped calling him Sonny, and who might also have had a better chance at reaching manhood if they hadn't made him a Junior, has been up to that Juvenile Court so many times they have a special defendant's chair there with his name engraved on it. He has been hauled in for shoplifting, burglary, petty theft, and the crime that made me give up on him, robbery and assault on an old lady. She wasn't too old to grab his collar and hold on and scream bloody murder till the cops came, though.

Each time before, he has gotten off with a warning, because Juvenile Hall is too crowded with murderers to have room for anything less dangerous, and because his parents are such responsible people—homeowners, no less; thank you, Zena; you're welcome—and they promised to keep an eye on him.

But unless I have miscounted, Sonny is no longer a juvenile. And I have run out of sympathy for him since his escapade with the old lady.

"Good luck," I say to my friend. "How is your sister doing?"

"Oh, Maggie's just fine, since you saved her from having her things put in the street. Only thing is, she got laid off from her new job. But I'll pay you back anyway, Miss Zena, don't you worry."

But I am worrying. I have not forgotten that session with Lucius about our expenses.

"You haven't told me who that was answering your phone."

"Ifa, of course," I tell her. "You remember Ifa."

"You mean that loudmouth African ho? She still at your house?"

"Yes," I say. I think *ho* is too strong a term, but I am not in a mood to argue.

"To tell the truth, I thought it might be her," she says, "but I was hoping I was wrong. Miss Zena, I'm worried about you."

"Why?" I ask.

"You better get that heifer out of your house before Lucius gets eyes," she says.

"It's not like that, Vy," I tell her. "I trust Lucius. Besides, she's just a child."

"Trust me," Vyester says. "Have I ever lied to you? She. Is. Not. A. Child. When is your guest leaving?"

"She's only supposed to stay another week."

"That's too long, Miss Zena."

"Well, a week is all her visa has left to run, and if Lucius doesn't get it extended for her, she'll have to leave anyway."

"I hope she does. Listen, thanks for the favor."

"Good luck on Thursday," I say.

"Thanks," she says. "If Sonny's hearing is over early, I'll come straight to work."

After I hang up, I find that I am still annoyed with my friend. She is looking for trouble where none exists. That kind of thing may have gone on at her house once or twice, but we live on a higher level around here. Vy has been known to take in alley cats. This girl obviously comes from a good background. She has education and culture. Besides, like I told Vy, I know my husband, and I trust him. So Vyester's remarks don't really get me worried.

Still, I start watching our guest as she moves around my house. In my old-fashioned opinion, she doesn't wear enough clothing in the house. Her shoulders are always bare, like her great, big, rough feet. And when she moves, she undulates and slithers, like a snake.

Snakes are not common in this part of the country, but I thought I saw one in the yard yesterday. I screeched and ran.

What the hell am I doing with a beautiful, slithery snake-woman in my house?

I ask myself that in the mirror, as I am checking my hair and my makeup on my way out the door to work. I wear a uniform coat in the shop, but underneath that smock I am always wearing a good tailored suit without its jacket, or a daytime dress. Today I have on a navy blue wool crepe suit that fits me perfectly and only cost me ninety-eight dollars. I won't lie and call it an Armani or even a Legmani—I buy my clothes at end-of-season sales at the kind of stores where the labels have been ripped out—but this suit is good quality, and I think it looks good on me.

I think paying a premium for clothes by designers who don't even respect us is stupid. I don't buy clothes for their labels, but for how they look. Label or no label, in a suit like this I am ready for anything—a luncheon, an important patron who wants me to come to her house, a business association meeting, dinner out with Lucius, or just plain working on heads. I wear sneaks in the shop, but I keep some good-looking sandals or pumps in my drawer so I can be dressed up in a flash if I need to be.

I check the rest of myself out. Not bad. I have a full face, tan skin with nair a wrinkle, large, wide-set eyes, and what Lucius calls delicious lips, but I think my eyebrows are my best feature. They arch naturally, and I have never plucked them. Since Ifa moved in, I have just about forgotten what I look like, though. I have a hard time getting to use a mirror around here. She is very fond of admiring herself.

There is a hissing sound, soft as a whisper, and a sort of a rustling down around my feet. I look down, but there is nothing there but my black hall carpet.

Then, without making a sound on her big bare feet, Ifa appears in the mirror behind me. "You should pluck your brows and arch them, Mum. And you should use more makeup. A little blush would do wonders for your face, even at your age."

I do not welcome this advice. I would not welcome it even if she put it more diplomatically. I know how to use makeup. I practically invented the stuff. At one time I even had my own line of Nubian Queen cosmetics. I have toned down my look lately, that's all.

"I don't have time, Ifa," I tell her. "I have to get to work."

She slinks and slithers away, and I let out a big sigh. I hadn't even known that I was holding my breath.

It helps me to remember that Lucius has a really serious snake phobia. The last time a snake handler came on our favorite talk show, he was so grossed out he shut his eyes and asked me to tell him when it was gone. I suspect that if he's alone when snakes appear, he turns off the set or changes the channel.

It also helps to take a few extra minutes, run to my room, and change out of my suit into a new slinky red dress I just bought last week that makes me feel young and sexy. My uniform will hide it, but I will know I have it on.

 SEVENTEEN

I WOULDN'T BELIEVE IT if I hadn't seen it with my own eyes. I went downtown the other day to take Sonny a comb and a toothbrush and some cigarettes, and after I left the Detention Center, there was that loudmouth little African ho, talking up a storm, hollering all up in Mr. Lucius's face. Then she flung her arms all around his neck and jumped up and kissed him! Yes, she did. She did it right out on the street in front of the Federal Building, which is next door to the jail. He didn't try to stop her, either; didn't push her away or nothing, and I believe I saw a little smirk on his face, which I wanted to wipe off for Miss Zena. But even though I work for her, that is not my job.

I am just so glad he didn't see me. I think Ifa did, but she cut her eyes away from me real fast.

Thank the good Lord my old car turned over, even though she coughs and stutters when it gets cold. Miss Thing and I roared out of there before I could see any more, or be seen. Even if I hadn't watched that little show, I had to get unparked fast and get away from those meter police around the Federal Building. They mean as toothless people with nothing but green apples to eat, especially the female ones. They'd as soon ticket you, and have you towed, as look at you. Sometimes I dislike women, and that's a shame, because they are my own sex.

I could hardly look Miss Zena in the face when I got back to work. I really felt bad for her. There she was, laughing and joking and styling hair, having a good time as usual, like nothing could ever possibly go wrong in her life. She's too trusting, that's what's wrong.

I'm worried about my friend. I'm afraid that this time she done set herself up for big trouble. If she don't get that little hoochie out of her house, Mister Lucius is going to get eyes for real, and somebody is likely to lose their life.

I know, because it almost happened around here. Fred's mama, who ought to know better, sent a hot-tailed hussy up here was s'posed to be Fred's cousin. Needed a place to stay while she was going to business college, Mother Sampson said. I wanted to know what kind of college only had classes once or twice a week, but she did help some around the house, so I didn't say anything.

Then one day I forgot my best curling irons, had taken them home the night before to do her hair with, as a matter of fact, so I came home on my lunch hour to get them. Found my bedroom door closed and heard some mighty suspicious noises coming from behind it. I sneaked and heated up those irons for a purpose that their maker hadn't intended. Then I kicked that door open, blam!

"Cousins, huh?"

The hussy rolled from under my husband and defied me, laying naked right there in my own bed. "We ain't really cousins. Everybody thinks we are, but his Uncle Isaac ain't really my father. My mama told me my father is Beau Robinson, the insurance man. So we ain't doin' nothin' wrong."

That's when I lost my mind. Put a burn on my own new sheets trying to brand her black ass.

She got out of my house so fast, she left all her clothes behind, even her shoes. Threw on a housecoat and ran down the street in flip-flop slippers, she was in such a hurry to get away from me, and caught the first thing smoking for South Carolina. See, that's another good thing about being ordinary instead of high-class. If people do you wrong, you ain't got no problem killing 'em.

Miss Zena comes from the projects same as I do, and I don't mean to say she's forgotten where she came from, because she hasn't. But she has raised herself up pretty high by her ankle straps, and she has got so many artistic ideas and fantasy notions, she might fool herself into loving a snake, and she might forget how to take care of business when some important killing needs to be done.

Well, if need be, I'll help her.

Luckily, Miss Idabelle So-called Cousin Sampson got away from me that day, because I was in a death-dealing mood. I packed up her clothes and sent Fred Sampson to the bus station to put them on the next bus south after hers.

After that, he was as agreeable and dependable as a woman could want—so full of apologies and meekness and make-it-up-to-me sugar I almost got sick of it and wished for the rotten, sneaky old Fred Sampson back. There's a type of man that, if you catch him wrong one time, he'll never step out of line again. My Fred is that type.

I only wish I could say the same for his son. Then, except for worrying about Miss Zena, my mind would be totally at peace.

 EIGHTEEN

I COME HOME EARLY one evening, and Ifa's voice is ringing and echoing throughout the house. She is talking excitedly. I hear some words that sound like "yabba, yabba" and another that sounds like "umgawa." When I walk into the kitchen, where she is shouting into the phone, she is grinning and her eyes are shining.

"Mum, Mum, you are wonderful!" she cries. "I love you, Mum!"

She is not talking to me.

I am flooded with an instantaneous rage that tightens my forehead and pumps up my blood pressure. I think it is because, even though we have forbidden it, she is still making overseas calls.

I snatch the receiver and yell at her about the phone bill. She says, "But, Mum, my people called me!"

I give her back the phone, but tell her to make it snappy, because I have to start cooking. I am still insanely angry. Much, much later I will realize that my rage is not because of our phone bill at all.

It is because I will never be able to make her eyes shine like that.

Ifa sets the table sullenly while I get dinner—grilled salmon, greens, and rice. We eat silently and get the meal over with quickly. As soon as I can, I duck out of Ifa's presence and follow Lucius into the Back Room.

We have a three-bedroom house, but we decided to give up the third bedroom so that we could have our Back Room. The Back Room is where Lucius mostly hangs out. It is the only room where smoking is officially permitted, and the only one I am not allowed to clean. It is cluttered with so much junk you can't see the dirt, anyway. I am dying to get my hands on the Back Room along with some soap, water, and disinfectant, but my husband loves it the way it is, and I try to respect his wishes.

I find Lucius stretched out in his lounge chair. The chair is much too big for the room, but Lucius is a big man, and I had it custom-made to fit him.

Usually Lucius relaxes once he gets in his chair, but tonight his face is all frowned up into a pile of wrinkles like a sharpei's. I take off the old uniform coat I use as an apron, hoping that he will notice me in my red dress. It is a really bright red in a slinky fabric, and it clings everywhere except down below, where it flares out into an A-line that camouflages my hips. I think I look pretty good in it, but Lucius is paying me absolutely no attention. He has a newspaper open on his lap, but is not really reading it. He is flicking the remote control absent-mindedly, but not really watching TV, either. In the ashtray beside him, an ignored cigar is burning down to a ghost of itself.

"What really happened downtown the other day?" I ask him, knowing that he has run into trouble in his quest for Ifa's visa, and wanting to hear the whole story.

He sighs heavily. "I may have offended some of my best contacts. Strike that, Zena. Ifa may have offended them."

This is terrible news. Why does my heart leap up and start dancing like Michael Jackson in "Thriller"?

I take the unread paper from his lap and deposit myself there in its place. "Tell me," I say.

"Woman, you weigh a lot, you know that? Watch out for my ole bad knee." But I am not on his bad knee, and he does not make me get up. He lets me stay where I am, and says, "I took

Ifa down to Senator Russo's office to see about her visa, and she embarrassed me. She treated his assistants like a bunch of flunkies. Worse. The people in there were trying to be nice to her, but she behaved like the Wicked Witch of the West. She kept waving her hands around and clanking those klutzy bracelets she wears and giving orders. When I left, she was stamping her foot and telling them, 'No, that is not what I want. This is what I want!' "

"You walked out and left her there?"

"Just for a few minutes. I had to go outside to take a walk and cool off. When I came back, it was really quiet in there. Like a funeral parlor. Senator Russo's secretary practically said, 'Lucius, if you want any favors, we're always glad to help you. Just don't bring *her* back here anymore.' "

"That doesn't sound like Russo's people are annoyed with you, Lucius. Only with her."

"No, but I should have had better sense than to risk my good relationship with that office by taking that ignorant girl down there. Senators don't grow on trees, you know."

I nod. I know. Lucius is a valued party worker, but he has just done a very risky thing. It's important to stay in the good graces of someone as high up as a U.S. Senator.

"Why didn't you take her to see Ambrose Miller?" Congressman Miller is a freshman, but at least he's firmly in Lucius's pocket. My husband played a big part in getting him elected. I helped by hostessing one coffee clutch and talking him up to my neighbors, patrons, and club members.

"Because Miller's a brother, and he's not too big on multiculturalism. He knows his constituents are mostly African Americans, and he has to keep them happy. Senator Russo's parents were both immigrants, so he's inclined to be generous to people who just got here."

I did not know any of this. I have been out of touch with party affairs for too long.

He smacks his palm with his fist. "Damn! I should have known better than take her there. She told me how corrupt the

Olori government is. I think she's used to bossing politicians because that's what her family did at home. All they had to do was wave their money around and give orders. I can't convince her things don't work that way here." He shakes his head. "I mean, they do in some quarters, but not at my level. Besides, it's more subtle here. Sneaky and under the table."

Asking Ifa to be subtle would be like asking a cat to bark, I think. She has told me that her family has a lot of money, acquired in some mysterious business enterprise, and that, because of it, they exert a lot of political influence. Their money and influence are no help to her here.

I wind my arms around my husband's neck and begin rubbing the knots back there, hoping to help him feel better. "Zena, I'm not in the mood . . ." he begins. But he does not finish the sentence, and he does not push my hands away.

"What is she going to do? Are they going to extend her visa?" I ask with my cheek against his.

"I don't know. Maybe, if she cooperates. But that is one hard-headed girl. That conversation we had about school was not the first one. All the way home, I was telling her she had better take some courses, so that she can get a student visa, if nothing else, and she kept telling me she is already a college graduate. I was surprised she finally seemed to be listening to me." He begins stroking my legs. "Are you wearing panty hose?"

"Yes."

"Damn."

"They come off," I tell him, and proceed to demonstrate. "See?"

"Yes, I see," he says, and takes the panty hose from me and tosses them into a corner. "What else do you have on? What is this?" He hooks his finger under something and pulls. It snaps back on his finger. "Ouch!"

It is my spandex body shaper. After a certain age, like fourteen, if a woman is going to wear a clingy dress, she'd better wear something underneath it to hold herself together.

"I guess I'll never understand women. Why would you walk

in here in a red dress like that, enticing me, and have all that body armor on underneath?"

I have no answer. I am just glad to learn that I have enticed him. I start tonguing his ear.

He tries pushing me away from him, and fails. "Stop that, Zena. Are you going to take that thing off?"

"Yes. But not here." I hate making love in the Back Room. Lucius refuses to part with his beloved old couch that opens into a sofa bed, but it has a steel rib down the center that cuts right into my spine. I say, why have a beautiful bedroom with a two-thousand-dollar queen-sized bed unless you're going to use it?

Once we are there, I undress quickly and jump between the sheets. I want to hide my fat, dimpled thighs, and I want to watch my husband undress. Lucius still looks wonderful for a man his age—not much belly, a long, lean, lovely back, and a shapely butt. Riding has something to do with it. He is always riding something—horses on weekends, a stationary bike on other days—while I am always sitting.

My poor husband has lost a lot of the hair on his head, though. Instead, he has grown new hair in a lot of interesting places. Hair sprouts from his nose and his ears, he has curly sideburns where there were none before, and where his chest was once bare, there is a tricolor triangle in equal amounts of white, black and gray. Also, while I am getting bald down below—something I try to hide—Lucius has grown a new forest around his cock and his balls.

After I have finished kissing his chest hairs, I love to go exploring in the woods. We are really getting hot and steamy, when there is a series of heavy knocks on the door.

"Mum! Dod! Please help me! I am ill!"

I throw on my green satin kimono and open our bedroom door a couple of inches. She attempts to push her way in, but I block the way. Oh, no, miss, I am thinking. I am not giving up the sanctity of our private space for you or for anyone.

"What is the matter, Ifa?"

"I do not feel well, Mum. I could not go to sleep. My heart is going crazy. Feel here."

I touch her chest where she indicates. It feels to me like her heart is knocking in a strong, steady rhythm. I wish mine were that strong.

"Have you ever been diagnosed with heart trouble?"

"No, but I have it now. I must see a doctor right away."

"You can't see a doctor at this time of night. What do you think is wrong?"

"I do not know. I went to sleep thinking about the angry people at home in my village who will be waiting for me if I have to go back there. I woke up thinking some of them were in the room with me. And they were. I saw their spirits."

My annoyance gives way to sympathy for the poor girl. She's scared as hell. I take her hand and lead her to the little bench in the hall. "Here, sit down, Ifa," I say, and pull her down beside me. "There is no one in this house but the three of us, so don't be frightened. How have you been sleeping? Do you like your room?"

"I do not sleep so well, but the room is lovely, Mum. I like it very much."

And then I make a dreadful blunder by saying, "I think it's a lovely room, myself. It was my mother's. I really tried to make it nice for her."

When she is scared, this girl's eyes grow so large they occupy her whole face. Nose, lips, all other features disappear to make room for those enormous eyes. "Is she dead?" she asks me.

"Yes," I say. "She died two years ago." I have almost gotten over it, but there are times when I still wake up wanting to run in there and tell Mama something, and then remember that she is gone.

Ifa has begun to tremble. "Did she die in my room? In my bed?"

"Yes, she did."

"Oh, my God!" she screams. "I am sorry, Mum, but I cannot sleep in that room. No wonder I am having the nightmares and waking up with my heart pounding. She does not want me in there."

I was glad that I could nurse Mama at home, and never had to send her to a hospital or a nursing home. She had a heart condition, one that did not require any special equipment, only rest. She passed away the best way, at home with her family, quietly, in her sleep.

But there is no quiet in our house that night, and for a while it looks like no one is ever going to sleep in it again. The terrified screams coming from that African girl bring Lucius out of our bedroom with nothing on but a pair of pajama bottoms. "What's going on? What's wrong?" he is hollering. "Doesn't anybody know what time it is?"

I do not like the way she stares at him.

She does not have much on, either—just a muslin shift that she sleeps in, one that is not shadowproof—and he is staring back, which bothers me even more.

"Let me get your robe before you catch cold," I say, and get it for him. It is an old, faded plaid flannel thing that he loves the way a baby loves its banky. He puts it on.

"I brought a robe for you, too, Ifa," I say, and hand her an old purple fleece thing of mine. She does not take it. Perhaps she does not notice it. She is leaning into my husband's chest and babbling like a drunken parrot.

"Oh, Dod, my room, it has a spirit, an unfriendly spirit, it does not want me in there, it gave me bad dreams, it will choke me or make me crazy." By now she is practically talking in tongues, words spilling all over one another.

"Ifa, Ifa, calm down, take it easy," my husband says, and puts an arm around her. I watch narrowly, but I think he is only being fatherly. "Zena's mother was a very sweet person. Her spirit would not harm you."

"No, Dod, you do not understand spirits, sometimes after a good person dies they turn into their opposite, and grow very wicked and dangerous. I must sleep somewhere else. I must have another room."

"There are no other rooms," I inform her.

"Then I will sleep on the couch in the little back room," she says.

Lucius and I glance at each other. The Back Room, Lucius's

home office, is also our sanctuary from the world. It is where we watch TV, relax, talk, have drinks, act silly, and never, never have company. It also holds a lot of memories for us. When we were a lot younger and more athletic, our passion couldn't wait for the bedroom, and we often wore ourselves out on that lumpy old leather couch.

He and I both say "No" at the same moment.

"That room has worse ghosts. Lots of them," I say.

"Then," she says, "I will sleep on the living room sofa."

"No, you won't," I tell her. "I never heard of such nonsense."

"It is not nonsense," she says.

"No, it is not nonsense," my husband agrees. He was raised by his Geechee grandmother, and he halfway believes in spirits and spells and all that spooky old stuff. "I mean, if Ifa believes in it, we mustn't call it nonsense. Come on, let's go check out this terrible, scary room."

Ifa hangs back, still babbling and terrified, but he coaxes her along and flings open the door.

I hardly recognize Mama's room. I almost scream myself when I see it. Our guest has transformed it into some kind of voodoo hut.

Mama's pretty flower paintings and her framed crewel embroideries have been replaced by reptile skins, hideous carved masks with raffia hair, and something I am afraid to inspect.

Over the bed, I guess as a nod to the Christianity she professes, Ifa has hung one of those creepy Jesus pictures with eyes that follow you around. A richly patterned snake that may or may not be dead decorates Jesus's frame.

Over the footboard she has draped a large python skin, and on the dresser is what appears to be a pile of small human bones. I do not go closer to check them out.

"Let's hold hands and pray," says Lucius. He goes into action and leads us in prayers for peace in the house and the repose of Mama's soul in heaven. He says another prayer for Ifa's peace and well-being, but none for us and our interrupted lovemaking.

We then sing "Precious Lord, Take My Hand," with Ifa joining in on the second chorus. Then we bow our heads and recite the Lord's Prayer, which she does know.

"That little service should make Ifa feel better," Lucius says. "She tells me that she became a Christian when she was sent to mission school."

"I do not feel better," Ifa says. Her eyes flash. "I still cannot sleep in this room."

Jesus's eyes follow me wherever I move in the room. The eyes of the masks follow me, too. They look more alive than Jesus, and they do not appear friendly. I avert my own eyes.

"No wonder she had bad dreams," I can't help saying.

"Now, Zena, please be tolerant," Lucius says. "Ifa has hung her religious objects to make her feel at home."

She grins happily, like a five-year-old. "Those masks contain the spirits of my ancestors," she says. "They protect me. So does the python."

Now I am the one who cannot stay in the room. I back out into the hall, while my husband tries once more to convince her to sleep in her bed.

"Leave the light on and the door open," he suggests.

"And will you leave your door open, too?" she asks him. "In case I have to call for help? I am sorry, Mum, Dod, but those spirits were going to strangle me."

He looks at me in appeal. I give a very slight shake of my head and mouth "No" silently.

He comes to me and takes my hands. "It's only for one night, Zena," he whispers, "so she can get to sleep. Remember, we are Christians, and she is a stranger, and Christians are supposed to minister to strangers. It says in Hebrews Thirteen that men have often entertained angels unawares."

I no longer think that Ifa is an angel, and I am not in a mood to hear Scripture quoted by my husband, or to listen to a sermon from him. What I want to hear is, "Baby, I'm sorry she interrupted us just when it was getting good. Let's go lock our door and see if we can get our groove on again." Instead, he preaches to me about what good Christians are supposed to do.

Personally, though Jesus is fine with me, I have not had good experiences with people who call themselves Christians. The ones who holler "Mercy!" the loudest are the ones who will talk about you the worst behind your back. The women in the church were the ones who gave Lucius and me the most trouble when we started seeing each other. It got back to me that they were talking a whole lot of garbage about how I was too worldly for the Deacon and how he deserved a consecrated kind of woman—like one of them, of course. All they accomplished was getting me to hurry up the wedding, before they changed his mind.

I am thinking that no matter what Lucius says, this African girl is no angel.

I am thinking that only some kind of devil would have known to knock on our door at exactly that moment.

And I am also thinking, if *she's* a Christian, I'm the Dalai Lama.

 # NINETEEN

WITH VY OUT on Thursday morning, the Curly Girl is a madhouse. By noon, three heads are under construction, and five customers are waiting. One head is under the dryer and another waits for her color to develop, while a pretty teenager waits patiently for her style. She has enough thick, healthy hair for three full-grown women. I hope Vy shows up soon.

On top of that, a customer that Vy forgot to mention shows up with a headful of dreads, half auburn, half black. She is a young woman in her late twenties—a teacher, she says. The appearance code for teachers has sure relaxed since I went to school! She is wearing a silver stud in her nose and a jazzy zipped-up suit that is knit with a silver thread in it. It looks good on her, and so do the dreads, but they are going to be a challenge to me. She tells me that Vy takes them out, washes them for her, and puts them back in every week. I can do dreads, but I do not have much experience, and I am hesitant about touching the heads of Vy's special customers.

I question this Miss Strickland carefully. She says that she takes the dreads out herself when Vy is busy, and offers to do it today. I accept gladly. Last week I interviewed a young woman named Tanesha who will do braids and dreads part-time, while her children are in school. I wish I had hired her. I wish she were here right now. I try not to panic. I should have become more skilled with dreads, but I did not, maybe because Dreadful Curly Girl (Pat. Pending) does not sound right. Maybe I can talk Miss Strickland into another style. Maybe, by the time her hair is washed, Vy will be in.

My other helpers, Bonita and Florine, are taking their time eating lunch, laughing and giggling over their shakes and french fries, right in the middle of the shop where all those patiently waiting women can see and hear them. I hate that when I go into public places and see it, and I will not have it in my shop. I have walked out of more stores than I can count because the clerks were more interested in taking their breaks and talking about their vacations than in helping me. The only thing that makes me walk out faster is being called by my first name instead of "Mrs. Lawson." As a race, we have fought too hard and too long for respect to put up with disrespect now. Unless I know my customers well, they are addressed as "Miss" and "Mrs." The same goes for my neighbors and acquaintances.

And my rule for employees is: If you must take a long lunch or have a long personal discussion, don't let the customers see you or overhear you. Go in the back room.

I take them back there and tell them just that. "You don't have to rush your lunch," I say. "Just finish it back here and come out ready to work. Let me see those hands."

Bonita's are scrubbed, with short, sensible nails, but Florine has long purple talons with designs embedded in them. I tell her, "Sorry, but those nails will have to go. You can't work properly in them."

Even though we do fancy manicures, I make it a firm rule in my salon that no worker wears them. I heard that the fad for those ridiculous long false nails started because they made convenient coke spoons. I certainly don't want to promote drugs in my place of business. We sell glamour, and there is nothing glamorous about drugs.

In five minutes, a pair of chastened hairdressers come out with their hands neat, their faces sober, and their attitudes on straight. Bonita, who has been with me a year, looks at the book, calls the next customer, and turns her over to Florine for shampooing. Florine is short and fat and inclined to be sullen, and should probably be in a different line of work. She doesn't come in on time, she takes long breaks every chance she gets, and she acts like sweeping the floor is beneath her, even though it's a job we all take turns doing. Now she's beginning to influence Bonita, who used to have an eager, efficient manner. I sigh. I am going to have to fire Florine. I hate firing people.

The smell of ammonia pierces my nostrils as Bonita squirts color on a customer's hair. I've insisted on using ammonia-free color in my shop for three years. I don't want problems with allergic reactions, or, worse, burns. I call Bonita over.

"But she asked for this," Bonita protests, holding out the package. "She brought it with her."

"Has she done the allergy test at home?"

"I don't know."

I go over to the woman and explain that these products have hazards, and we would rather not apply them to her head. If she wants to use them at home, of course, that's her prerogative.

She describes the effect she wants. Blonde or something approaching it, something like Mariah Carey's hair color, no darker than chestnut brown. The model on the package is young and has blue eyes. Now, in age and other specifics, this woman in no way resembles Mariah Carey, and she does not have blue eyes. I take a deep breath. Now is the time to call on all my skills of persuasion and diplomacy.

"Ma'am," I say, "a subtle effect is what we want to achieve, not one that will startle people. I want you to see how soft and appealing this shade is on you." I have a stock of wigs I keep on hand for just such occasions, and I pull out a medium brown one that matches the customer's skin. "Permit me," I say, and adjust it on her head. "Now imagine yourself going out in the daytime for lunch, or in the evening to a club, or on vacation." I do not mention work or the need to be conservative there. Practically all of my patrons work, but they do not want to be reminded of it when they are in my shop. They want to feel like pampered ladies of leisure, and that is how I treat them.

"Imagine," I say, "how this color would go with all of your outfits and all of your moods, not just some of them. Look at yourself! See your natural beauty in all its glory!" I spin her to face herself in the mirror. The woman, of course, is delighted.

It is not my place to have an opinion, but I am so tired of black women coming in here wanting to be blondes. Nappy blondes, straight blondes, wavy blondes, dreadful blondes—it's all fashionable these days, thanks to Dennis Rodman, and it's all unnatural. I know I am a businesswoman, but I want to give women something that is flattering, which is usually something near the shade that God gave them. When I know light hair will not become a woman, I try to talk her out of it. But I don't try too hard, because they pay me very well for hair lightening, and I understand where they are coming from. I know they're trying to fit into a society where blonde is the ideal.

I used to go platinum myself, back in the days when I was screaming silently for attention. I bet people were laughing at me behind my back, and if they were, I deserved it.

I am glad that black skin, natural hair, and the Afrocentric styles that go with them are becoming beautiful again. But let's not get carried away with this love-of-the-Motherland stuff, shall we? We don't get much income from naturals, and lately, I don't feel like embracing everything that comes from Africa as much as I used to. Ifa looks like the young Eartha Kitt, as I may have mentioned. And Eartha was one hot hoochie. She still is.

Lucius has explained that the girl sees him as a surrogate father, nothing more. In Africa, he has told me, a girl is very vulnerable without a father to act as her protector. Besides, he says, Ifa and her father were very close. She was his late-life child, Daddy's baby girl. He spoiled her rotten, and after her father died, she was inconsolable. So she is drawn to my husband as a father figure. I can understand all that. Sure. What bothers me is that I did not ask my husband for all of those explanations. They do not help me to understand why, when I caught them with their heads together last night, they jumped apart a little too fast.

Nor do I understand why Ifa felt compelled to tell me again

that in Olori the man is in charge of the household, while Lucius sat there with a pleased smirk on his face. I felt as if they were ganging up on me. They looked like a pair of fat cats who had just eaten a juicy bird meal and still had the feathers sticking out of their mouths.

I turn the customer back over to Bonita while I get to the teenager's hair. So thick. So healthy. I remember when I had hair like that. Ifa's is not as thick as it ought to be at her age. Probably her diet before she came to us is at fault. She eats ravenously now. Last night I baked a chicken, and when I looked up, the wing I had in mind for my second helping was gone, along with all the rest. Tonight I'd better cook two chickens. I will halve them and broil them with lemon, pepper, and sage.

I think our food bill alone has doubled as a result of her stay. I don't want to think about our telephone bill. Lucius has purchased locks for the phones.

"How do you want your hair?" I ask the girl, whose name is Latasha. I think that maybe she is the age I should think of adopting. Neither an infant nor an adult—just a shy, sweet thirteen.

"I don't know." Latasha could use some of my Nubian Queen Charm School lessons in confidence, I think.

"Well, do you have something special coming up, like a prom?"

"Proms ain't till May."

Ouch. She needs grammar lessons, too. "Anything else big on your schedule?"

"I'm going to sing a solo in church."

Prodded and pressed, Latasha admits that she will be singing her solo, "Great Is Thy Faithfulness," for Women's Day this Sunday, and that she's scared to death. Maybe looking nice will help her to be more confident when she gets up to sing. I suggest a Corkscrew Curly Girl (Pat. Pending) style, even though it takes a lot of time, because I want to give her some self-esteem. I don't recommend corkscrew curls for anyone over thirty, but they are wonderful with young faces.

I braid extensions into Latasha's hair because, even though she doesn't need them for length, they will hold the style in place. I curl the extensions tightly and leave them tight for that bouncy effect. I start to show her how to tie them up with ribbons, remember just in time that ribbons are for age ten and under, and suggest scrunchies instead, to keep the curls off her face for school and sports. I even give her three gold scrunchies, one for the top of her hair and two for the sides. The Corkscrew Curly Girl (Pat. Pending) runs fifty dollars and up, but I don't charge her any more than I would for a regular press and curl.

Little giveaways like this do more than keep my business thriving. They're a kind of spiritual insurance, as Lucius's pastor explained one Sunday. When you yourself need a favor, you will get one from an unexpected source if you are an abundant giver. I'm not big on church, and I didn't put anything extra in my envelope the way Reverend Haskins probably thought I would as a result of his sermon, but I was, as the kids would say, down with his message.

I take Latasha's much-folded ten-dollar bill. After a glance at herself, she leaves, curls bouncing, skipping on air. She knows she's been given a present. That's enough of a return on my gift already.

My feet are hurting. No wonder. I have been so busy since I walked in, I didn't take even time to change my shoes. I kick off my dress pumps and work in my stocking feet. I have bunions on my big toes and corns on all my others, which are hammer-shaped, and I wear sneakers and slippers whenever I can. I'll get into my lovely soft Pumas in due time.

"Psst! Miss Zena!"

The whisper comes over the partition between our booths. Vy has arrived, just in time to save me from putting in some dreadlocks backwards. I knew she was here before she spoke. I heard her dumping her purse on the counter and sliding her stool into her favorite position. I have tried and tried to get Vy to call me simply Zena, but I have never succeeded. She insists on keeping a barrier up between us, whether of age or class, I don't know.

I don't think it's age.

But, since we started out in the same projects, I don't think she should use formality with me. Just because I ran away from the James Weldon Johnson Homes a little faster than she did, and got a little farther away from our starting point, should make no difference between us. Try as I may, though, I can't break her of the habit.

"What is it, Vy?"

"Let me finish rolling this lady's hair, and I'll come around."

Her usually smooth, round face is drawn. "You know Sonny lost his case. The judge gave him—"

I hold up one hand to silence her. I do not want to talk about personal problems and scandals while customers are present. My hair looked so raggedy this morning, I almost tied it up in a scarf, but that brings back past miseries. "Listen, Vy, my color needs a touch-up, and I could use a set tonight, too. Okay?"

She nods. "You're on."

"Later, then." I will get an excellent color and set after we see the last customer out of the door, and we will talk about her son's problems then.

I am not looking forward to hearing Vyester sing her new blues. She probably needs to borrow bail money for Sonny, and while I don't mind lending it to her, I don't want the amount she owes me to get too high. She already owes me for keeping her sister off the streets, and another loan could make things tense between us and spoil our friendship. She might even start avoiding me if she can't pay it back.

I am, however, looking forward to my shampoo and set and the old-fashioned scalp scratch she always gives me first.

She forgets to scratch my scalp, though. Damn! She must really be upset. I know I am. Or at least *aggrieved*. (I am forever improving myself, and one of my self-improvements is to learn a new word every couple of weeks and use it as much as I can.)

"Uh-oh," Vy says as she parts my hair.

"What's wrong?" I ask.

"A whole lot of new grays coming in up here."

"I don't want to know about them," I tell her. "Just hide them." Especially right now, with that beautiful young woman at home with my husband, I do not want to think about my gray hairs.

"Okay. How you want it, Miss Zena?"

I have to change my hairstyle fairly often, so people will notice it and be inspired to come to my shop. But I have run out of ideas.

"I don't know, Vy. Be creative."

She is very still for a moment, thinking. Then she starts teasing my hair out with the rattail of the comb.

"What are you doing, Vy?"

"Surprising you. Say, Miss Zena, what you think about this? I had the radio on in my car today, tuned to Jazz 106, and I heard this woman call February Multi-ethnic Diversity Month. I thought, oh no, I didn't hear that. I couldn't be hearing that, not after Medgar died and Malcolm died and Martin died, too, and my own Uncle Purvis spent three weeks in jail for civil rights protesting and lost four teeth, not to mention his mind. He ain't been right at all since them head whippings he got from the cops for fighting for our civil rights. Oh, no, I didn't hear her say that about February."

Vy sounds very aggrieved at having to share Black History Month. I am aggrieved, too. "That's too diverse for me," I say.

"Me too. February is our month. Let them other people get a month of their own, or else go to jail and get their heads beat like we did, before we include them in ours."

I tell her how disturbed I was by the arrival of Miss Strickland and her dreads.

"You should have made her wait, Miss Zena. She knew better than to show up that early, just because she got a half a day off. She had an evening appointment."

"Still," I say, "I need you to teach me how to deal with dreads. I ought to learn, before that happens again."

"Sure I'll teach you," she says. "But you know, you have enough to do already, Miss Zena. Why don't you hire that braid expert, Take a Leash, or whatever her name is?—Okay, I'm done. Take a look at yourself."

I am indeed surprised, and pleasantly. She has given me a headful of short corkscrews that spring from three inches back on my forehead. Most of them are my natural dark brown, but she has tied in a few dark red ones. The effect is not at all too young for the woman I see in the mirror, who is maybe thirty-five, tops.

"Do you like it?"

"I love it." I can't wait to get home and see how Lucius likes it. I plan to jump into one of my satin nightgowns and surprise him. "Vy, you know I don't mind helping you bail Sonny out, if that's what's on your mind."

"I'm not going to bail him out."

"You're not?"

"No. Fred and me, we talked it over, and we decided we done all we could for Sonny. The judge gave him six months. If he wants to appeal, we'll help him pay his lawyer, but that's all. Meanwhile, let him sit in there and stay out of trouble, and think about changing his ways.

"It's hard, though, Miss Zena. I know we decided on the right thing, but I keep wanting to jump up and run down there and get him out."

"I know it must be rough on you, Vy."

"It's hard," she repeats. "It's like letting someone you love die."

I pat her arm and sit quietly for a minute, sympathizing with her in silence. I would feel better if I could get mad right now about the injustice of the system and rant and rave about the unfair way it refuses to give young black men a break, but though I believe that is true, it simply does not apply to Sonny Sampson. He's had more breaks than a cat has lives, and he didn't deserve them any more than his parents deserve such a rotten kid. No, I cannot get aggrieved over Sonny.

"Anything else, Miss Zena?"

"Yes. Lend me an eyebrow pencil, and some blush if you have any."

She watches while I do a lot of repair work and decorating on my face.

"You put that girl out yet, Miss Zena?"

Vy has known me so long she can read my mind, or maybe my actions.

"I'm working on it," I tell her.

"Don't take too long," she warns. She seems to be thinking for a minute before she adds, "If you want, I could kill her for you."

"What did you say?"

"I said, I'd be glad to kill her for you if you want me to. I wouldn't go to jail. I'm not responsible. I had a nervous breakdown one time and had to go talk to a doctor for a whole six months. I never told you about it, because I needed this job, but now I know you won't hold it against me."

"When was this, Vy?"

"Oh, a long time ago, right after my mother died. I threatened to kill myself, so they put me in the hospital. They still got a record of it somewhere. That's why I know I could kill her and get away with it. They don't put crazy people in jail, they just send them away for a rest, and I can prove my head ain't right."

Now, that's what I call love. I have to get up and hug her then. "Oh, Vy, things aren't that bad yet. I don't know what's going on. Maybe nothing. Sometimes, though, I think Lucius might be getting ideas about being a dog."

"Any man will be a dog," she says, "if you leave him around a bitch long enough."

I give my friend another long hug. She feels good, but she feels different, too. I step back and give her a good long look. "You're gaining weight," I inform her.

That is when she drops the ton of bricks on me. "That's because I'm pregnant," she says.

I shriek and yell and holler questions for about five minutes. "How long? Why didn't you tell me? When did you find out? When are you due?" I am jumping up and down like a jackrabbit on a trampoline.

She gives me a sheepish smile. "I've known for a long time,

but I didn't go to the doctor till last week. He says October, but I think sooner."

I put my hand on her shoulder and press her down into the chair. "For God's sake, sit down, Vy. I don't want you working so hard."

"See, that's why I didn't tell you. I have to work. I need the money. Besides, you need me here."

"But not all the time. Not as much. I'll work longer. I'll hire Tanesha right away. I'll hire another operator, too." I am babbling. "I'll teach Ifa to do hair."

"No you won't, not unless you want me to quit."

Life is strange. Not too long ago, I would have chosen Ifa over Vyester. Now I feel the opposite way.

"Boy or girl?" is my next question. I mean to ask, does she want a boy or a girl, but she has the answer already.

"Girl," she says. "I knew it was a girl all along, before they did that test on my amnio center. Calm down, Miss Zena. I am not sick. This is a normal condition. I can still work. And if you need some killing done, I still got my knife."

I am so excited, I can't talk. A baby girl! Another chance to buy frilly little clothes!

At the same time, though, I feel a hollow sadness inside. I missed my period a couple of weeks ago, and for half a minute, I got excited and thought, well, maybe it could be. Miracles do happen.

But I was just having fantasies again. It was just another sign that I am getting old.

 TWENTY

AFTER MY LONG, hard day, I know I won't be up to cooking, so I do something that's against all my usual rules. I buy a large bucket of fried chicken and take it home.

This time, the living room looks like a disaster area, with newspapers and magazines strewn everywhere. The kitchen is worse.

Ifa and Lucius are sitting at the table talking intensely, with cold cups of coffee between them. It looks like they have been sitting there since breakfast. The sink is piled up high with dirty dishes, and coffee grounds, bread crumbs, and eggshells are everywhere.

Lucius gives me that big warm smile of his that always makes everything all right. "Ifa and I have been talking about life in her village," he says, "and the political situation in her country."

"Yes, it ees terrible. I have been telling Dod. Everything ees corrupt. Everything." She jabs her long, maroon-tipped finger at me as she makes her points. "You can buy a judge, a governor, anyone you want. The government ees in a terrible mess."

"So is this kitchen," I can't help saying.

"Oh, Mum, I am sorry," she says, "but our discussion got to be so interesting, I forgot about the dirty dishes. Dod is really a very interesting man. In Olori he would be a great chief, with many houses."

"And many wives and children in them, I suppose."

"Yes," she says, and stares at me defiantly. She is wearing a length of blue cloth wrapped around her at armpit level, and nothing else. Her boobs are covered—barely—but her skinny shoulders are bare.

I plop the bucket of chicken and the triple side order of coleslaw on the table and pass out plates, banging one so hard I break it.

"Well, this is dinner," I state. "If you look in the refrigerator behind you, Ifa, you'll find some Pepsi."

She does not move. "I prefer juice or water," she informs me.

"Fine. But there are two other people here who want Pepsi."

"Colas are bad for the teeth and the stomach, Mum. Water is better."

"Thank you for the information," I say, and get up and get the bottle of Pepsi myself. "I thought you were going to do some more housecleaning today."

"I was, but Dod and I got to talking, and—eek! What kind of chicken ees this?" She is holding one of the Colonel's Original Recipe thighs aloft and staring at in horror.

As she raises the chicken, I catch a whiff of odor from her armpits that almost knocks me out. My gentle hint about using deodorant has done no good, then. I will have to be rougher this time.

"Colonel Stewart's Fried Chicken," I say. "Very famous. Very popular here. No one has been known to die from it. Try some."

"This piece ees so beeg! Eet looks like some animal!" she exclaims. She takes a cautious nibble, and then a bigger bite. Three more bites, and she is down to the bone, which she also waves, almost asphyxiating me. "You see thees bone? It ees black. That means this chicken has been frozen and thawed and frozen again. Very bad."

And then she proceeds to crunch the bad bone with her large, white, splendid teeth until it disappears.

"I love chicken bones," she says. "They are so sweet."

Lucius and I watch in amazement as she rapidly devours five

or six pieces of chicken, bones and all. Then we wake up, realizing at the same moment that if we don't move fast, there will be none of that no-good chicken left for us. I have to settle for two wings and a biscuit, while Lucius grabs a breast in each hand.

Before Ifa gets up from the table, she also drinks half a liter of Pepsi, and finishes her meal off with a loud belch.

"Ah, that felt good," she says, and stands up. "I will do the dishes now, Mum, unless Dod wants another massage."

"Ifa gave you a massage?" I ask him.

My husband begins coughing and harrumphing like a small-time crook on the witness stand. "Well, er, you see, Zena," he says, "I complained of a headache, and she offered to, uh, work on my pressure points. Really amazing, how much it helped. Amazing."

"I think Dod has a lot on his mind, and it gives him tension," says the masseuse.

"Yes, well, I'll give him his massages from now on, thank you, Ifa," I say, feeling my slow burn rise rapidly from simmer to boil. "Why didn't you get dressed today?"

"But I am dressed," she protests. "This is what we wear all the time in our village."

"You are not in your village now," I tell her. "Here, we wear more than a pareo, or whatever you call that thing, especially when we are around gentlemen. I have given you clothes. Please wear them."

Lucius coughs again and leaves the room to go smoke a cigar.

"But this is perfectly modest," she says, turning and modeling the wrap, which mostly falls to her knees, though it separates pretty high up in back, almost, but not quite, up to her booty.

"I am sure you think so, but tomorrow I want you to wear more clothes."

She has returned to her chore. I think that the Seven Dwarfs were probably plumbers, since all American plumbing is standardized to their height. As our visitor bends her long spine over our sink to wash dishes, the rear separation in her garment rises. My God.

"Ifa!" I shout. "Stop! Forget the dishes. I want you to put on more clothes, unless you are going to bed. And before you change, I want you to bathe and use plenty of that deodorant I gave you."

"Oh, Mum, you are always picking on me," she complains. "I think I will just go straight to bed."

I relent just a little. "Were you able to get any sleep last night?"

"Yes." She gives me one of her radiant sunrise smiles. "I did my python dance. It summoned my protector, the python. He chased the evil spirits and allowed me to sleep. You must allow me to perform my dance for you and Dod."

"What is the reason for python dancing?" I ask her.

"The python is my family's patron," she explains. "He helps and protects me. Every village in the bush keeps a python."

"Do you mean a real live python?" wonders Lucius, who has come back into the kitchen to pour himself another Pepsi.

"Of course," she says condescendingly. "I am the only person who is allowed to feed the python all by myself."

"And where does the python stay?" I wonder.

"Wherever he wants," cracks Lucius.

She is very serious. "Yes, but mostly in the best room in our house."

I remember that when Cecelia invited us to visit the Olongos in Olori, she said that we would have the best room. I shudder.

Ifa runs to her room and comes back with a number of items that include her python skin and my cassette player. "Watching me dance is a great opportunity," she informs me. "I am the best python dancer in Buruku State." As far as I am concerned, she is welcome to her titles: Official Python Keeper. State Champion Python Dancer.

Ifa dabs makeup on her face, arms and legs, mostly white dots like a snake's markings. She wraps the eight-foot snakeskin around her and starts a tape of intricate drumming playing on the boom box. I hear big conga drums, small bongos, and an occasional trill from a flute.

Now Ifa begins a series of slow weaving and undulating movements that make her look exactly like a snake. She smiles sleepily as if she has just swallowed a large mongoose and is digesting it. Her chest heaves up and down slowly like a python's coils. Her hips rise and fall, too. She is no longer a woman, she is a python—fat, well fed, sleepy, but still dangerous.

My husband watches her as if in a trance.

She weaves toward him and holds out her hands.

At the height of the drumming, he suddenly leaps to his feet, takes her hands, and begins weaving and twisting in an exact replica of her movements. And all these years, I thought the man couldn't dance.

I also thought he had a serious snake phobia. In fact, I was counting on it.

Now, though I cannot believe my eyes, there my husband is, dancing with the snake-girl, circling the room in a glide and mirroring her movements.

Then, with a visible struggle, he breaks the spell and drops her hands. "Girl," he says in a husky voice, "you need to stop dancing like that in front of people. There are limits to what a man can stand."

Instead of yanking him away by the ear and then slapping her silly, like I ought to do, I retreat to my bedroom. A giant snake that looks like a truck tire is coiled on my gold damask bedspread. I blink, and it disappears, but I saw it. I know I saw it. I have a feeling I will see it again before this nightmare is over.

Lucius is in the hall when I come out, looking feverish. He starts trying to explain himself, talking fast. "You know, Zena, when a man is getting close to the kingdom, that's when the Devil finds the most powerful ways to tempt him. And the Devil always shows up as a serpent, you know that."

He follows me toward the living room. "Zena, the girl is a heathen. It's not her fault her family taught her pagan beliefs. And you know what we are supposed to do for the heathens. Convert them. Have a care for their souls."

"Go ahead, try to convert her," I tell him. "While you at it, you better call some of your good Christian church folks and see if they will take her in. Because I'm going to put her out in the morning."

"You can't do that, Zena. She's our charge. Our Christian responsibility."

"I can, and I will." I push past this Christian fool I married, and head for my little secretary desk in the living room. I hunt for my phone book, find the numbers Cecelia left with us, and start dialing.

I get one wrong number, one disconnect message, and one operator's recorded voice telling me I have made a mistake.

She's sure right about that.

 # TWENTY-ONE

MISS ZENA IS having troubles at home. She don't have to tell me. I can see the pain in her eyes. All the makeup and curly-cues in the world can't hide that. I have troubles, too, but not that kind, thank God. Not anymore. When the judge gave Sonny that sentence, my knees began to buckle, but Fred was right there by my side. He gripped my arm by the elbow and held me up. My steady Fred. My solid rock, my good, dependable man.

Together, we have been through too much with that boy— truancy, driving violations, lost license, petty thefts and not-so-petty ones. We have talked it over and decided to see can we cut him loose, at least while he's away. Alone, I couldn't do it, but together we can be strong.

Maybe we gave Sonny too much, and that is the reason he turned out wrong. He never wanted for anything, and if he asked for things, even stuff he didn't need, we found a way to get it for him, even if we couldn't afford it. Trains and model airplanes, electric cars and a trail bike, skates and a moped. And sneakers. Especially sneakers. Now I think, if I had my way, all kids would have to go barefoot until they could buy their own shoes. If they step on a tack or a piece of glass, let their parents put a Band-Aid on. I know, if I had it to do over again, I wouldn't buy my son so many pairs of high-priced sneakers. All he did was run out and steal more. I guess we made him feel he was entitled to a whole storeful.

Oh, that boy had everything he wanted, and a lot of stuff he didn't want. Video games and a Nintendo and a whole army of little G.I. soldiers. Expensive little suits in every color, with shirts and ties to go with them—and they just hung in the closet, because we didn't take him to church except on Easter. Hand-knit sweaters in designs like Bill Cosby wears, and heavy socks to go with them. And all he wanted to wear after he turned ten was a hoody sweatshirt and some baggy pants that hung low enough to almost fall off his butt! If I had it to do over again, I'd send him to one of those schools where they make the kids wear uniforms.

Another thing I wish I'd done was listen to his teachers more, instead of copping an attitude every time they sent notes home or called me on the phone. I just refused to believe my precious, perfect little boy had done all the bad things they said he did.

The first time Sonny was expelled for fighting, they had to expel me, too—for fighting the principal. After that, I think, they stopped telling us what he did wrong— they were too afraid of me. Now I wish I had kept my cool and listened to what his teachers said. If I had a chance to do it over, I'd tell those teachers, "You are in charge of him while he is with you. Do anything you have to do to make him behave and learn, and if that means swatting him, you have my permission."

Fred and me, we made plenty of mistakes with Sonny, but we have decided his problems are not all our fault. Sometimes a bad apple just crops up in a family tree that is otherwise full of good fruit. When you see that happening, you have to toss that apple out before it spoils the others. We decided we should stop throwing good money after our bad apple, and start saving for our new one.

We are just grateful to be getting a second chance to raise a child right. We have made a pact already not to spoil her. We have agreed to use a "Stop" signal when one thinks the other one is spoiling our little girl. This signal will be, "Do you smell spoiled fruit?" As for our son, we have to put him out of our minds, at least while he's away.

To tell the truth, I'm kind of happy to have Sonny out of the house. I don't have to hear his rap music pounding away, I don't have to see his dirty, sneaky friends, and I don't have to put up with his nasty mouth and his rotten moods—his whining, for instance, when I won't let him drive my car, even though he hasn't got his license back. Oh, I'll take him cigarettes and snacks and let him call us collect once a month, but I can't let myself get upset over him the way I used to. For one thing, he's grown. For another, I can't afford to put any stress on my old body now that it's pregnant again.

I didn't want to tell Miss Zena my news, but it just slipped out. She's got too much on her mind and too much trouble on her hands at the moment. Trouble she went out looking for and found, I'll have to admit.

What makes it worse is, Mr. Lucius is a Christian man. They the worst kind. They can convince themselves it's all right to steal a blind man's money and drink the baby's milk and beat up on their own mamas, because there's a verse somewhere in the Bible that says it's all right to do those things. Worse, if you accuse them of wrongdoing, they'll start proving to you that you're a bigger sinner than them for saying so—and what's more, they'll believe it. I'd rather have a whole barrelful of snakes than have Miss Zena's troubles. I'd also rather have a snake, dog, and weasel combined in my house than a holy, hypocrite Christian man.

My Sonny is a lowlife and a thief and a junkie, but at least he ain't never claimed to be holy. And my Fred has also done some low things, like screwing that Cousin Idabelle and trying to get his brother drunk so he would sign over his share of their father's insurance, but he never said Jesus told him he was supposed to do any of them.

Whereas, along with all her other troubles, I bet Miss Zena's husband is trying to lay some Scripture on her right now and tell her to be a Good Samaritan to that girl—so he can keep on having the spice of variety in his house.

But if she's falling for it, she's not the Miss Zena I know.

Oh, my Fred got religion one time. Yes, he did. He went to this Pentecostal church and got happy, started testifying, and even joined church. Then he started working on me to go with him. "Girl," he would say, "you know we ain't been livin' right all these years. It ain't right for a married couple to be unequally yoked, and besides, I'm concerned about your soul. Now I got myself saved, you need to go and get saved, too."

Well, I know some Holiness folks. They stay in church hollering "Praise the Lord" all day and never get their houses cleaned or their kids fed or their laundry done, so I knew I would have to give up a whole Sunday to go with him. Finally, after he had pestered me for a month, I got all my housework done the night before and went with him to this service in a storefront that used to be a thrift store. That didn't impress me. Usually a thrift store is the last stage in a building's life, and after that it dies and gets boarded up or knocked down, but these True Vine Disciples of the Word people believed they could resurrect it.

Well, this raggedy little church Fred had joined had a five-piece band in there every bit as good as the Apollo orchestra. Drums, guitar, bass, sax, and piano. It had a choir of about five people who, if you shut your eyes, sounded like fifty. They got into "You Don't Know Like I Know What the Lord Has Done for Me" and really tore it up. I mean, feet were patting, hands were clapping, tambourines were jangling, drums beating, and cymbals clashing. The choir turned the music inside out, upside down, backwards, and sideways, and really *exhausted* that song. Everywhere I looked, people were leaping to their feet, shouting and moaning. By the time the choir finished singing, everybody was on their feet clapping and dancing, and half the congregation, including Fred, were talking in tongues. It gave me the creeps, so I slapped him. "Stop that gibberish," I told him. "Talk English, or I walk out right now."

The Pentecostal minister was the fattest man I ever saw, but he skipped and glided back and forth across that stage like an ice skater. Smooth and swift as Surya Bonaly. One time, I even thought he was going to do one of her back flips. Skip, glide, and shout. "Hallelujah!" Skip, glide, and shout. "Oh, help us,

Holy Ghost!" Skip, glide, and shout. "Come hither, Paraclete! With Your help, we gonna do some healing today!" I wondered why he was calling on a parakeet to help him heal folks, but Fred explained the word to me. It was another term for the Holy Ghost. Skip, glide, and shout. "Now, who needs to be healed?"

After staying up half the night mopping and vacuuming and ironing so I could spend all day Sunday in church, I could feel my old bad knee acting up. So I raised my hand and went up front along with the blind, the maimed, and the seriously lame. When I saw the ones in wheelchairs, I got ashamed and started to go back to my seat, but when I saw Fred looking so happy to see me up there at the altar, I stayed where I was.

When it got to be my turn, the Reverend said, "Show me where it hurts, daughter."

I pointed to my knee.

"Praise the Lord," he said. He knelt in front of me and got up under my skirt and commenced to rubbing on my knee.

I heard a rumbling sound from Fred behind me, like the warning that comes at the beginning of a volcano erupting.

The Reverend closed his eyes and began praying and rubbing higher up on my leg.

"Not way up there, Reverend. Just my knee."

But I hadn't needed to say anything. Fred snatched the minister's hand away and dragged me out of that church so fast, I didn't even feel my feet touch the ground. All the way home, I was imagining that minister's poor wife and what she had to put up with. All that weight on her. She probably said, "Not tonight, Rev," a lot of times, not wanting to be squashed, and that was why he was so horny. I've heard ministers are all that way, though, even the skinny ones—though I've never seen a skinny one. The church sisters cook too much chicken and macaroni, and bake too many cakes and pies, that's why.

All the rest of that day, Fred was cussing and calling the Reverend all kinds of dirty low-down stepfathers and fat so-and-sos and describing what he ought to go back there and do to him.

I don't know if he did them things or not. I don't think so. But one thing I do know, he never went back to that church, and he never said nothing to me about getting saved again.

Church can't help Miss Zena, not right now. If I know those jealous church people, they are rejoicing right now to see her brought low. Same thing with those fancy ladies in that Divas club. She thinks they're a step above her with their money and their education and their fancy airs, but I know they're just another bunch of jealous females, because Miss Zena and Mr. Lucius are happy, and most of them ain't. What good is it to have a husband who makes big money, if he's never home? What good is it to be married to a doctor, if you're sick at heart all the time?

I got to see if I can think of some way to help Miss Zena. Maybe I can look around and find that African girl a job, a live-in job if there still are some. She looks big and strong, and folks who need help around the house aren't too particular about green cards. They'd rather not have to take out Social Security, anyway.

If I can find her some folks to live in with, she won't have to stay at Miss Zena's house except on her days off. And maybe, with her pay, she can rent herself a room someplace else.

She'd have to come down off her high horse, though, and keep her opinions to herself. White folks do not be wanting to hear what you think. They want you to listen to them and say "Yes, ma'am," so they can tell their friends, "My girl agrees with me." That's how white people get to be experts on us. They express their opinions to their help. The help keep quiet, because they want to keep their jobs, and the employers think their silence means agreement. Truth is, they do not want to hear anything at all from you, unless you can sing some spirituals. That, they like.

That girl do not look like she can sing at all, and I doubt if she knows any church songs. However, I will call my friend Verniece and see if she knows of any openings. We used to be part of a circle of houseworkers that traded off jobs so we could each get a day off once in a while to breathe and take care of our own business. One of us would call in sick, and say that the other would take her place. Sometimes we didn't even bother to call, because we all looked alike to most of them people.

The best jobs were where the people were never home. It was easy to trade days on them. Once I got caught when I stayed home to take care of Sonny, and this woman tried to say I had done something dishonest by letting Verniece take my place. I said, "You got your house cleaned, didn't you? What do you care? Shut up." She shut right up, but I never worked at that house again. She told Verniece she was scared of me.

Now ain't that something? This woman and her husband got all that money, a house big as a hotel, and a pair of dogs that look like horses, plus real horses, plus three cars—and she scared of me! She owns all the property, she has all the money, she probably owns the police and the politicians, and she thinks one little black woman can do her harm. We sure must be some powerful people to scare someone like her that bad.

I was glad that lady didn't want me back. She had a habit of hiding all the mops to make me scrub the floors on my knees, and I mean she had her some floors! White tile stretching so far it looked like a beach in Florida. Then, too, she was always try-ing to get something extra out of me. If I finished a half hour early, she wanted me to do some ironing or clean the stove. I would tell her real polite, "Ma'am, that isn't part of the job." And she would say, all whimpery, "Yes, but look at the clock, you have time."

Then there was another one wanted me to keep her kids, so she could go out to lunch or go shopping with her friends. Keep them and clean her house too, while my Sonny was home with-out a baby-sitter—just a neighbor who promised to listen for him. They was some bad little kids, too, so wild I had to shut them in one room to get my work done. When I let them out, they said they was going to tell. I said, "Tell. I don't care." I never went back to that house again, either. The kids were too bad, and the job was too hard. Talk about nasty! Her dust bunnies were big as rabbits, and they had multiplied.

I got out of the mop brigade, thanks to God and my late mama, whose insurance money paid for my beauty school, but I hear they are still making their rounds.

A little hard work would not hurt that big, spoiled African girl at all. I believe I will see if I can find her some.

 TWENTY-TWO

GIT UP OFF MY TRUMP!" shrieks Vera Marshall, my partner, and slams a diece, ten, king, queen, and ace of diamonds down in front of her. She pulls in five tricks at once with those cards.

"We gone rub their heads good, Zena!" Vera exclaims. Both of us begin rubbing our heads at the same time, to signify a head rub. That is a hand in which the opponents never get to make a single trick. The one trick they might have grabbed is in clubs, which I trump with a jack of diamonds. Her diece, the nine, takes my only other trump, another diece, but it's okay. We win briskly, with my spades taking up as trumps where her diamonds leave off, because our opponents are out of spades. Oh, I do love pinochle—especially when I win!

"We did it, partner!" Vera squeals.

There's nothing like winning a good, vicious hand of pinochle. I needed that.

"Put it over here," I say to Gloria Shepherd, on my right, and knead her scalp with my knuckles, while Vera messes up Phlora Wilson's wig.

Gloria looks ruefully into her pocket mirror. "Good thing I got a hat to wear to church tomorrow," she says. "When can I come in and get this mess fixed up, Zena?"

"Just call for an appointment," I say gleefully, and reach out like I am going to rub her head some more. But what I do instead is sweep her loose hair that I have disarranged around and up to one side, and fasten it with a banana clip I have in my purse. I do this for her because she's a good friend. She looks better than she did before, anyway, because, after forty, hair that's pulled up always looks better than hair that is hanging down. At our age, with gravity winning its victory over our faces and bodies, we need all the uplift we can get.

That win at cards was sweet. I am savoring it because, after last week, I needed it.

I decided not to throw Ifa out, after all. She hadn't really done anything to deserve it, other than getting on my nerves and dancing too sexy and looking too good in some of my cast-off clothes. But I would sure like her out of the house part of the time. Say, at a job. She is expensive, plus, like Visa, she is everywhere I want to be—in the living room, in the Back Room, and especially in the bathroom. But she can't go to work, because she still doesn't have that green card. All she has is the hope of getting a student visa.

Not so long ago, the first two fingers of my right hand were sore from being crossed so tightly behind my back. The two fingers helped keep me from losing my temper when Ifa wouldn't clean up her room, wouldn't put on enough clothes around the house, wouldn't stop looking adoringly at Lucius, who kept beaming back at her. They stood for all the time she had left to stay in this country—two weeks. But the two weeks have passed, and she is still here.

When I confronted her about the phony names and phone numbers her sister left with me, she really looked surprised. I believe her sister tricked her as well as me.

Ifa said, "But, Mum, there must be some mistake. Cecelia would not mislead you."

"She did mislead me. Those people who are supposed to be expecting you do not exist. That means she has deposited you with us, with no money and no other place to go. Why did your sister dump you, Ifa? Is she mad at you for any reason?"

She hesitates. Her voice is low. "Well, Mum, I was the baby, and Cecelia always felt that my father was more fond of me than of her. She always claims that he spoiled me."

To me, that's not a good enough reason to dump your sister on strangers in a foreign country. "Anything else she might hold against you?"

"Well, Mum, I told you, she had that operation, and I did not. It was very painful, she says. It makes intercourse uncomfortable and childbirth horrible. That may be why her husband—" She stops and covers her mouth, as if she has said something she did not mean to say.

"What about her husband?"

"Mum, I stayed with them once, and he came into my bed."

Okay, there it is. A reason for dumping someone overboard if I ever heard one. Ifa is lucky she came here by plane and not by ship.

"Mum, in our culture, that is not such a big thing," she explains. "Men often have several wives, and very often they are the sisters of the first wife. I was his guest. I could not refuse."

"Weren't you your sister's guest, too?"

"Mum, you do not understand, it is not the same as here. Women do not have any say about what men do. Cecelia is a highly educated woman, a college professor, but she has no rights at home. Oh, she is in charge of the meals and the children, and she also handles the money, but her husband is in charge of her."

"How do the women feel about their husbands taking extra wives?" I ask her.

She shrugs prettily. "What can they do? They accept it."

I feel my back stiffening and my head tightening, something that has been happening a lot to me lately. Sometimes it develops into a migraine headache. It makes me wonder if I am getting high blood pressure.

I know one thing—I am on the Middle Passage, something like my ancestors, and it is rough to be rounding the bend of forty-nine and sighting fifty, getting swamped by waves of sweating and nervousness, and taking on water. Headaches. Feverish spells. The end, the absolute end, of my dreams of motherhood. I said good-bye to youth long ago. Hello to old age is next. Having this young temptress in my house does not make the prospect easier.

"Well, just in case you were wondering, Ifa, women do not accept it here. Men have one wife at a time, and that's all they are allowed."

"I know that, Mum." She hesitates, then begins to stutter. M-mum, I, I, I hope—I hope you do not think I am attracted to Dod."

"Why wouldn't you be? He is an attractive man."

"He is an old man. He is like a father to me, that is all."

This should be reassuring, but I am irritated because, as usual, she has phrased it the wrong way.

I was glad the Divas were having one of their old-fashioned card-playing meetings today, not an afternoon to sit and soak up culture. I needed to play some hard hands of pinochle and let off steam.

At our last cultural meeting, we had a Muslim woman who spoke about the joys of man-sharing. When I remember her talk, I still get upset. I don't care if man-sharing is a solution to the able-bodied–man shortage, and I don't care if it does help when you're on a lecture tour to have your husband's Wife Number Two at home to baby-sit. I don't want any parts of it, and I said so.

What made it worse was, some of the women in this club got catty on me. Monica Lewis said, "I thought you would be the last person to object to man-sharing, Zena."

"What the hell do you mean?"

"Don't you have an arrangement like that at home?" asked Lenore Wilkerson, my neighbor, who probably started all the gossip about me among the Divas.

"All I have is a grown daughter," I said, and Monica laughed.

"I hear your husband goes to a lot of medical conventions," I added. "Of course Doctor Wilkerson doesn't go, they are for real doctors," I say to Lenore, "but I'll bet Doctor Lewis isn't lonely while he's away."

Monica turned ashy under her pancake makeup. "Tell me, what are the sleeping arrangements at your house, Zena?" she had the nerve to ask.

"We have two trailers and a portable john in the front yard," I said. I believe she thinks she's better than I am because I work for a living. I felt like going upside her head, but something kept me from doing it. I would like to say it was my own ladylike nature, but it was Gloria Shepherd pinning my wrists behind my back.

I thought I had a lot of friends in this club, but Gloria may be the only one. Vera Marshall is all right, but our personalities clash—she is too pushy for me. Possibly Laura Tyson would be my friend, too, if she were younger, but she's over sixty. I don't have that much in common with the older women in the group, who tend to be richer and more conservative than I am, or with the younger ones either, because they are more militant. There is no one here I can talk to about my problems. The only one I can talk to is Vyester, and she isn't here, she's at the shop. But I can release some of my fury by playing hardball pinochle.

Taking a break after our head rub, Gloria, Vera, and Phlora all light cigarettes, which I hate, but what can I do? It's a free country, and this is not a "No Smoking" house. I get up from the table to move away from the smoke and to search for something to drink. I stand at our hostess's buffet stirring sugar into my tea. Then I feel my back stiffen again.

At the table behind my back, two women are talking.

"Well, I think it's a shame," one says, "the way that foreign girl is hanging all over Lucius, after Zena was good enough to take her in."

"She was a fool to take her in, if you ask me," says the other. "Where did you see them?"

"Oh, they've been seen all over, but I saw them downtown, in the Two Thousand and One Cafeteria—you know, that place behind the courthouse where the lawyers and politicians all eat lunch. She was so busy putting her hands all over him, I don't know how she managed to eat."

"Um, um, um."

"And when they left, she had both her arms wrapped around one of his, like a snake. To Lucius's credit, he pulled his arm loose. But she went and grabbed it again, and kept on talking all up in his face."

"Um, um, um. Did you speak to him?"

"Not me. If I let on that I saw them, I'd have to tell Zena. You know I don't want to get in the middle of something like that. I practically crawled under my table to keep him from seeing me."

"Well, it's a shame," says the other voice, which I recognize as belonging to Monica Lewis, "but then, Zena deserves it, doesn't she? I mean, nobody forced her to take that girl in. I've heard these Africans have no more morals than jackrabbits."

"I wouldn't put it quite like that," her companion says. "I would say, their morals are different from ours, because they come from a different culture."

"No morals," Monica repeats as if she hasn't heard a word, "and besides, they steal. I hope Zena is counting her silverware and keeping an eye on her jewelry."

"What they are stealing," the other woman says decidedly, "is our jobs."

"And sometimes other things," says Monica darkly.

I feel the blood rushing to my face, and am glad I am too brownskinned to blush obviously. If I were light-skinned, my face would look like a tomato right now.

"Let's hope not. You know, I wouldn't mind if they would just settle for a few trinkets. James's father is retired, of course, but he had a part-time hustle as a bellhop in a hotel downtown. Nothing big, but it kept him busy and paid for his beer and his cigars. Well, last month he showed up for work, and his job was gone. Management had brought in fresh slaves. Africans had taken over the place."

"They work for less, that's why," Monica said. "You would think these companies would care more about their loyal American employees than about saving a few cents on salaries, but they don't. My own father used to work for the hotels in Florida, until those Cubans came in and took over."

"We were talking about Africans, not Cubans."

"Same thing. We were talking about *foreigners*, and how they come here and take all our jobs. Everett has not been able to get affiliated with a single hospital, but he told me that some Pakistani doctors who just got here last year are already on the staffs of the best teaching hospitals. How do you think that makes him feel?"

Monica's husband is a doctor. That's why she can afford to have so many diamond rings. She is planning to have extra fingers grafted on so she can wear them all.

"Terrible," the woman says, and now I recognize her voice. It's Laura Tyson, who must be back from her safari in Kenya. Her husband's a doctor, too, but she doesn't brag or show off like Monica does. "I don't understand it, but it probably has something to do with money. Everything in this country does."

"Oh, of course," says Monica, who wears fur coats even in hot weather, and sometimes wears one coat and carries the other, to let everybody know she owns two. "Our government sells some bombs to the Pakistani government, or more likely gives them to them, and they sell them to somebody else, so then they can afford to endow some research on beriberi at one of our hospitals. That research money buys staff positions for three or four of their doctors. How much research can black Americans endow? How many bombs can we buy?"

"I don't know, but I think we'd better start saving up for some," says Laura, proving that the situation in this country is so bad it will sometimes make even the most gentle people get violent.

I forget and glance over my shoulder at Laura to see how her Curly Twist (Pat. Pending) style is holding up. Gray and all, it looks fine, like I just put it in this morning, and I am glad, but she sees me, and there is no way she can pretend our eyes didn't meet. She gives me an embarrassed little wave, and I wave back.

I pray, but the floor doesn't open up and swallow me.

Laura invites me to join them at their table, of course. I like Laura, and I tolerate Monica because she is a fool and can't help herself, but after overhearing the conversation, I would rather climb into a mud pit and wrestle a bunch of alligators than sit down with them.

I mumble some excuse about a Crock-Pot I forgot to unplug, and rush home. I hope they don't think about my excuse too much. That's the whole point of Crock-Pots—you can plug them in and walk away, and hardly ever have to worry about them. I left some beans and smoked turkey necks going in one this morning. And suddenly those plain old lima beans I am cooking at home look a lot better to me than the tropical fruit salad and banana bread and margarita and screwdriver cocktails our hostess is passing around. Even if the salad does have mangoes and coconuts in it, as well as passion fruit and fresh pineapple, as I heard someone say.

# TWENTY-THREE

BEFORE I EVEN turn the key in my door, I hear the sound of shekeres and pounding drums. Once it would have made me want to dance. Now it only makes me want to leave.

We have company, I see when I walk in. Lucius is sprawled in one big chair and Charlie Matthews in the other, and Ifa is giving them a private performance of her snake dance.

I think I see a big python coiled on the sofa. I blink, and it is gone. Instead of sitting down where it was, I remain standing while Ifa goes through her coiling and uncoiling movements, hypnotizing the men. She does not have on her python skin. She is wearing a print fabric bra and a matching short skirt that hangs low on her hips, and nothing else, except for a crown of feathers in bright colors and a hip girdle made of feathers like her crown. Her eyes are closed and she seems far, far away. She raises her arms gracefully over her head, and I see that a razor has never come near her bearded armpits. Neither, I suspect, in spite of all my scolding, has deodorant. The men don't care.

Our live-in python turns her back and does a sort of lazy hula, flipping up first one hip and then the other, the long graceful line of her spine wriggling like a snake. Charlie leans forward and grips the arms of his chair—to keep from leaping out of it and grabbing her, I suspect.

I am furious at my husband for turning my home into a

hoochie-coochie parlor. But, because Charlie is present, I keep my cool. When the entertainment is over, I go to the kitchen for snacks to munch with the large drinks the men are holding. Ifa does not offer to help.

When I come back with the tray, the men are still applauding.

"Thank you," says the star after a deep bow. Too deep—her bra is just a small strip of cloth. "But really, you know, you should not applaud. That was not supposed to be entertainment. It is a religious dance."

Charlie guffaws, but Lucius is more sensitive. "You are right, of course, Ifa. But your performance was so wonderful, we could not help ourselves."

"Help yourselves to these now," I say, passing around pretzels, wheat crackers, and cheddar cubes. "I am sorry I didn't know you were coming, Charlie. I would have had a better menu planned than a pot of lima beans."

"Ain't nothing I love better than lima beans, Zena," says our friend, mopping his brow with a big white handkerchief. "You know I'm a country boy. I was raised on beans. But I didn't come to eat. I came to take you all out to dinner."

"What's the occasion?" I ask, though I know. He has come, this nosy old hound dog, to satisfy his curiosity about Ifa. She has obliged him by performing her snake dance, and now he is panting and sweating, his tongue practically hanging out.

"Bob Sanders, the guy that used to have the jazz club, has opened a new restaurant out on the county line that I want to try. I also have a new car that I want to try before I buy it. I need your opinions of both."

"How thoughtful of you, Charlie," I say, though I know he just wanted a chance to see Ifa again and try to figure out where she fits into our household. In my opinion, most men are not only dogs, they are also worse gossips than women. Several of Lucius's other men friends have already happened, conveniently, to be in the neighborhood and have dropped by, they claim, just to say hello to us. I want to believe them, but, if this is so, how come they never dropped by before? All of these guys are married, but that hasn't stopped them from being interested in Ifa.

Staring pointedly at Lucius, I say, "Who asked Ifa to dance?"

"I volunteered, Mum," she says. "Dod mentioned that he had seen me dance, and Mr. Charlie said he would love to see it, too, so I offered." She sounds so innocent I feel briefly sorry for her.

"You say it's a religious dance," Charlie says. "What are some of the features of this religion of yours?"

"We honor all river creatures, because the river brings life and fertility, but especially the python, because he is the king of the reptiles and rules over all of the others. We believe that the spirits of our ancestors sometimes live on in reptiles. I believe that my father has become a python, because he was a great chief. In my dance, I am imitating the python to honor him."

"I see," says Charlie.

Very seriously she adds, "Usually I wear a python skin when I dance, but I did not put it on tonight, because I did not want to upset you. I have discovered that most Americans do not like snakes."

Lucius grew up with snakes in swampy Georgia, but he never got used to them. To him they are just something to be killed as quickly and efficiently as possible. He does not, however, cover his eyes when Ifa does her snake dance.

Charlie laughs. "You think they're ready for this at Solid Rock, Lucius?"

"We have a very enlightened pastor," my husband says, "but I don't think he'd let us keep snakes in the baptismal pool."

Ifa's eyes flash. "You are making fun of me."

"Not at all, my dear," says Charlie. "We are only commenting on cultural differences."

"Well, I am also a Christian," she informs him. "The Anglican missionary priest baptized me. I do not like missionaries, though. They come into our country and try to destroy our culture. What gives them the right to do that?"

Lucius, who is head of the Missionary Board at our church as well as a member of the Deacon Board, looks as if he is in great pain.

Charlie coughs and looks at his watch. "I have a seven o'clock reservation, so we have to leave in about twenty minutes."

"I think I want to change," I say. "And I know Ifa is not going out with us in her dance costume."

"Am I invited?" she asks.

"Of course you are," Charlie says, flirting shamelessly. "You are the guest of honor."

She blossoms immediately with this attention, smiling her best smile, the one that comes with dimples. Then she looks down at herself, and the smile disappears. "But I have nothing to wear for dinner."

I sigh. I think that nothing is exactly what Charlie—and, I am afraid, my husband—would like to see her wear. But it will not happen while I am around, and the clothes I bought her are all casual, so I must play fairy godmother to this Cinderella one more time.

"Come with me, Ifa," I say.

I spend quite a lot of time hunting through my closet for something to lend her. Most of my things are too tailored to wear to dinner, or too dressy for all but formal evenings. Finally, after she has tried on and rejected a white wool suit and a long black skirt with a gold tunic, we find a deep garnet wool crepe dress with a skirt that is too long for me, one that I have not had a chance to take up. On Ifa, the length is perfect. She will probably end up getting to keep this dress, along with all the other things I have given her, because I don't have time to hem clothes these days.

It takes me so long to outfit Ifa that I do not have time to change out of the purple dress I wore to the club meeting. This is the sort of thing real mothers go through all the time, gladly, but I am not really this girl's mother, and I resent it. I have to settle for adding a scarf at my neckline and a spritz of Boucheron behind my ears. Then, remembering something Monica said to

Laura at the meeting, I rummage through my jewelry box. I do not have time for a thorough inventory, but I see immediately that my gold snake bracelet with the emerald eyes is missing.

There is no time to talk to Ifa about this, only time to hear the men lavish compliments on her when she descends the stairs in my garnet dress, with matching fingertips and lipstick that looks suspiciously like mine.

"Splendid," says Lucius, trying to sound paternal and conservative.

"You look ravishing, young lady," says Charlie. "You take my breath away."

She smiles. "That," she informs him, "is because I am a goddess."

"You see, man," Charlie says, punching Lucius in the arm, "I knew you needed my help. I knew you had to be under a strain, trying to keep two women happy. But a woman and a goddess—wow! You really have your hands full."

I take my husband's arm. "Please inform our guest that there is only one goddess in this house."

"And only one God," adds Lucius.

I resist the custom, universal among our friends, for the men to sit together up front, and insist on pulling my husband into the backseat of Charlie's new steel gray Town Car. Charlie helps the goddess into the passenger seat before he slides behind the wheel. He is wearing a black suit and a bright red bolo tie. He probably has a conventional black tie in his pocket in order to be ready instantly for business, which is always picking up.

"Tell me how you became a goddess, Ifa," Charlie asks her, easing away from the curb.

"I do not like to talk about it," Ifa says, "but my mother went to the priest to ask for me. Not the Anglican priest, who would simply have told her to pray, but our traditional priest. She wanted another child to comfort her in her old age, but she had become barren. She paid much money to have certain things done, and I was born on schedule."

I wonder if this would work for me. I think briefly of asking

Ifa about it, then cancel the thought. That time is past. In spite of the story of Sarah in the Bible, in spite of reports of miracles everywhere, that possibility is over, gone.

Ifa continues, "Because of the ceremonies that were performed to help my mother become pregnant, and because of the time of my birth, and certain other things, they say at home that I am a goddess."

"Indeed you are," says Charlie, and turns on the jazz station.

This car rolls along smoothly to the soft music. I sink into the rich-smelling leather cushions, which overcome the smell of my perfume and some less pleasant odors wafting my way from Ifa, and check out the accommodations in the backseat. Boy, do undertakers make big money. I mean, we have a Mercedes, but it's old. Lucius bought it with part of his retirement package, and we're not likely to get another one. He tends it like a baby, but the upholstery is cracking, and it has none of the conveniences of this car, which is really a limo. The backseat has a bar stocked with miniatures, separate temperature and speaker controls, and a nine-inch TV. I turn the thing on just to see if it works, and enjoy five minutes of *Access Hollywood* in full color. Then I turn it off, since I do not care how many children Michael Jackson has—he is still a fairy in my book. I take a look at Lucius. He is frowning.

Married folks learn quickly that neutral subjects are sometimes best. I ask him, "Do you think Michael Jackson should be allowed to have children, since he's supposed to be a child molester?"

"That decision is up to the Lord," my spouse pronounces.

Oh, so he's taken refuge in holiness again. I am getting awfully tired of these pious Sermons on the Mount from my husband. I lose my neutrality. "Was it the Lord's decision to have Ifa dance for Charlie?"

"She offered to do it. You heard her say so yourself."

"Yes, but you could have stopped her."

He is silent. He didn't want to stop her, that's the problem. He wanted to watch her.

"You have no idea how our house looked when I walked in. It

looked like a hoochie-coochie parlor. Booze, cigars, and dancing girls. You better be glad the Wilkersons didn't call the vice squad. Somebody would probably have gone to jail."

"Zena, maybe it looked bad, but it was completely innocent. You know she's just a big old missy girl who likes to show off."

I am silent. I am thinking about Vy's insistence, on the day we had lunch with Ifa, that she was not a child. It also occurs to me that I don't usually leave the Divas' meetings as early and abruptly as I did today. "You thought I would get home later this afternoon, didn't you, Lucius?"

"What does that have to do with anything?"

I let out a heavy sigh. "Your little floor show wasn't meant for my eyes. I guess I should be glad you don't go to topless bars. Does Charlie?"

"I have no idea," he says stonily. "He hasn't mentioned it to me."

We ride in stiff silence, except for smooth jazz, until we reach Sanders's House of Blue Lights.

This new restaurant just outside the city is named for a song that was popular back in the fifties. It has murals of jazz musicians, all done in shades of blue, and big blue chandeliers, and booths and chairs with blue upholstery, and little blue lamps at each table, which make it hard to read the menus, but probably hide the fatigue in my face. Good. A quartet is performing at nine, a poster on an easel informs us. Until then, more smooth jazz from the FM station soothes our ears.

Lucius and I decide on chateaubriand for two, preceded by smoked oysters.

Charlie orders grilled salmon, with pâté for an appetizer.

The men order more of the bourbon they enjoyed at the house while watching the private floor show. I order a champagne cocktail.

Ifa has two champagne cocktails, three appetizers—stuffed mushrooms, shrimp cocktail, and smoked oysters—and two entrees—a T-bone steak and crab cakes. Between her drinks and her appetizers, she demolishes the bread basket, leaving us with one bread stick apiece.

Charlie, who is paying, does not seem to mind her appetite. He watches her with sly satisfaction, as if he is fattening up a goose for his personal Christmas dinner. And he flirts with her outrageously.

"So you are a goddess," he says. "Are goddesses built differently from other women?"

"Not at all," she says, reaching for one of the olives in his salad. He does not mind that, either.

"Can only gods make love to goddesses, or do mere mortal men have a chance?"

She, too, is amused. "Mortal men have a chance, of course, if they do not mind being compared to gods."

"And do goddesses ever marry mortal men?"

"Of course they do," she states, sucking the marrow from her steak bone.

"I love the way you do that," he says, watching her suck the bone. "I find you fascinating. Will you marry me?"

"I will consider your proposal," she says coolly.

Lucius raises one of his nervous eyebrows, and I feel a giggle escape my lips. Charlie already has a large wife and four robust children. Marilyn Matthews is as tall as Ifa and twice as wide, with arms as big as my thighs and hamlike hands, strengthened by swatting her kids around, that could give Mike Tyson problems. I think of her likely reaction if Charlie were to bring Ifa home, and hide my laughter in my napkin.

Suddenly, I stop laughing. I am the fool who has let an African temptress move into my house. Marilyn would not put up with it for one minute. If Charlie tried to move Ifa into their home, Ifa would shortly be at rest in one of the mortuary's coffins. And so, probably, would he.

"Does this restaurant have steak sauce?" the goddess demands.

The waiter, who has been kept busy satisfying Ifa's other requirements, returns with some A-1, which she pours so liberally one can no longer see her steak. Meanwhile, Charlie has ordered an after-dinner drink.

"I have witnesses," he says, raising his stinger, "that I intend to marry this woman."

"You have witnesses that you are drunk," says Lucius, laughing.

"But I do not know this man who is proposing to me," Ifa, perfectly serious, says to Lucius. "I know nothing about him except that he likes to play cowboy. What is his occupation?"

"I think I will let him tell you that," says Lucius

"Guess," Charlie says, taking one of her hands.

"I think you are something like a doctor," she says slowly. "Not a medical doctor, but a man who works with herbs and can consult the spirits. In our village they are called juju men, and they are greatly respected."

"Close," Charlie pronounces.

"He's an undertaker, Ifa," I tell her. "He takes care of the dead."

She drops her fork with a great clang. "My God!" she cries, and pulls her hand back. She eats no more. She doesn't even order dessert, and she is quiet for the rest of the evening.

Until we get home.

Then she confronts Lucius with raging fury. "Dod! How could you do it? How could you sell me to that man?"

He looks at her in utter amazement. "What on earth are you talking about, Ifa?"

"Oh, I know what that dinner was all about, that is why I ate everything I could. I have no power, I am just a helpless girl, but at least I could make that man pay. I know what kind of car that is. I have seen cars like that before. That man is rich. He must have paid you a lot of money for me."

By now I am collapsing with laughter.

"Go ahead, Mum, laugh at your poor daughter in her misery. I am the one who will have to go with that man. My God! A juju man who works with the dead. How could you do it, Dod? How can you even be friends with a man like that?"

It is true that Charlie does not have many friends. Undertakers and cops seldom do. But Lucius, because of his life in politics, has come to know and appreciate many people, including men in both occupations. Charlie Matthews is one of them.

"How could you do it, Dod?" she repeats over and over.

"How could you? I know you had to do something about me. My visa just expired. But this is a terrible thing to do to me."

By now I am helpless with laughter. But Lucius, at least, is not laughing. "I didn't sell you, Ifa. Men don't sell their daughters here."

She looks at both of us suspiciously. "Then why did he propose to me?"

"I don't know, since he already has a wife," I say. "He was drunk. He was probably just flirting with you."

Now Lucius does laugh. "Wait till I tell Charlie to come here and get this woman he bought."

"Wait till I tell Marilyn he bought her," I say.

"Ifa," Lucius says, "I don't mean this unkindly, girl, but why do you think anyone would want to buy you?"

"You are both making fun of me! You are treating me like a joke! You think I am a joke, because I am an ignorant girl from the African bush."

"No, no, baby, we don't feel that way," my husband says. He goes to Ifa and puts what I am supposed to think is a fatherly arm around her shoulders. "We don't think you're a joke. We're very fond of you."

"Ifa, let's go to your room," I say abruptly. "I want to ask you about something."

I follow her to her room. "Where is my gold snake bracelet with the emerald eyes?" I ask her.

"I borrowed it." she says sullenly.

"Where is it?"

She points to her dresser. Her scariest mask is guarding my jewelry. And not just my bracelet, but the matching earrings, and several gold chains as well.

I have heard somewhere that African women have a craving for gold trinkets that is as powerful as an alcoholic's craving for liquor. I also understand why Ifa would find a snake bracelet irresistible. This does not move me to forgive her.

I hold out my hand for my things, and she drops them into my palm. "Have you borrowed anything else?"

"No, Mum," she says.

I look around. She has moved my best lipstick, two bottles of my nail polish and several bottles of my perfume to her dresser. My cheval glass sits at the foot of her bed, I guess so that she can wake up admiring herself.

"Give me back my dress now," I tell her. "In the morning, I want all of my other things returned to my room."

Her face crumples like a baby's, signaling the start of tears. "Oh, Mum, you are so mean!"

"And, I think, if somebody had been as mean to you as they should have been, I would not have to raise their spoiled child."

 # TWENTY-FOUR

IFA LOOKED LOVELY TONIGHT. Her student visa came through, and she can stay in the U.S. for as long as she needs to complete her studies. She was all dressed up for school in a pair of black slacks I bought her, a white oxford shirt I gave her, the large gold hoop earrings she brought with her, and one of my gold chains. I started to snatch it off her, then relented, deciding to wait till she got back home. But I let her know I noticed it.

"My chain looks well on you," I told her.

"Thank you, Mum." She raised her hand to her throat, and her cuff slid down and revealed my snake bracelet coiled around her wrist.

An "Ohhh" escaped my lips, and she looked with surprise, first at me, then down at her arm.

"M-m-mum, you m-must let me wear this, it is my p-patron, he will bring me good luck on the first night of my studies. I p-promise I will return your things."

"When?"

"Tonight."

It is not good enough. I want my bracelet back now, before wearing it gets to be a habit with her. It took me a year to pay for it, as I recall, a foolish year when I sometimes lived on pinto beans in a dark house because I lacked money for food and the electric bill.

"Give me back my bracelet now."

"But why, Mum? You never wear it."

Rage rises to my forehead and signals the beginning of a dreadful headache. "Because it is mine, whether I choose to wear it or not. Maybe you do not understand the idea of property, but it belongs to me."

Then Lucius is in the room in his trench coat, in a hurry to drive her to school, because he has other things to do, other places to go. He looks up at her, pauses, and grins. She does look lovely. The relaxer I put in her hair is holding, and she has brushed her hair around her head in an elegant conical upsweep. I believe she is wearing mascara, her lashes are so thick, and also my new Plum Nelly lipstick.

No, she does not understand the idea of property. Not when she wants something.

She returns Lucius's smile radiantly, as if she is seeing the sun rise for the first time and her face is reflecting it.

He grins a little wider, and holds up his hand to help her down the steps. She steps down daintily, like a princess. Then she rolls her eyes at me, waves her wrist with my bracelet in my face, and switches out, with my husband holding the door for her.

I walk around the house gritting my teeth for a while after they are gone. But then, I relax. I realize that I enjoy having my house to myself for a change. I never noticed until Ifa came how small our house is. The presence of this large female guest has begun to cramp my style and overshadow my life. Not until Lucius has taken her out of here do I realize how much the crowding has been getting on my nerves. I feel myself unwinding now. I still have to deal with her musky odor, which seems to be hanging in the air, but I am grateful for the sudden silence, the space, and the peace.

I can breathe. I can stretch. I can expand. I can work on the shop's books, which I do for an hour, and on my craft project, some mudcloth place mats, for another hour. I can play a Lionel Richie album and samba along to "All Night Long." I can do a load of laundry and lay out my clothes for the next day.

I can also wonder, as the fourth hour begins, where my husband is and what he is doing.

I know, of course, that he is very busy these days. Lucius has a new candidate he is launching, a young man who made a sensation on TV late last year by rescuing a baby from a burning house, and who has since appeared on a couple of local talk shows. This young man, Booker Brown, has done his homework. He knows what is going on in the city, and he is quick on his feet when he is asked serious questions. He was already Ambrose Miller's assistant, so he is not new to politics, but the unexpected publicity and a suddenly available seat in the state legislature have combined to launch his career early.

Booker's candidacy means many meetings with the party committee, many visits to bureaucratic offices, and a lot of strategic public appearances to seek votes and contributions. Sometimes these meetings and affairs go on until late at night, so I am, once more, a campaign widow. I should be used to it by now, but I never am.

I pick up the phone and call my husband's office at party headquarters.

It rings and rings, until the answering machine, with Antoinette Harris's voice on the tape, picks up. Net is no one I have to worry about. She is about seventy-five years old, as wrinkled as a dried apricot, and has outlived several of the candidates she worked for, including the ninety-year-old incumbent whose seat just became available. She has a memory like a computer and a gift for charming and cajoling people, including candidates' wives.

It is after ten. I am not worried yet, but I miss my husband. I go to the Back Room to be close to his presence. I smell his cigar smoke pungent in the air. I stretch out on the greasy old couch and soak up the scent of Lucius himself—sweat, Polo, cigar tobacco, Bergamot hair pomade. I breathe it in deeply and am comforted.

Then I notice a slip of paper fluttering from Lucius's cigar box I pull it out and read:

Dear Dad,

Mum is mean to me. I feel that she is angry with me. Please do not let her send me away. I am very happy here with you.

Remember what I told you. The man is in charge of the household.

Love,

Your daughter Ifa

All's fair in love and war, which are sometimes one and the same thing. The first thing I do is tear the note into tiny pieces, put it in the ashtray, and light it with Lucius's beloved old Zippo.

When nothing is left of it but ash, I stretch out on the couch, close my eyes, and think. I will have to be careful. Ifa has cast me in the role of the Wicked Witch of the West, and herself as the helpless Dorothy. Anything I say against her will be interpreted as cruelty. Lucius loves to take the part of the underdog. Also, she obviously adores him, and men loved to be worshipped and adored. Come to think of it, who doesn't?

As I have already observed, she does not respect property. She grew up under a communal system, in a family where everything belonged to everybody. Including husbands.

Yes, I will have to be careful. The enemy is within my gates, and she is cunning. But she may have left one thing out of her calculations.

This is America, where women do have some say about what goes on in their households. And furthermore. . .

The glare of the overhead light in my eyes jolts me awake. I must have drifted off to sleep. My husband is bending over me.

"Wake up, Peaches. Go to bed. You'll be all stiff and sore if you spend the night here."

"Whoa," I say, coming out of a brightly sunlit dream in which he and I rode horses, bareback, bare-ass, bare-everything, on a private beach. "What time is it?"

"One o'clock," he says. "I am afraid the meeting went on very late."

Ifa is grinning like a jack-o'-lantern over his shoulder. "Politics is very interesting, Mum. You should try it." Even in my sleepy daze, I am angry enough to smack her for this remark.

"There wasn't time to bring Ifa home, Zena, so I took her with me to headquarters," my husband says.

I would much rather he didn't explain. I swing my legs down from the couch, smooth my skirt, and ignore Ifa. "Where were you, Lucius? I called your office, but there was no answer."

"Sorry. We used Ambrose Miller's office. We needed the space."

"Good night, Mum," Ifa says as I head for my room. She hands me my chain and my bracelet as I pass. "Thank you for letting me wear your things tonight. I do not think I will wear them to class again. The school is in a very bad, very dangerous neighborhood. I am glad Dod says that he will continue to drive me there."

I am suddenly wide awake, and I do not like the direction my mind is taking. As befits a congressman, Ambrose Miller has a spacious, well-appointed office with fine, handsome furnishings.

Including a couch.

 # TWENTY-FIVE

IFA GOES TO SCHOOL only one night a week—Monday. The rest of the time, she has nothing to do. When I drop a hint about helping out around the house like she once did, she complains that she has developed a back problem.

I let my cleaning service go when she began to clean our house. Now that she has stopped doing housework, I refuse to hire them back. I am aggrieved by the idea of paying house-cleaners to work while Ifa does nothing. It reminds me too much of Sonny Sampson, whose parents paid a boy to rake their leaves while their son slept late on Saturday mornings.

I am too tired at night to clean, so the dirt is piling up around here. Dust bunnies hop around our rooms, and mate under the furniture and make more, and a coating of dust flours the tables, and the kitchen stove needs a lot of elbow grease to get rid of the other kind. It is disgusting.

I will get to the dirt when I can, though it will aggrieve me further to clean the house myself while that big, lazy girl does nothing.

Gone are the days of scented baths and massages for me. Gone, too, the days when the house was neat and clean before I arrived home. Now I have a busy business, a filthy house, and a lazy goddess lounging in my front room.

The living room sofa has become Ifa's favorite parking place.

Every evening, I find her lolling there, clicking the remote from the Style Channel to MTV and back again. When I get home from work, the first thing I see is her big bare feet hanging over one arm of the sofa like a pair of turtles. When I leave the house to go to work, there they are again, looking like loaves of pumpernickel bread tipped with burgundy nails.

"What is planned for dinner, Mum?" Ifa asks languidly as I stumble through the door laden with groceries and other packages.

"The menu for tonight is root, pig, or die a poor hog," I tell her.

She sits up, startled. "Root and pig? What does that mean?"

"Oh, just an old expression. It means, Every man for himself, and every woman, too. There are groceries in this bag. I suggest that you take them to the kitchen and unpack them. If you get hungry enough, I expect you will find a way to eat them, too."

I let the door slam behind me as I go out.

Fifteen minutes later, I am at Vy's, watching as she cleans her kitchen. Sometimes I want to cry out, "Why, why are women expected to do *everything*?" We cook and we clean. We wash and we iron. When there's a funeral, we go. When someone is sick, we go. When people are very old or very young, we care for them. When thank-you notes and Christmas cards are due, we write them. When bills come in, we pay them. When someone calls with a problem, we listen and try to help.

I know Lucius keeps busy with his campaigning, his constituents, and his meetings, but I still feel like I carry two-thirds of the load, and the dead weight of Ifa in the house makes it twice as heavy. I work more than full-time running a business, plus I take care of the house, Lucius, Ifa, and our social life. And I do it, most of the time, with a smile. But tell me, where, where is it written that I am supposed to?

"I am tired a lot lately, Vy," I tell my friend. "A lot of the time, I feel like I want to break down and cry."

"It's menopause," Vy says.

"Oh, shut up," I tell her. "I'm not that old."

"Yes you are, Miss Zena," she answers. "Wake up and smell the roses."

"Whatever you say," I reply. Vy confuses me sometimes with her comments.

"You ever notice how much of a woman's life is devoted to cleaning up crud?" I ask her next. "When I think about it, it makes me sick."

I am watching her as she cleans the top of her stove, sweeping blobs of black gunk into the palm of her hand. It makes me guilty, because my stove is in even worse condition. But I simply cannot work in the house while that lazy girl lounges around and watches me. Watching my friend bend her back, I wonder again why all plumbing fixtures are the right height only for children and very short adults. Lucius says it's because most plumbers are short European men. So are tailors, which is why he is limited to only a couple of stores when he shops for clothes to fit his six-foot-three frame.

Vy sprays her stove top with one of those new citrus-scented cleaners to loosen more of the gunk. But those products don't really do the work for you. There's no such thing as Quick Kleen or Grease Free. There's only scrubbing, digging, and elbow grease, which Vy applies to her stove with a scrubber sponge after pausing to flick some more black gunk off the cute ceramic kitty cats that sit on a shelf above the sink. Me, I'm sick of cute stuff. I am getting rid of everything that is not useful.

"Yeah, I know." Vy sighs heavily, the way I do sometimes over the same sort of job. "But at least it's my crud. Mine and my family's. I'm not working in some white woman's kitchen, cleaning up behind her. White folks is nasty. They drink milk right out of the carton, and pick meat off a chicken with their hands. They eat ice cream straight out of the carton, too."

"They even do it right after they've kissed and petted dogs."

"I know. It spreads germs. I wouldn't eat behind them. I used to take my lunch to work in a bag, even though it bothered the lady I worked for. Every time she saw me take out my lunch, she said, 'You're welcome to what we have, Vyester. Just help yourself.' I told her I was on a special diet for my liver. I said I had to have plum skins and pecan dust from down home."

I laugh. "What did she say?"

"She just kept saying, 'Well, you're welcome to what we have. Just help yourself,' " Vy mocks.

I sip my coffee, remembering those days. I don't like to think about them often. Yes, compared to those times, cleaning up our own kitchens is a luxury.

"I remember this one lady," Vy continues, "who didn't want me to use paper towels. Too wasteful, she said. Bad for the planet. She had all this concern for the planet—none for me. She gave me these teeny little rags, her kids' outgrown underwear, that she wanted me to bleach and wash and hang out every week. She didn't want to give people an excuse to cut down more trees, she said. The planet needs trees. I needed more money. I quit because she wouldn't give me a raise. She said she couldn't afford it. But she had just sent a hundred dollars to save the whales."

"White folks are something, all right," I chime in. "It used to get me, the way they love animals more than they love people." I have told Lucius that I think Booker Brown would have a better chance of getting elected if he had rescued a dog instead of a child. I continue, "I worked for one woman who spent a fortune on her dogs. They had their own soft flannel beds and jeweled collars. Blankets with monograms and eating bowls made out of porcelain. They even had mink coats, can you imagine? Mink coats on dogs, when they were born with fur! And this lady let them kiss her on the mouth and lick her face. Ugh! She said her dogs were members of her family. But when I asked her if my little niece could come and spend the day with me while I was working, because my sister-in-law was in the hospital, she said she felt her employees should leave their personal problems at home. Her dogs were members of the family, close enough to kiss, but my niece, a person, was a problem."

Little DeeDee, Deirdre, is twenty-four now, a college graduate with a job in TV, and I haven't seen her in years, but whenever I think of my brother's child, I think of my reasons for quitting domestic work.

"Sounds like that lady needed to have her a baby," Vy comments.

"Oh, she couldn't have children, she told me."

"She could adopt one."

This reminds me of one of my pet grievances. "Speaking of that, Vy, have you noticed lately how they will go all over the world looking for children to adopt instead of taking in black American ones? Chinese children, Russians, Rumanians, those children with pointed ears and big eyes and little werewolf faces who come from all those Dracula countries—anything but Africans."

"Uh-huh," Vy says. "It's the Devil at work. It's that devilish racism that makes them adopt them Dracula kids instead of ours. One morning they gonna wake up and wonder why they got tooth marks in their red necks. They deserve it, I say.— Speaking of strange people from overseas, is that African girl still at your house?"

"Yes," I say. I have been hoping to avoid the subject of Ifa. I am at Vy's house to escape thinking about her. Last night, like the week before, Lucius and Ifa got in late from school and meetings. Three times in the past couple of weeks, I have touched my husband in our special secret way, and three times he has pushed me away. Finally I asked him if he thought he should try that new men's medicine, Vigoro.

He got mad and asked me if I had gone out of my fucking mind. It shocked me, because Lucius seldom curses.

"You mean Viagra," he went on. "I do not need it, but that is the name of the stuff. Vigoro is a fertilizer. What use would I have for that? Nothing can fertilize you."

Lucius has never before commented on my inability to have children. It is a measure of how much I hurt him that he said something about it after all this time.

I have not brought up that medicine, Vigoro, again, nor have I touched him intimately, since it makes him so angry. But I am not happy.

"That girl got a job yet?" Vyester asks.

"No. She's going to school. Lucius was only able to get her a student visa, not a working visa."

"Uh-huh. And you and Lucius still feeding her and putting clothes on her back?"

"Yes."

"Uh-huh. You still okay with that?"

"No," I admit. "Hell, no. I am sick of seeing her around my house all the time. I am beginning to hate the sight of her, the sound of her, and most definitely the smell of her." I am surprised by the vehemence with which the words come out of my mouth.

"Then why don't you put her out?"

"It is still cold outside, and she has no other place to go. Her sister left us a bunch of names and phone numbers that were supposed to belong to people who were expecting her, but they were all phonies. Wrong numbers and numbers that were out of service."

"Sounds like something some of my family would do." Vy pauses. "Reason I was asking is, I heard of a live-in job out in the suburbs. Housekeeping and looking after an invalid old lady. She wouldn't have to take care of kids or cook."

Ifa would not keep a job two days if she had to cook. The one time she attempted to fix an African-style meal for us, she put something on our plates that was like loose grits without any seasoning, except for the weevils in it. There was more of this mess all over the stove than on the table. Soup, she called it. Seminola soup. Boiled weevils, I called it. She had brought it with her, weevils and all, from Olori. I threw it all out.

A job that does not require cooking sounds like a great opportunity for Ifa. But I have some questions. "Are they nice people?"

Vy shrugs. "They rich white folks."

In other words, I have asked a stupid question.

"Who's paying for her schooling?" Vy wants to know.

I haven't thought about this. Our adult evening schools are

cheap, of course, but they do charge something, especially for courses that prepare people for jobs. Unlike immigrants, who have been lied to, Vy knows that nothing in America is free. I answer slowly, "Lucius, I guess."

"That means you paying for it, along with the rest of her keep. These foreigners all think we're rich, Miss Zena, but we don't have to prove they're right. Let her earn some money, so she can pay for her classes herself. If she lives in, she can save everything they give her. Besides, you will be getting her out of your house."

This sounds wonderful to me.

I did ask Lucius yesterday if he thought he ought to get a checkup. Of course, I didn't say why I thought he needed one.

He snorted and said, "Are you kidding? Go for a checkup to Sawbones Jones? I might as well take my carcass to Jiffy Lube."

I didn't argue with him. Our doctor, Wardell Jones, is okay for healthy people, but I wouldn't go to him either if I thought I had something wrong.

Vy says, "You know these rich white people don't care anything about green cards, Miss Zena. They just want somebody to clean their big old houses, and nobody's coming in there to check and see if the help has the right I.D. Course, these people live pretty far out in the suburbs. Without a car, it would be hard for her to come and visit you on her days off. She ain't got a car, does she?"

"Of course she doesn't have a car."

It is unholy, the joy that starts down at my toes and spreads upward until I am tingling all over with happiness. This job opportunity that Vy has found for Ifa is sounding better and better. I once scrubbed other people's floors, and so did Vyester. Before me, my mother also did her share of floor-scrubbing, as did Vyester's, probably.

People who wonder why I work and push myself so hard probably didn't start out cleaning houses like I did. At one point, I decided I'd do anything to get away from that—so I sold cosmetics door to door, did hair in my kitchen, and sold clothes and jewelry out of my living room. I let people think my merchandise was hot, even though it wasn't. It sold faster that way.

I think now about my grandparents, how they struggled to make a living sharecropping in South Carolina and never did better than break even, according to the man who owned both the land and the store where they bought on credit. All that labor and nothing to show for it!

And I think about my mother, spending her entire life cleaning for other people so I could have food, shelter, and clothes. The smile that spread across Mama's face when I finished high school. The wrinkles that were there at only forty-five.

I remember my own struggles to be independent and make Mama proud of me. My day's work was different from my mother's, though, because I knew it wouldn't go on forever. As she said, "You are just doing this to make a point." And I was. I was doing it to pay my tuition at beauty school and business school—so I would have to scrub floors no more. That's the main reason I still work so hard—so I'll never have to clean other people's houses again, or wait tables. It's a fear that haunts me. My feet couldn't stand it now.

And now my hard work is going to support a lazy African princess who probably thinks she is better than I am, because her folks sold mine into slavery! It sets my teeth on edge.

It's Ifa's turn, now. Let her get a domestic job and find out what it's like. And if that sounds like I want revenge, maybe I do.

Bur I also think, maybe Ifa needs to take her lumps, as my ancestors did. Endure her oppression, feel her pain, and fight her way to freedom, just as they did and we did. It's her turn to go through it. Only then will her freedom mean something.

Vyester ties up her garbage bag and heads for her back door.

"Let me do that for you," I say. Vy moves more slowly than she used to. She is really showing now. I want to take her out to eat, so that she can enjoy a meal without any kitchen cleanup afterward.

"Nah. It isn't heavy. Fred would do it, but in the time it takes to remind him, I can do it myself."

I wrest the bag away from her anyway. "Did Sonny take out the garbage when he was home?"

"No. I should've made him, but he groaned and whined and complained so bad, I didn't. Wish I had. Wish Fred had made him cut the yard, too, and get a job after school. I would wish a lot of things, but it's too late."

I dispense with the garbage and come back. I recall, now, being here at Vy's house and hearing Sonny groan and moan when asked to perform a chore. Seeing his parents give up asking after the third request, and watching them carry out the trash or cut the grass or wash the car themselves. I thought at the time that they were spoiling him.

But at least, I am thinking now, they were spoiling their own child, not someone else's.

Vy takes a cloth, soaks it in a bucket of cleaner, and begins wiping down her cabinets. "See, it feels good doing this. I don't mind, 'cause this is my kitchen."

"Yeah, your kitchen and not Madame Queen's."

"The kitchens were bad, but the bathrooms were worse," she remembers. "Talk about nasty! Some of those children never got toilet-trained, not even when they were ready to go to college. Still and all, we had to clean up behind their nasty asses, and not say a word. And the dogs, shedding dog hair all over the place! Working for Madame Queen sure was a bitch, wasn't it?"

Go in any private place where struggling black women gather, and you will hear this conversation. Some of it is true, some of it is just angry stuff we say to make ourselves feel better after a lifetime of grueling work and "Yes, ma'ams," but we all know it by heart.

"Sure was," I say. We seldom talk about it, but I realize that our shared past of domestic work is part of the bond between my friend and me. That, and the liberation of getting out of days' work and into something else. We have come quite a distance, Vy and I. Like the rest of our people.

"Shoot, it didn't kill us, and it probably wouldn't hurt your visitor none to try it. Let her scrub some floors, wait on some folks, sweep up some nasty dog hair, and get paid. It would get her out of your house while she waits for something better."

Vyester is a true friend, and psychic besides. She knows, for instance, how desperate I've been lately. I have tried calling all the numbers Cecelia left, and gotten nowhere. I have tried calling long distance information for Olori and also gotten nowhere, because they speak English over there, but not American. I have even tried calling the I.N.S., but I always chicken out and hang up when someone finally answers the phone. I am not angry enough to report anyone to the government. Vy's idea is the best one to come along yet.

"These people's name is Macintyre. I'll call them this afternoon if you want."

"Do that," I say.

 # TWENTY-SIX

BEFORE LUCIUS GETS HOME, I practice what I am going to say to him. When he walks in the door, I don't jump on my subject right away. I give the man time to hang up his coat, take off his shoes, and put on his slippers. I bring him a weak bourbon and water. Then I ask him about his day—about his meetings and how things are looking for Booker Brown in the primary.

Good, he says. I congratulate him.

After that, I sort of ease my husband to the Back Room and tighten up his drink with another splash of bourbon. Then I give him a shoulder and neck rub that has to be better than Ifa's, because I know his muscles as well as I know my own.

"A person has to be self-supporting to be self-respecting, wouldn't you say, Lucius?" I ask him as I work my way, half inch by half inch, up the back of his neck.

"That depends on who the person is," my husband replies. "That is the same argument the welfare reformers use, and you know I don't agree with them. If the person is a mother with young children, I'd say no, at least not until we get better child care. Oh, that feels good right there. Don't stop."

"But what if the person is not a mother with children?" I say, starting over on his neck at the spot where his spine intersects his shoulder bones.

"Then I'd say yes," my husband says, "unless you are talking about a child still in school."

Men are so unsuspecting. They love to talk about abstract subjects that have nothing to do with real life, and will do it for hours, never dreaming that you are moving in closer and closer to your target and are about to hit them up close and personal with something solid and concrete, like a brick.

"I agree with that, too," I say, making my voice soft and soothing. "If I had a child in school, I would most certainly support it. At least until it reached the age of eighteen. Then I might say, 'Get a job. Pay your way.' "

"And I would agree with you," my husband says. "My parents told me college would mean more to me if I paid for it, and they were right, even though I only went for two years. Could you rub this spot right here a little bit more?"

I do as I am asked.

"Then you won't be upset," I say, "when I tell you that Vy and I have found Ifa a job."

I feel him tighten under my hands like a fighter facing Mike Tyson. He turns his head suddenly. "What kind of job?"

"Don't do that, Lucius," I say, gently but firmly adjusting his head as I would a patron's. "You'll spoil all the work I've done on your muscles, twisting and tensing them up like that. Take your shirt off so I can get to your back."

No one can resist my good back rubs. He obeys and bends forward over a pillow I have placed in his lap. "She ant urk," he says in a muffled voice. "Ee ah no green ard."

She can't work. She has no green card, I translate.

"She doesn't need a green card for this job," I say.

"Whuh kine shob?"

"It's private. Health care and household management," I say, and start tapping up and down his spine with my knuckles. I add quickly, "Don't you always say an idle mind is the Devil's workshop, Lucius? Ifa has been idle for a long time. It is bad for her mental attitude." I don't add that it is bad for my mental attitude, too, to watch her lounge around here while the dirt and the bills pile up.

He lifts his head. "She has to stay in school, or she'll lose her student visa."

"She only has classes one night a week," I say, and push his head back down. "I'm sure she can manage to get to those."

I add, after a long pause, "Of course, she will be living pretty far away from the night school. But it's time she learned how to get around."

"You didn't say she was going to live somewhere else, Zena," he says, and sits up. Uh-oh. Our cozy time is over.

We have a long back-and-forth after that, with him talking about the dangers of a young woman going out in the world on her own, and me saying she is grown and has to get out there sometime. I am losing in this discussion until I purr sweetly, "Of course, if you are going to miss her all that much, dear, I'll forget about it. "

"I won't miss her at all."

He is lying. And I am hurting, thinking of her youth and beauty and my growing signs of age. Of her perfect skin and tight jawline, and my jowls and dark blotches. Of her long, smooth legs and my own cellulite-pocked thighs. Of her boundless energy, bolstered by rest, and my fatigue, increased by too much work. Of her slim build, and my spreading hips and jiggling arms that I keep covered with long tops and sleeves.

Of course I could work on some of this. I have a cute set of pink weights that I bought last fall, but I don't even remember where I put them. Wherever they are, they are as dusty as the rest of the house.

"I just want to make sure she will be all right," Lucius is saying. "She's a young person, and I feel responsible."

"So do I," I say. "And I think we would not be responsible if we let her go on believing that she does not have to work. Let me check on dinner."

I have a mustard-seasoned chicken roasting in an oven bag with onions, apples, and carrots. On my way to the kitchen, I see an ugly thing that looks like a big, dusty pile of old truck tires occupying my sofa. I move closer to inspect it. It is a giant python. Its white-patterned, dusty, gray-and-brown sides expand and contract with its breathing. I approach it, but I can't stand its smell. It is horrible, like something that has decayed in the refrigerator until it is past recognition. Then it opens its mouth, yawns, and grins at me.

I go to the hall closet for a stick to beat the thing with. At this point I am not afraid, just angry that this creature has somehow moved in without paying rent.

When I come back, it is gone. Instead, on my couch, I spy a flash of gold and green. I bend down and pick up my emerald-eyed snake bracelet. Instantly, an electric shock goes through me, though I have not touched anything that is plugged in. It is a strong, terrifying current that knocks me backward so hard I almost fall.

Though it cost a year out of my life, I put the bracelet in the garbage can. Only then do I feel the shock drain out of me. At some point, I think I scream, because Lucius comes running.

"Baby," he says, "what's wrong? Tell me, Zena. What is it?" He puts his arms around me, and all of a sudden the doubts about my attractiveness and the tensions and suspicions that have separated us are dissolved in a mist of tenderness. We are a couple again.

"S-s-snake," I manage to say. "There." I point to the couch. "Her snake god was there, grinning at me."

He goes on holding me, and does not try to convince me I've been seeing things. "It's gone now, baby. It's gone."

"I know. But, oh my God, it was horrible." I am still shivering, so he wraps me in a big plaid blanket and gets me some hot tea. The blanket smells horsey. It once belonged to Pickett. But I don't mind.

When I stop shivering enough to talk again, I say, "Lucius, do you think that girl is working some magic? She has decided that I am her enemy, you know, and she's into juju like all of them."

Our sofa is vacant now, but just behind my eyes I can still see that *thing* coiled on it, heaving and waiting. Ifa's god. The monster that kills by embracing.

I do not go near the sofa again. I have always liked it, and we paid a lot for it, but I am already making plans to have the Salvation Army pick it up.

Lucius falls into a chair and covers his face with his hands. "It's my fault," he says.

I go to him to give comfort. "How is it your fault, Lucius? I was the one who brought her here. Though she was supposed to stay for dinner, not forever."

He holds up his hand to stop me. "It's my fault, I said. I should not have encouraged her in that profane dance to her heathen idols." He bangs his fist into his hand, angrily socking himself. His voice is sad and guilty, and his face is as long as Pickett's. "She was supposed to have been converted. I should have been bringing her soul back to Christ, not letting her dance to her serpent god."

"Religion sure can complicate things, can't it, Honey?"

"What are you saying?"

"I'm saying the reason you should have stopped her from dancing has nothing to do with Jesus. It has to do with you liking to watch her."

"Zena, are you accusing me—?"

"Just tell me I'm wrong. Tell me I'm a liar." And I start doing a little dance of my own around the room. "Tell me I'm wrong. She's beautiful, isn't she? It's been a long time since you stared at me the way you stare at her."

Finally he admits hoarsely, "I'm as susceptible as the next man, I guess."

"Is that all you're going to say, Lucius Lawson?"

"Yes." The boss man has spoken. The subject is closed. "Where is Ifa, anyway? Is she in her room?"

"No. I dropped her at Vy's." She is there getting prepped for her job interview tomorrow, but why go into details?

My husband is not stupid. He knows why she is there. "Where did you say this job is?"

"I didn't say." I study my French manicure, which I believe was invented by Frenchwomen to hide the dirt under their nails. "It's out in the suburbs, that's all I know. I'll find out exactly where it is tomorrow."

"And she's going to live there, you say?"

"If she's hired." There is a silence between us so deep, nothing could touch its bottom. Lucius doesn't want Ifa to leave our house, but he doesn't dare say so.

Finally he says, "Zena, I think you could have investigated this position more thoroughly, and you could have talked to me about it sooner." Translation: He doesn't want her to leave.

"No, I couldn't. It came up suddenly."

"Well, Ifa could get in trouble if she works without a green card, you know. She only has a student visa. If she doesn't go to school, she'll be an illegal."

I have heard all this before, and I am getting tired of it. "Her employers don't care whether she has a green card or not. I'll pick her up on Mondays and take her to school myself."

I think I have taken care of his objections, but he raves on, "Who are these people she will be working for, anyway? How do you know they are all right? How do you know she will be safe? I've got to talk to her. I'd better go and pick her up."

"Vy will bring her home," I say. I am sick of talking about Ifa. "Know what, Lucius? This is the first night we've been alone in this house in ages. It's all ours for a couple of hours. Let's enjoy it, shall we?"

I have some Cordon Negro on the bottom shelf of the refrigerator. I turn off the oven, put the split chicken on two plates, and bring the wine, along with two goblets, and pour. "Here's to us."

While Lucius sits at the table and nibbles, I put on some smooth, romantic sounds, an album of fifties and sixties love songs. Our song, Jerry Butler's "For Your Precious Love," flows sweetly through our four speakers. I wait until Lucius puts his chicken down, then hold out my arms and walk toward him. "Dance with me, dear."

He holds up his hands to block me. "There are some things you haven't told me, Zena. I don't know everything that's going on."

"You're just spending an evening with me. Old, familiar, comfortable me," I reassure him. I refill his goblet.

The second track is Marvin Gaye's silky, sexy "Let's Get It On." I dim the lights, which I should have done in the first place. Easier than exercise. I take off my dress, in slow motion. Then I remove my half slip. Lucius is watching me. I pull off my panty hose and begin some slow, dreamy movements. He is really staring now. I am glad I am wearing my new leopard-print bra and panties. I step out of the panties and sway toward him. I am glad the room is dark. Last time I looked, my coochie was almost bald! It was bad enough before that it was going gray.

Then we are dancing, but not for long, because he dances me into the bedroom.

My husband is large and strong and warm, and I have never been needier, and we have never been closer. As it turns out, he did not need Vigoro after all. He just needed fewer distractions.

After he rolls off me the second time, I say "Wow!" He doesn't even seem winded.

I decide to confide my deepest worry. "Lucius," I whisper, "I am bald down there now. I hope you don't mind."

He chuckles. "If you're afraid it will catch cold, I guess you could buy a little wig for it. It's still pretty hot, though."

Well, that's one less thing to worry about. After we have finished laughing, I say, "Baby, if you're this strong now, past fifty, I hate to think what you could do when you were twenty-five."

He chuckles. "Oh, I kept pretty busy, as I recall. Turn over." He changes positions to take the slow and easy ride home.

I do, too, but Lucius is not Superman, after all, nor is he a teenager. Before things even get started for the third time, I hear him snoring softly behind me. I chuckle. I have had more than enough loving for one night, anyway. Once more, and I would be sore.

But I will want more tomorrow night, probably, or the night after that. So that young hussy had better get the job.

Later, much later, I wake up in the dark thinking that Lucius is embracing me again.

"That feels good, honey," I say. "But not so tight, dear. Don't hug me so tight, please. You're squeezing me so hard I can't breathe. Ow!"

Then I smell that horrible smell again, like rotten vegetables that have stayed in the bottom bin of the refrigerator too long.

And I scream.

 # TWENTY-SEVEN

WELL, I CALLED THOSE Macintyre people and set up a date for an interview. Then I told Miss Zena to bring that girl over here on Sunday night and again on Monday morning, and never mind telling her why. She came swishing in here wearing a red coat and some black tights, with a false ponytail attached to her head like she was going to model clothes at Sir John Strawbridge Bloomingdale's.

She is getting too heavy to be a model, though. She has gained weight staying with Miss Zena and Mr. Lucius. I guess she likes having regular meals, with enough on the table for second help-ings. When I first saw her, she was so skinny she looked like they didn't have enough food back where she came from. She is funky, too—Miss Zena is right about that. I will have to give her a talk about those armpits, so she doesn't mess up the people's uniforms. She is also built like temptation, stacked up like sin, and has a walk like trouble. If Mr. Lucius hasn't been eyeing her when she walks around in those tight pants, he's made of stone.

Sunday night didn't go like I had planned. Just like the first time I met her, Ifa clammed up and didn't want to answer my questions. I never even got around to telling her about the job. Finally it was time for me to put dinner on the table and call my family. Ifa grinned then, and looked like she didn't know which she wanted to devour first—my son, or my pot roast with mixed vegetables.

I have just stopped throwing up all day long, and now I have another reason to feel sick. Sonny is back home after serving only one week of his six-month jail sentence. The judge decided to let him come home with one of those beeper bracelets fastened around his ankle. If he leaves the house, it goes off, and he gets picked up. This is called house detention. The reason for it, his lawyer says, is that they only have room up at the jail for the worst offenders.

"Oh, Lord, no," is what I said when I heard. If they can't find room for a boy who has been convicted of assault and armed robbery, because they need the space for serious criminals, I'd hate to see what they're keeping in that jail. I didn't want him to be there, but Fred and I got used to him being away. I do not need that great big no-good boy hanging around here right now. But he's my son, and this is the only home he's got, so he lays around here all day. We can't put him out, and he can't go nowhere.

He's not supposed to associate with criminals, but the friends that come here to see him do not look like choirboys. Most of them are the same old crowd, the ones who helped him get in trouble. I just shooed a couple of them crows out of here before Miss Zena and Ifa came.

It was just three days ago that Sonny's lawyer called and said, "I have good news, Mrs. Sampson." But it was not good news. If they were sending Sonny upstate or out of state, that would be good news to me. Overseas, even better.

My nosy old next-door neighbor, Thelma, said, "I guess you are glad to have your son back home so soon." I said, "Hell, no, I am not glad!"

How can I be glad to have a son at home who doesn't think about his mother, doesn't think about his father, doesn't think about anything except new ways of breaking the law?

I am so disgusted, I don't know what to do. The justice system ought to have arrangements to straighten out a loser like my Sonny. He needs to be reformed by professionals, not amateurs like his father and me. We don't know what else to do for him.

Miss Zena tried to tell me that the jails don't reform criminals, they just punish them, but I didn't want to hear it. It don't make sense. If you gonna lock somebody up, why not try and change their lawbreaking habits and give them new ones?

It's a sin to say it, but he's my son, and I don't want him. He's here because there's no place else he can go—the same reason Ifa is at Miss Zena's house.

At the table, Miss Africa introduced herself to Sonny. "My name is Ifa. It means 'life,' " she said, and held out her hand.

"My name is Fred. It rhymes with 'dead,' " he told her, and gave her hand a shake. But he was grinning like he planned on living for a while. My son is handsome like his father, with perfect teeth and wavy hair—not that his looks have done him any good. He has a bright, beautiful smile, but it does not reach all the way up to his eyes. He is only eighteen, but his eyes are hard and dead-looking. They scare me.

After Ifa wolfed down half the pot roast, she disappeared into the basement den with Sonny. They got interested in a movie on TV, and complained when I tried to call her upstairs. That kept me from giving her a thorough interview like I'd planned. After the movie was over, it was time to take her back to Miss Zena's.

When Miss Zena brings Ifa back on Monday morning, the girl looks around my house real suspicious, and starts complaining. "But, Mum," she says, "I thought you said we were going shopping. Is Auntie Vyester coming with us?"

"How can you go shopping, if you don't have any money?" Miss Zena asks her.

"I don't know, Mum, but you said—"

"I brought you here because your Auntie Vyester knows how you can earn some money. After you've done that, we can go shopping."

I am proud of Miss Zena for standing up to her like this. Once she would have given in, mumbled something about "Well, okay, since I promised," and gone digging in her purse for some plastic or some shopping dollars. But this time she holds her ground.

The glamour girl immediately starts pouting. I can tell she is used to having her way. She looks from one of us to the other, like a person in a trap who is trying to con somebody into letting her out. She crosses and uncrosses her legs, taps her feet, and acts like she has the seven-year itch. She wants to get out of my house fast.

But I am in no hurry, myself. I want to take my time and talk to this girl, see if her personality has improved any, though in my experience this seldom happens. I don't want to let down Verniece and the rest of my friends down by taking her on an interview if she doesn't know how to act.

"What courses are you taking in school, Ifa?" I ask her.

"I am studying ventilation, air conditioning and refrigeration engineering. They are very hard subjects."

"I'm sure they are," I say sympathetically. "You won't need to know all that for this job I have in mind. All you will need to know are broomilation, mop conditioning, and bucket engineering."

"A scrubwoman?" She is shouting. "You want me to be a scrubwoman? Me, Ifa Olongo?"

"How would you like to have your own room, your own TV, your own private bath, and a hundred and fifty dollars a week?"

"I had all that at home, as well as servants and plenty of clothes. I had my own telephone, too. Would I have that?"

"We'll have to ask," I say. Behind her back, Miss Zena is shaking her head vigorously, No. She has told me about Ifa's expensive phone jones. I nod, to show that I am hip.

But I can't help asking her, "Well, if you had it that good at home, why did you leave?"

Her face closes up like a door. "I left for private reasons. What do I have to do to get all those things?"

"Not much," I tell her. "Miss Zena tells me you know how to clean house."

Her face gets all pouty. "Yes, I do. But I am not going to be a housecleaner. I am going to be a movie star."

And that is when I get so creative, I surprise myself. "Of course you are. That is how all stars get discovered in America, cleaning houses. The rich man who owns the house you are going to take care of is a big Hollywood producer."

Her eyes get so big, they spread out and cover the rest of her face. "Are you serious?"

"Absolutely. I have already told him all about you, how beautiful and talented you are. That is why he wants to hire you."

She smiles and turns to Zena. "You see, Mum? I knew big things would happen for me soon."

Miss Zena is frowning. I can tell she is bothered by these lies I have made up on the spot, but they are getting the results I want, so I go on. "All he wants you to do is keep the upstairs part of his house clean and look after his mother. She isn't sick—just old and feeble. He is very busy, but he has promised to arrange your screen test."

This big overgrown bush baby starts leaping around my room and screeching with joy. "A screen test! Oh, thank you, gods and goddesses! Thank you, ancestors! Thank you, Jesus!"

I don't know what kind of mixed-up religion this girl practices, and I don't want to know. I put my hands on her shoulders to calm her down before she starts talking in tongues for real, and maybe spitting up snakes. "Now, Ifa," I say, "this is very important. Do not bother Mr. Macintyre about your screen test. He knows you want to be a star, and he knows he has promised me that he will give you a chance. But he hates to be reminded of his promises."

"I understand. I will be patient. I will not remind him," she says.

I let out the deep breath I have been holding in. It looks as if this is going to work. I am glad. It is one less thing on my mind, and I have a lot on my mind these days.

Miss Zena said, "Hello, Sonny," when she came in, and my son hardly answered her from the couch, just grunted something while he kept on clicking through the TV channels. She looked at me with a lot of sympathy, and said, "I'm sorry, Vyester. You deserve a break."

I saw that African girl cutting her eyes at Sonny, and him

looking back, and their eyes locking while signals went back and forth between them. Neither of them said anything when she walked in, but I could feel the electricity they generated charging up the air in the room. I sure hope them two aren't planning on getting together regular. If they did, that would really be bad news.

"Come on, Ifa," Miss Zena says, and pulls her toward the door.

And that is the end of that, I hope.

# TWENTY-EIGHT

THE RIDE UP to the Macintyre mansion is not pleasant, but once we get there, Ifa is so impressed she behaves beautifully. I begin to think that there is hope for her and that she may make a life for herself here in the United States.

On the way, though, she lets her bad attitudes about African Americans show. First, she has too much to say about Vyester's car. Miss Thing is no late-model high-ticket item, and she groans and complains a lot, which she has a right to do after twelve years on the road, but still, she runs.

"Why do you have no seat covers back here?" Ifa complains when she gets in. "There are holes and rips in this seat. They will tear my stockings and hurt my legs."

"Move over, then," says Vy.

"I can't. There is too much trash back here."

Vy turns around and addresses her directly, taking her eyes off the road for so long that she frightens me. "Do you want to walk?" she asks.

"No."

"Then keep quiet about my car, and just ride." Vy turns her head around just in time to avoid hitting three pedestrians. We rumble our way up a main street, belching and backfiring as we go.

"You drive like a madwoman, Auntie Vyester."

Really angry now, Vy wrenches Miss Thing into the left-hand lane, narrowly avoiding the fender of a pickup truck, runs one red light, and screeches to a halt at the next. "Damn ignunt powhite drivers," she says. "Damn ignunt cops, messing with the lights and changing the timing. Used to be, I could always make that light in thirty seconds." She turns to Ifa. "Now, what you got to say?"

"Nothing," Ifa replies. I look back and see that she is shaking. After that, she remains wisely silent about Vy's car and her driving, and I make sure my seat belt is fastened.

Next, though, Ifa comments on the condition of the streets we are traveling. "You can tell block people live around here," she says. "It is a very dirty neighborhood. Why do they not clean it up?" She points. "Look at those steps. They are filthy. And those children on the steps, they are not clean, either. This is America, the land of opportunity. I do not understand why block people do not do better."

"You are here with no money and no job, living off the charity of my friends," says Vy. "Since this is the land of opportunity, I do not understand why you are not doing better. Explain that to me, please."

"I am not a charity case!" Ifa cries.

"What are you, then? Tell me."

While Ifa splutters and coughs worse than the car, we jerk and struggle our way from the ghetto to the lower suburbs, through some Archie Bunker neighborhoods with tiny yards that have plastic deer standing on them, and on to streets of bigger houses with brick fronts and larger yards. Finally we turn onto one of those streets where the noise ordinances are so tough the birds use sign language and the wind doesn't dare make a sound in the trees.

Vyester pulls into a driveway about as long as my whole block. It curves in front of a stone mansion that appears to have about forty rooms, with a porch roof that is supported by white columns. Vyester brazenly parks her beat-up car squarely in front of the porch, between a Rolls-Royce and a convertible Beamer, and screeches to a stop.

Ifa is silent. She is taking everything in, wide-eyed, and I can tell she is impressed.

"Will I live here, Mum?" she asks

"Yes, if they decide they want to hire you."

Her eyes are shining. "I feel as if I am a movie star already!"

"Ifa—" Suddenly, I feel so sorry for her I almost blow the whole thing. Vy, sensing my attack of conscience, grabs my hand so tightly I think it will fall off. I keep quiet.

A white woman with a face full of wrinkles Estée Lauder cannot help answers the door in a black uniform and white apron. When she sees us, she pulls the door toward her until it is almost closed again, and talks to us through a three-inch space.

"Are you Mrs. Deutsch?" Vy asks.

"Yes," she says cautiously.

"I'm Vyester Sampson. I called you about the job." Vy gives Ifa a shove forward. "This is the girl I talked to you about. Her name is Ifa."

"Come in," the woman says, and opens the door wider. She addresses Ifa. "Do you speak English?"

"I am a graduate of—" Ifa begins in her haughtiest tone. I pinch her skinny arm. Lucius told me he had the same trouble stopping her from reciting her academic credentials when he went to register her at night school. I am glad the girl's people didn't clip her clit, but sometimes, I swear, I wish they had clipped her tongue.

She is a little more hesitant now, after enduring my prolonged pinch. "I mean, yes, I speak English."

"Good, because I'll have to train you. You look strong and healthy. Do you have references?"

"She hasn't been in this country long enough to have references," says Vy.

"We will vouch for her," I add.

The woman looks dubious, then sighs. "I guess that will have to do."

"When will I meet the master of the house?" Ifa wants to know.

"Heaven knows," says Mrs. Deutsch. "He's always on the road. Right now he's in California."

"Ah," says Ifa, imagining, I know, that the master of the house is busy producing a big picture. "Do you know his schedule?"

"No, I don't. Why do you want to know? You won't have any business with him. Your main job will be taking care of his mother, old Mrs. Macintyre. As for the rest of your work, you will report to me."

"I will need to see him when he returns," Ifa says. She sounds like a queen who wants one of her subjects brought to her. I regret that Vy and I did not have time to train Ifa in correct servant deportment. But then, no amount of training could make this haughty girl exhibit humility. "Now," she declares, "I want to see my room."

"Follow me," says the white woman. She is obviously the executive housekeeper of this place, which probably requires a staff of at least six. All three of us trudge up some stairs, and then up some more stairs, and then down a long hall. Mrs. Deutsch throws open a door.

Ifa's room is really quite nice. It is large—these old houses do not stint on space—and has double windows on two sides. It has old-fashioned wallpaper with a gold stripe, and light fixtures that probably date back to Thomas Edison. I wouldn't mind having those brass sconces and that bowl-shaped Tiffany ceiling shade in my dining room. One wall has a large closet, the other, a medium-sized TV. The bed is placed catercorner between the windows. Even though it is a full-sized bed, this placement does not make the room look small.

Ifa's eyes dart around until they spy what she is looking for. She sits on the edge of the bed as if testing it, but what she is really testing is the white princess phone by the bed. She picks it up hungrily. Evidently, by the size of her grin, she gets a dial tone.

"This will do very nicely," she pronounces.

I feel for her employers, but I say nothing. Next, we go to meet the old lady. Mrs. Macintyre has shrewd eyes, but has been left speechless by a stroke. She seems amused by Ifa, but I have the feeling that, if she could speak, she would turn thumbs down on hiring her.

After that, Vy and I leave, promising to come back with some clothes and some toiletries.

"I feel like I just got a huge load off my shoulders," I say, "but I also feel like I have abandoned a child."

"Go with the first feeling," Vy advises. "I have told you and told you, she is not a child. 'This will do just fine,' " she mimics. "How did she get used to such luxury, anyway?"

"Her folks are rich, but they can't bring money out of the country. It's oil money, I think."

"What good is their money, if they can't bring it with them? I think they were conning you, Miss Zena. We haven't been over there to see how they really live. What I want to know is— how come all the Africans I've met claim to be related to kings and queens? That can't be, Miss Zena—unless, over there, the king is just the one with the most goats. I bet that's the way it works."

"Maybe so," I say.

"If a man barbecues enough goats, they crown him king for that week. Especially if he lets them drink the goats' blood."

"You may be right."

"I know *my* family would let anybody be king if he gave them all they wanted to eat and drink. At least until someone else gave a party."

Vy is fantasizing, of course, and in her fantasies as in life, she takes no prisoners. But sometimes, I myself don't know what to believe. Actually, Ifa's people do drink blood, as part of their traditional religious observances. In one of her more relaxed moments, Ifa has shown us her ceremonial wooden blood-drinking cup. "Put it away," I said. I thought the whole idea was gruesome. I don't even like taking communion in church. Ugh. No wonder AIDS is spreading like crazy over there.

The Curly Girl is closed, because it is Monday. As we bump our way down one of the city's potholed streets, I think about how to use what is left of my day off. Part business, part pleasure, I decide.

"Vy," I say, "let's go check out that new beauty supply warehouse that just opened. What do we need?"

"Weave hair. We always need weave hair, in red and blonde but mainly in dark brown and black."

"Real hair or false hair? Wavy or straight?"

"Faux, of course."

Faux it is. Fee, fi, faux, fum. I forgot. Hardly any of our customers will pay for real human hair these days.

"Mostly straight hair," Vy continues, "but some wavy—about three to one, I'd say. We need gold and silver frosting, too, and paint for temporary hair streaks. And moisturizer, and hairbrushes, and conditioner, and hot oil treatment packs, and some of that new lavender-color nail polish that's coming in. Customers have been asking for it. They're tired of darks and metallics. Oh, and a couple of wig stands, and some big-tooth combs."

"Okay. We'll go shopping for salon supplies. After that, I'm taking you to lunch."

"Josephine's?" Vy asks quickly.

I agree without a fuss. I have been avoiding the Mad Mango lately. Desmond Jenkins, the owner, has been telling me that his niece is coming to the States from Barbados, and saying that he has no more room at home, and needs to find a place for her to stay. I am wise enough not to comment, but he is hinting more and more heavily that he wants me to take the girl in.

Last year, I remember, Ann Worthy put up some guy from Kenya as a favor to her husband, who has investments there, and practically had to use dynamite to get him to leave.

Not long after that, Monica Lewis fell for some flattery from some Pakistani women whose husbands work with hers, and when she looked up, she, too, had a female guest—one whose long hair smelled like rancid butter. That should have taught her not to talk about me, but it didn't.

It's becoming an epidemic. This is the Land of Opportunity, true, but we are the most disadvantaged people in it, and we cannot afford to have all these other people riding to their opportunities on our backs. As that businessman writer James Clingman says, we are at the bottom of the economic ladder, yet we stand there holding it for all and sundry and saying, "After you." Life in our communities these days feels tight, like we were just getting comfortable enough to breathe in a house that was big enough for all of us—when the new arrivals poured in and our house began bursting at the seams.

Who conned us into this? Nobody. We did it ourselves, probably because our churches talk so much about helping Africa, and maybe also because we want to feel like Lord and Lady Bountiful. After being guests in the white folks' country for so long, we want to be hosts. We want to believe that we are higher on the heap than these new people, and that we have surplus to share—when, really, we have nothing.

And as soon as the new people acquire something, they learn to discriminate. I heard Phlora Wilson talking recently about how some East Indians and then some Viet Cong refused to rent her daughter a house. That's a crime and a shame, even if Phlora does have some bad grandkids.

As for me, if I have truly gotten rid of Ifa, which I doubt, I will never open my door to anyone else from the Third World again, not even if they come riding up to my house in the Publishers Clearing House Sweepstakes van.

Josephine's Soul Food is a good place to relax. Miss Thing does not look out of place on her parking lot, where other beat-up cars and trucks, mostly Fords, are parked along with a couple of Japanese motorcycles. Black folk do not buy Harleys, because they are preferred by Rebs, just as, until recently, we did not buy GM cars, because their maker was not known to hire us, and Ford did, and also gave to the U.N.C.F. and the N.A.A.C.P. But our memories are short, and Miss Thing is a Buick, of late eighties vintage.

The odor of frying fish greets us before we enter, blown our way by the huge exhaust fan above Josephine's door. Once we are inside, it mingles with the aromas of simmering ham hocks and frying chicken. I settle at the cleanest-looking table, the one on the far wall. Flies from last summer still cling to the flypaper hanging from the ceiling fan. I try not to look at them. A roach rushes under a crack in the linoleum, but not fast enough. I catch it with the toe of my shoe and crush it. It's little details like this that made too many of us rush through the suicide door marked "Integration." But Josephine herself and her kitchen, which is in plain view, are clean.

"Hey, girlfriends," says the owner, leaning on her round brown arms at the counter. "How you two feelin'? I've missed you." Josephine feeds a brother, two sisters, five natural children, two adopted children, and twelve grandchildren out of this restaurant, and says "Praise the Lord" a lot, and calls herself blessed. I guess she is.

"How you doin', Josephine?" Vy greets her.

"Just fine, praise the Lord. I keep runnin' from Arthur, and he ain't caught me yet."

She means, of course, Arthur Itis.

"Somebody caught you, to give you all them kids," Vy signifies.

"Yeah, well, I forgot his name, but it wasn't Arthur. Got somebody else chasin' me now. His name is Oliver, and I ain't runnin from him too fast."

I believe Oliver is both real and lucky. Josephine is over sixty, but I can testify from personal knowledge that her white skunk stripe is the only gray in her hair, which is otherwise pure, pretty black. Her bifocals are in purple harlequin frames, chosen because her wardrobe, from slacks to evening gowns, features a lot of purple. She has dimples when she smiles, which is often, and her warm personal welcome makes up for the defects of her decor and her housekeeping. You just don't get that kind of a greeting at T. G. I. Friday's.

After putting a tray of biscuits in the oven and slamming the door, Josephine turns back to us and asks me, "Where you been keepin' yourself, Zena? You look skinny. Been on a crash diet? Rabbit food and air sandwiches?"

This is news to me. I didn't know I'd lost weight. If I have, it's from the stress of living with Ifa. Well, it's an ill wind . . .

"No, just doing without your good cooking, Josephine."

"Well, we 'bout to put an end to that bad habit. What'll you have?"

"Fish, corn bread, lima beans, rice, and greens," I say.

"Make that two," says Vy, and races to the ladies' room. When she comes back, her tan complexion has a green tinge. "I thought I was through with that nasty morning sickness. I guess I better take my platter home."

Her belly is getting so big it turns a corner before she does. At least once a day I fuss at Vy for not telling me sooner that she was pregnant. She always reminds me that I have had my own problems, which she hopes she has just solved.

I thank her, and we clink glasses of Sprite in mutual congratulation, Josephine not having ginger beer in her refrigerator.

I don't care if she doesn't have ginger beer. Her fried whiting is wonderful. Besides, I can relax here and be myself. I don't have to keep up a bright, bubbly front of success and happiness, the way I feel I must at the Mango or, for that matter, at Divas meetings. I can say, "Girl, these shoes are killing me," which my shoes usually are, and kick them off and rub my toes, which look like rock gardens. I can belch, the way you always want to after drinking some soda, and it doesn't have to be a delicate little ladylike burp, either. I can cry if I need to, or holler, or curse, because this place is like home, and its owner is like family.

It feels so good to be back here, I want to cry.

Josephine comes over with my platter and a big white rag. She hands it to me so I can wipe away my tears. Then she takes it back, mops the sweat off her forehead with it, cleans the table with it last, and sits down to catch up on the news. She is full of motherly advice for Vyester. Vyester listens. She promises not to go to any funerals or watch any scary movies or look at any fires, lest they mark her child. She declines to have a diviner who is a friend of Josephine's swing a crucifix over her belly to determine the sex of her infant. She already knows it is a girl, she tells her. She has some Jell-O and nibbles on a biscuit, then accepts her platter, wrapped in foil and a brown bag, to take home. When the check comes, we both reach for it.

"You always pay, Miss Zena," Vy says. "Let me."

Something tells me I'd better let her pay this time, if I want to keep her friendship, and maybe stop her from always putting "Miss" in front of my name.

I settle for leaving the tip. Then, after I can't possibly eat another forkful of fish, I let her drive me home.

TWENTY-NINE

OUT OF SIGHT, out of mind. I have no more nightmarish snake encounters, and my memory of the hideous thing on the couch fades. Instead, I enjoy the peace and order of home without a grown Olori daughter. No more loud demands. No more rude, insulting comments. No more borrowed jewelry or missing cosmetics. No smeared makeup on the mirror, no scattered tissues with dark red lip prints, no trails of face powder running from the bathroom sink to her door. No dramas about ghosts. And enough food to go around, and no more constant waiting to use the phone.

My rule forbidding Ifa to make phone calls was short lived. It was abandoned after Lucius saw her using the pay phone across the street in her short red coat and dark leggings, and promptly went to get her.

"She looked like a streetwalker, Zena," he complained. "Think of the neighbors. We'll just have to let her go on making calls here."

So we did. Once I had to pull the jack out of the wall, because she had been screaming *"Yobba! Yobba! Umgawa!"* at someone for an hour, and I had a headache. And our phone bill climbed again, to the point where I told Lucius either he or Ifa would have to get a job.

But now our phone is always available. I call Vy to see how

she is feeling and to thank her again for finding the job for our guest. I simply can't thank her enough for that.

I also invite Vy to the Divas' annual fashion show. It's a big event—all Ann Worthy's idea, of course—which features a new African American designer every year and provides art scholarships for talented high school students. Sometimes I miss the days when all we did was get together and run our mouths and play cards.

When I invite Vy, she says "Miss Zena, I got a family and a living to earn. I ain't got time for all that fancy antsy stuff."

"It'll do you good, take you out of your world for a few hours. I know Sonny must be getting on your nerves. You need a break."

"Arty farty."

"It's for a good cause—scholarships for art students."

"Airy fairy."

"We will have three different designers and ten models."

"Fancy antsy. When do I get to wear designer clothes? I tell you, it ain't my scene. I'm a plain Jane."

"Look," I tell her, "we're each responsible for ten tickets, and I've only managed to sell eight. I'll treat you."

This puts an entirely new spin on the discussion. "Okay. What are we wearing?"

I pause to think. "I have a black crepe coat dress that should do for me. Do you still have that black two-piece dress you wore last New Year's?"

"I think so. It's pretty big. It has an elastic waist. Maybe I can still get in it."

"I have a sheer duster I'll lend you to wear over it, in a gold-and-black print. It'll cover up your condition."

"Why should I want to hide my condition? I'm proud of it." But she likes the idea of the duster, I can tell. Our call-waiting beeps. It seems louder and more insistent then usual. Vy promises to call me back after she checks her closet, and I take the other call.

It is Ifa, of course. "Is Dod there? Let me speak to him, please."

Callers who start off like that always annoy me, even when they aren't Ifa. I think that, if they have met me, people ought to at least have the courtesy to say hello to me and inquire about my health before asking to speak to my husband.

"No, he's not here, Ifa. Can I help you?"

She doesn't bother to hide her disappointment. "Awww. Well, maybe you can help me, Mum. I need to see a doctor."

"Why?"

"I am worried about the condition of my heart. You remember. Also, my employer wants me to have a checkup."

I am glad I took the call. Even though I have begun to convince myself that nothing was going on between her and Lucius except my paranoid imaginings, I don't want to give him an excuse to be alone with her.

I can take her to the doctor, of course, because it is Monday—my day off. Still, there are other things I'd rather do—like call Rose Cooper's Day Spa for an appointment and get a massage. The Cowboys' hoedown was Saturday night, and I am still sore from all that do-si-do-ing and promenading, and the spurs grazing my shins, and the cowboy boots stepping on my toes. Once, I remember, a great big boot—heel and all—came down on my foot when I was curtseying to my corner and my partner forgot I was there.

But they raised the money they needed, and my husband had a ball with his big ole corny country self. He especially loved the fiddler and the competition for the gaudiest Wild West glad rags. He had a new red bandanna for the occasion, and some oxblood boots, and a white hat, and a pair of white chaps with three-inch fringes. He looked gorgeous. He would have won, too, if he'd been by himself. But I wore my shabby old brown suede cowgirl outfit, which I tried to hide under a huge cape when I left the house, and the judges had seen it before.

Now, every time I move my left foot, the one that got stomped, it radiates hot zingers of pain and cries out for more aspirin. Maybe I'd better call my podiatrist instead of Rose's spa. The next time I hear somebody holler "Circle right!" I intend to circle my right arm in their direction—with a fist at the end of it. We women sure put up with a lot to keep our husbands happy—or just to keep them.

"Yes, I can take you, Ifa," I tell her. "Can you be ready in half an hour?"

"I am ready now, Mum," she informs me. And, sure enough, when I pull up to the mansion, she is standing under the portico, leaning against one of the white columns like Scarlett posing at Tara.

"I need a ride to school tonight, too, Mum," she informs me. "I missed my classes last week, and I do not want to get too far behind in my studies. I have to keep my visa."

I agree to take her to school, too. I am guilty about getting rid of her, though I can understand and sympathize with Cecelia a little more now.

"I will not have to ask you for favors like this much longer, Mum," Ifa informs me. "I am getting a car."

"Oh, really?" They must like her a lot at the Macintyres', I am thinking. Maybe they want her to take the old lady out for rides. "Do you like your job?"

What comes out of her is an outpouring of anger. "Mum! How could I like it? I hate it! I have never been a servant before. I can clean, but I was not brought up to be a servant! We are taught to take care of our elders, but that old lady is no relative of mine! She wears messy diapers, and I must change them as if she were my child." She sighs, and her voice drops with resignation. "It is all right, though. It is a job. It was time I got one and stopped being a burden to you and Dod."

She must have received a paycheck already, a pretty good one, I think, judging by the new dress she is wearing. It is a rust-colored A-line with a matching coat and some interesting fringed appliqués. It had to cost at least—well, never mind. More than I ever spent on an outfit, that's for sure. I am not going to ask where she got it from or what it cost. It had to be hot, I am thinking. But how would Ifa, new to this country and isolated in the outer suburbs, know where to make contacts for hot clothes?

Mind your business, Zena, I admonish myself. "You look nice," is all I say.

And "Thank you, Mum" is her only response. So where and how she got her outfit, which on my second inspection I recognize as by a designer whose show I saw on CNN, remains a mystery.

There are five people ahead of us in Sawbones Jones's waiting room. I am astonished. If that many people come to him, the shortage of doctors I keep hearing about must be real.

When her name is called, I do not recognize it. Who, I ask her, is this "Teresa Olongo"?

"Mum, that is my Christian name. You will remember I told you that I was baptized by the missionaries. Auntie Vyester thought it was best that I use it because it is a name Americans understand. My sister does the same thing. Her real name is Wura, but she goes by her baptismal name of Cecelia when she comes to this country. I hate to talk about her. I miss her terribly."

She grips my wrist so tightly it is painful. "Mum, will you go in with me, please? I have never been to one of your doctors before. I don't know what they do."

What Sawbones Jones mainly does is talk. Not about you, his patient, or about your symptoms, which have brought you to his office, but about himself and what he imagines are his brilliant ideas and revolutionary thoughts.

I love black men, but I do not love black doctors. First of all, let me explain that, to me, black men are fine, fine, fine. I don't mean the wrecks that have been steamrollered by this society, but the survivors who are more or less intact. When a black man is sure of himself and is doing his righteous thing, whatever it is, and doing it well, God has no finer creation. Black men's voices have a different tonal register than white men's—deeper and more thrilling. Their hands are more sensitive. Their facial expressions are more serious, because they know how serious the situation is. You never catch a black man with that blank, goofy white-boy look on his face. If black men get goofy, they get dead very quickly. So they stay alert and aware.

Black doctors may be all that, too, but when I go to see a doctor, I don't want a man, I want a skilled body mechanic, and a patient listener who is interested in my symptoms. The doctors I know are too involved in themselves and in expressing their ideas to be either.

Lucius excuses black doctors by saying that they are smart people who do not get to talk to too many other smart people in the course of a day. When they do get that chance, the talk just spills out of them. Well, I may be smart, but I get sick, too, and I want a doctor to pay attention to me and my problems—not vice versa.

I have to remind Sawbones Jones that he is supposed to give Ifa a checkup, not just quiz her on Olori politics and the effects of the latest coup over there. See, she loves to talk, too, so this visit could take all day. She has a fine time with him until he deftly swabs the inside of her elbow with some alcohol and says "Make a fist for me." Before she knows what he is about to do, he has stuck a needle in her arm and taken out about a pint of blood.

Her eyes get big and frightened. She quizzes him suspiciously. "Why did you take so much of my blood? What are you going to do with it?"

"Send it to the lab for some tests, Miss Olongo. Do you think there will be elections in your country this year?"

"Where is the lab? I will take it there myself."

"That won't be necessary. They pick up our specimens twice a day. You have no heart problems, just a tendency to be nervous. I am going to prescribe a mild tranquilizer for you. Is it safe to travel these days everywhere in Olori?"

"I am more interested in whether my blood will travel safely to your laboratory," she says.

He laughs, and she is offended.

"Mum, he had no right to laugh," she tells me as we leave. "I have enemies. If the wrong people get hold of my blood, I am dead. Worse than dead. Compared to the results of their curses, death would be a blessing."

Her religion, as I have noticed before, seems to be heavily into flinging evil curses back and forth, like a game of volleyball.

"I am not impressed with your doctor," she adds. "He does not seem to do very much for his patients."

It's funny how, when she criticizes Americans, especially African Americans, I am moved to defend them, even if I privately think that they could stand improvement. No doubt she wanted Jones to dance around her and shake an animal tail. My mental picture of him doing this makes me chuckle.

"What is so funny, Mum?"

"I am not impressed with your juju," I tell her. "The snake has left my house. It did not harm me."

She ignores me except for a slight smile. "Why did he take so much of my blood, anyway? Does it have something to do with this note my employers sent him? It was sealed, so I did not read it before he did." She pulls a note from her purse—a very nice burgundy Coach. This juju baby is wearing at least a thousand dollars wholesale in merchandise—pretty rich for a maid's salary.

I open the note and read it. The Macintyres wanted her tested for AIDS.

At first I am indignant at the implied racist assumptions. Then I grow thoughtful, and tuck the note in my coat pocket before she has a chance to read it. I am grateful to the Macintyres for thinking of an angle that hadn't occurred to me.

Just in case Lucius has been fooling around with this hot young foreign stuff, I want her tested, too.

 THIRTY

TROUBLE IS WHAT I got in my house. Every time I turn around, trouble. Every place I look, trouble staring me in the face like my own old age on the way in the mirror. Them hoods from the corner hanging around my son like flies round a garbage can. Crazy people banging on the door all hours of the day and night and screaming. The phone ringing all the time—when I answer, I just get wrong numbers, in deep voices with foreign accents, or hang-ups, or heavy breathing.

Last night it was a girl from up the street knocking on our door, hollering and screaming for my son until I thought all of us in here would lose our minds. Everybody knows this girl is a junkie, has been one for years. She had two crack babies— neither one lived six weeks. I guess Sonny finally let the poor thing in and helped her, cause she quieted down and went away.

I hate calling the cops, because, number one, he's my son, and number two, he's under house arrest, and number three, I know they take it out on small fry like him and let the big ones at the top get away. But this is no way for a person to live, especially if she's trying to stay sane and grow a normal, healthy baby.

Trouble. If it ain't Ella Mae from up the street, it's that Olori hoochie calling up every day, or showing up nights and lounging on the sofa with her legs sticking up, and draping herself all over my son every time I turn my back. She is one brazen hussy, not that all the young girls ain't these days. She won't be the first hooch I chased out of here, and probably won't be the last.

When I said something to her about showing some respect for me and my house, she said, "Why should I respect you, Auntie Vyester? You lied to me. I met Mr. Macintyre, and I talked to him. That man is not a movie producer! He is a manufacturer of dog food!"

I said, "He has a lot of money, and he told me he was going to invest some in a movie. That is producing, isn't it? Whether he is a movie producer or not, you have to behave yourself around here, and do what I say. If you don't respect me, respect yourself. Put your feet on the floor and keep them there." And she does—but only while I am in the room.

I ain't bothered Miss Zena about her—this is my house, and it's up to me to straighten it out and keep it straight. But I have a feeling Miss Mumbo Jumbo has a lot to do with all the other bad stuff that's been happening around here. Things were pretty quiet until that ho showed up. And another thing. I would sure like to know where she got them clothes she has on. Silk blouses and gold chains. Real suede jackets and leather skirts. They don't sell those things at the One Price Clothing Store. They aren't giving away slick little red cars like the one she is driving, either.

I guess I had no business trying to help her. When you help the Devil, he don't stop doing his dirt just because you did him a favor. Dirt is his nature.

I just took another one of them foreign-voice calls. I think it was from a car phone.

I look outside and see a big black Lexus with smoky windows. The phone rings again. This time, Sonny picks it up right after I do.

"Man, you know I can't leave the house. You got to wait till my African bitch gets here. All right?"

The voice at the other end rumbles something.

"Nah, you have to wait till she gets off from work. She has this job way out in the burbs, and I told her to keep it, it's a good cover. Don't worry. She does whatever I say. When she shows up, she'll take care of business."

There is more rumbling at the other end of the line. It sounds like a threat.

"Man, don't even go there. Don't even think like that. This ain't my house, it's my parents'. Just chill for a few more minutes, will you? Be cool."

Five minutes later, she pulls up in her shiny little red car and gets out. I see her lean in the window of the Lexus and do some business. When she bends over, her skirt is so short I can see all the way up to the North Pole, plus everything below the Equator, not that I'm interested in her geography. Sonny's friends on our steps are suddenly quiet, except for some soft whistling. One of the windows in the Lexus slides partway down, and somebody sticks his head out and spits—right on the toe of her shoe.

She stomps into the house, and right away she and my son start to arguing.

"Ifa, what you mean, you spent some of the money? Are you out of your mind? Do you know what kind of people you are dealing with? Those Jamaicans don't play, and neither do your Olori friends. If you short-change them, they will kill us! I want you to take these clothes back to the store and bring me the money."

She laughs. I hear more yelling, then a scream and a crash downstairs. Nobody has to draw me a picture. I taught my son never to hit a woman, but he has ignored all my other teachings, so I guess he forgot that one, too.

I really didn't want to know what is going on—that is why it took me all this time to figure it out. But where is the I.N.S.? Where are the D.E.A. and the A.T.F.? Where is Sonny's probation officer? Where is my husband? Why do I always have to be the cop on this beat?

The phone rings again. I pick it up at the same moment my son does. The foreign voice calls Sonny a name, and tells him, "Just put this on ice, you so-and-so. Chill this."

I have already decided to call the cops after all, when the brick comes through the window, followed by the firebomb.

 # THIRTY-ONE

THE SPLENDOR OF the Divas and their guests almost blinds me when I walk into the ballroom of that downtown hotel. Oh, the coats—fake leopard, real mink, cloth with Afrocentric appliqués, fabulous flowing knock-offs of Rome and Paris, Tokyo and London, Rykiel and Karan. Oh, the hats, ribboned and feathered and veiled, and the ones for church with brims the size of flying saucers! The fur turbans and the gilded crowns! The kente gelees, the satin baseball caps, the Arab burnooses that look like my Aunt Maybelle's kitchen tablecloth! Skirts so long and skinny their wearers are hobbled, pants so wide and full you could shoplift a month's groceries and tuck them up there. Caftans that could shelter both your grown children.

We are assembled to watch a fashion show, but the real show is coming through the doors.

We take our places at the tables, but no one stays seated for very long. Women table-hop and speak to everyone they even think they might know, just so their outfits can be seen. Here comes Monica Lewis in a burnished dress and coat of copper satin, with a tall fez to match. She even has copper-colored shoes. Too much.

There goes Fast Fanny Davenport, wiggling from table to table in so much green velvet she looks like a caterpillar.

They ran out of places to sew sequins on Vera Marshall's

velour outfit, so they stuck one extra sequin on her forehead and a couple of others on her cheeks.

Speaking of velour, here comes my next-door neighbor, Lenore Wilkerson, in purple velour slacks and cardigan and a silver blouse with purple trimmings. On her head is a snug helmet of silver sequins, trimmed in—you guessed it—purple sequins! Actually, as much as I dislike Lenore, I have to admit that she looks good. Our women really love dramatic fashions—and they sure can carry them off.

I feel almost too low-key in my little black coatdress with its self-covered buttons, plain black crown-style hat, and pearls. I take off my white gloves and put them in my purse, and start in on my salad. At least I have wild silver fingernails for the weekend, with suns, moons and stars stuck on. It is possible to carry this ladylike look too far. I am married, but no one says I have to dress like a nun. Vyester is not only married but pregnant, and even she looks dramatic in my sheer georgette duster, printed in wild gold-and-black flowers.

"I want to thank you for lending me this coat, Miss Zena. See, I have a problem. None of my bras fit anymore, so I didn't wear one. I don't think people can tell as long as I keep this coat on, can they?"

Vy was once a 34A, but pregnancy has boosted her to a 36C, she tells me. She flips her lapels apart and flashes her bosom. It jiggles.

"People won't know, Vyester," I lie reassuringly. "You better button up, though, to be safe."

"I can only button the top button, Miss Zena. The rest doesn't reach. I didn't have time to change into something else. We had a little excitement around the house today."

This sounds serious. "What kind of excitement?"

"Oh, just a little fire. Fred took care of it." She makes it sound so unimportant, I brush it off.

"You look fine," I say, and mean it. I wish I had worn something wild and dramatic, too.

Vy, bless her professional little heart, is not noticing the clothes. Only the hair. "If that woman over there walks in the shop and asks me to bleach her Afro one more time, I'm going to hand her a wig, because she's 'bout to be bald," she says of one woman in a short blonde style. "Takes too many chemicals to lighten her type of hair. She has that Dago hair—dey go one knot, dey go another."

Her whisper is too loud, but I am enjoying it too much to shush her.

"You see that girl there, the one with the red streaks painted on her bangs? I had to work on her three hours last week to build her hair back. She had just about killed it with some home-made Behave-Yourself."

She adds, "I wish somebody would teach these women to stop putting their wigs on crooked. They make me think *I'm* cockeyed. And just look at that wild weave over there, Miss Zena. It's gonna come loose if she tries to comb it, which I don't think she did today."

By now she has me laughing so hard I almost choke on my salad. "Vyester, stop!"

"I will, but you see that ho over there in the white satin? She got so many curls wove into her head she looks a porky-pine. She ought to break down and let her baldhead boyfriend have some of them curls. She definitely has enough for two heads. And all those different colors! Green. Did I see green? Yes, I saw green curls, and blue ones, and purple, too."

I do choke. The entrée is dry chicken sprinkled with some-thing gritty that turns out to be cheese, wild rice, and string beans with some sliced almonds. I leave most of it and wipe the cheese off my chin. I am going to give Ann and the other orga-nizers a piece of my mind. Fifty dollars a ticket is too much for a fashion show and luncheon with inedible food. I suppose the hotel is keeping most of it. We could have used a school or a church, and gotten Josephine to cater.

As lime Jell-O—yecch—is served for dessert, a heavy bass beat assaults our ears. A rainbow of spotlights bathes the stage, and I remember that we are here to see the show—not be the show.

The first models strut the runway in skimpy bathing suits, plus little bitty tie-ons and throw-ons that somebody has to be kidding to call cover-ups.

Vyester says, "Don't that model reminds you of Ifa? I think she looks a lot like her, specially round the mouth and the eyes. You know, I don't know whether or not that ho is still working. She's at my house an awful lot."

"What's she doing at your house?"

"Visiting my son, which she got no business doing. One day last week I came home early and caught them, and ran her out of there, because them two are definitely bad news for each other. But she comes by other times, specially when I'm at the shop.—Look at that open-work dress! She ain't got nothing on underneath it! Where would you wear that, Miss Zena?"

The item in question is a little black mesh A-line number that hits the model halfway up her legs and shows all of her secrets.

"Nowhere but in the bedroom," I tell Vyester, and then fall silent, thinking. We know some pretty fine people, and we have introduced Ifa to them and their sons. Through us, she has met Air Force cadets, medical students, even the son of a congressman. But she has ignored this select group. Instead, she is interested in Sonny Sampson, who is a thorough hoodlum, rotten to the bone. This says something about her that I would rather not consider.

We are now into evening wear. The model Vyester mentioned is back, swishing extravagantly in a full-length gown of red raw silk that is cut high in front and low in back. Apparently her resemblance to Ifa is something other people notice, too, because I overhear a woman at the next table comment on it.

"Look, there, modeling the red gown. Isn't that the African girl that stays with the Lawsons?"

"Yes, I think so. Look at that walk of hers. The brazen hussy! If she swung her hips any wider she'd knock the walls down."

"They say she's sleeping with Zena's husband, and Zena doesn't know. Isn't that a shame?"

I feel around in my purse for my little pearl-handled pigsticker.

"I heard she does know. I heard she approves. I heard the girl is accommodating both of them."

I find the knife, take it out, and open it.

"Oooh, I always thought there was something kinky about Zena."

I take a deep breath, because I did not come here planning to cut anybody, push back from the table, and begin to rise.

"For real?"

"Yeah. You ever notice how she gives you all them extra little pats after she's through with your hair? I can't say for sure, but I don't like being touched by her all that much."

I am on my feet, reaching for the nearest head. "Well, just let me touch you with this," I say. "I will give you a permanent wave for life." I slice, and a rain of sequins comes pouring down. The head has turned out to be Lenore Wilkerson's elegantly hatted one. With glee I remove more sequins from her hat and a few inches of velvet from her jacket. Then I turn and slice the top off of Monica Lewis's fez.

"Since when did you join the Masons, Monica? I thought they didn't let fools in." I reach into the sliced hat and pull hard. Some hair comes away in my hand. Probably a badly attached weave, but I hope it's real.

It would feel so good to really hurt Monica, maybe maim her permanently. Just in time, though, I remember the lesson I learned from my battle with that other Monica ages ago, back in grade school. I knocked her down and bloodied her nose, but she still won. I never got over her calling me ugly. This time, I only cut clothes—not people. But Vyester is at my side, flailing away. She does not play. She has a really big knife, a kitchen eviscerator that would clean out a goose and ready it for cornbread stuffing in two swipes. With it, she succeeds in removing the seat from Monica's satin skirt, air-conditioning her backside.

Those gossip-mongers aren't getting in any licks. All they are doing is screaming and turning the air blue with curses. I want to stop, though, because things are getting out of control, and I have just remembered Vyester's condition. I brought her here to relax and enjoy herself, not get all wore out in a fight, and she is not looking so good. Her hair is disheveled and her color is bad. Besides, I have run out of breath and have cooled off somewhat. I am still swinging, though, when Ebony Morris shows up and pulls me off of Monica. Ann Worthy is behind her, clucking like a nervous hen.

"Why are you sisters beating up on each other?" Ebony wants to know.

"Ask them," I say.

"We are supposed to be about sisterhood and unity, especially in public," Ebony informs me.

"Then ask them why they were talking about me."

"Terrible conduct. Simply not worthy of a Diva, Zena, dear. I expect better from you," Ann clucks. She is just too much of a lady to deal with anything that is not refined.

"Fine," I say, "because I just decided I am not a Diva anymore. I will go home and write out my letter of resignation if you need one. What good are your club members to me, anyway? If they thought I had a problem in my house, why didn't they come and tell me about it, instead of gossiping about me behind my back? You used to be a down-home bunch of pinochle players, but now you're a silly gang of snobs and hypocrites. Well, I don't have to put up with all that. I don't have to be liberal and love Africans, either, and I don't have to share my home with them, and I don't have to do anything else you say do. I'm in charge of my own black ass, and if you don't like that, you can kiss it."

"That's tellin' em, Miss Zena," Vy applauds.

I feel glorious. I meant every word. I pick up my white gloves from the table and throw them at the Divas' feet.

"Come on, Vy," I tell my friend. "I've got to get you home. And if you don't stop calling me Miss, I'll never speak to you again."

"I don't think you better take me home, Miss Zena," she says. She bends double, clutching her belly. Her beautiful copper-tan face has suddenly gone gray. "You better take me straight to the hospital."

# THIRTY-TWO

THIRTY-ONE WEEKS. Thirty-one weeks. Babies are supposed to grow inside a woman for forty weeks. All of us require at least thirty-six weeks to get all of our little parts complete, to get our lungs and our hearts working well, our blood vessels all the way grown and connected, our fingers and toes distinct and wiggling. The lucky ones among us get forty weeks. Thirty-one weeks is better than thirty weeks, but it is not as good as thirty-six, thirty-eight, or forty.

Vy is thirty-eight. That is not too old to become a mother, but twenty-eight is better. For the mother's age, that is, not the baby's. The baby ought to be thirty-eight, thirty-nine, or forty. Weeks, that is. I think I may be going nuts.

Thirty-one, thirty-two, thirty-three, thirty-eight, thirty-nine, forty. This is the kind of numerical nuttiness that runs through my head as I pace the waiting room on the maternity floor of Holy Redeemer Hospital, which is now called John F. Kennedy, like everyplace else. Thirty-one weeks, not forty. Not thirty-four or even thirty-two, but thirty-one. Thirty-one hours, that's how long it seems it's been since Vyester was taken to emergency surgery. It has only been four hours, though, I see when I look at my watch. Four hours and twenty-eight minutes in surgery to bring forth a child that has only been growing for thirty-one weeks. Vyester is thirty-eight. When I brought her in here, she looked a lot older than that.

Fred, her husband, looks about a hundred and fifty sitting over there across from me with a worried stare on his face. We have both given blood for Vy, and I like to think that my blood will now be in their baby's veins. Fred drops his face into his hands. Good. That face was terrible to look at, droopy and sad and with as many sagging wrinkles as a basset hound's.

I go over to him.

"Fred," I say, "I think the luncheon was too much for her, I'm sorry. I shouldn't have asked her to go."

"It's not your fault, Zena," he says.

"I got in a fight with some of those uppity women. She jumped into it, too. I'm sorry."

He looks at me then and does an amazing thing. He laughs. All his wrinkles turn upward at once into glorious smile lines, and he drops twenty years, and suddenly I know what Vy sees in him. "You got in a fight? You, Zena?"

"Yes, and it probably upset Vyester, and I'm sorry."

He laughs again. "Never knew you had it in you. Vy, now, she'll fight at the drop of a hat."

"I know. I wish she hadn't."

"You couldn't stop her if you tried. Told you it isn't your fault. It's that rotten boy of ours who upset her. He's up to something. He's always up to something. People coming round day and night. Kids. Junkies. Hoodlums. Foreigners. The phone ringing all the time. Funny deep voices on the phone with foreign accents. Police cruising by all night. Last night there was a drug riot on our block. 'Bout thirty kids, all wild and crazy and stoned out of their minds. They kept banging on our door. Then this morning we got fire-bombed."

"What?"

"Yes, fire-bombed. I put the fire out before it spread. Always keep fire extinguishers around, Zena; they come in handy."

"Vy did say you had a fire at the house, but I thought it was just an accident."

"Other people go crazy living around drug dealers. I have to have one in my own house. Why couldn't they keep him locked up, Zena? Why?"

I put a hand on his shoulder. "I don't know. Can't you work with him?"

"I've tried. I can't talk to him. He's like a block of ice. I don't know who he is anymore. Aw, it's my problem, not yours. I gave up on it this morning after the fire. I cleaned house. I found some guns that African girl brought my son, a Glock and a couple of .38s, and I turned him over to the police so they would lock him up before somebody kills him. Then I put your African queen out."

"She was there today?"

"She's been at our house a lot. She and Sonny have become a hot item. I think he put her on his payroll to run errands for him. But I don't think she'll be back, after what I said to her.

"All I'm trying to say is, don't blame yourself, Zena. Your little fashion show wasn't the problem, even if it did turn into a ladies' wrestling match." He smiles. "Wish I could have seen it. I don't think it brought on the baby, though. We've been having worse troubles."

I like Fred. He's like most of us, trying to do the best he can in a world that has gone bad, struggling gamely on in spite of impossible problems. And right now, in the midst of his terrible troubles, he is being most gracious. "You want me to go, Fred?"

"No. Please stay a little longer."

Finally a doctor comes in and talks to Fred. From the relieved smile on his face, I know that things are getting better, and that maybe they are going to be all right.

"It's a little girl. Just like she said it would be," he tells me. And we hug, long and hard, as if I were the baby's grandmother. Which maybe, sort of, I am.

But there are hairy times ahead for little Miss Sampson. I go with Fred to look at her in the Neonatal Intensive Care nursery. She is terribly tiny, just a little over five pounds, and she is hooked up to so many machines. All those big machines for such a tiny baby! She has a mask over her face, and tubes go in and out of her chest, her stomach, her tiny arms. Beepers and monitors tell about her blood pressure and breathing and such.

It makes me scared. But her face is nice and red from crying, and they let her father go in and hold her for a few seconds, and I snap a picture through the glass.

Her name is A'Zena Lucia. She is named for both of us—for me, and for Lucius. I have to run and tell Lucius right away. I leave Fred with his family, and rush home.

# THIRTY-THREE

MY HUSBAND NOW spends most of his free time hunched over the computer he has recently installed in the Back Room. I am jealous of this machine. It is my new rival. Sometimes he is up half the night playing with it.

"Turn off that thing and listen to me, Lucius," I say, giving my rival a light slap on the top of its monitor and flinging myself on the couch. "Vyester had the baby. It's a little girl."

"That's nice," says Lucius, as excited as if I have just said that the price of chicken is going down. "Send her some flowers, will you?"

"This is important news, Lucius," I say. "We are going to be godparents. We have to pray for the new baby. She is a preemie, and she is having a hard time, and she is named for us. A'Zena for me, and Lucia for you."

Even while hearing this news, my husband sneaks in a few more taps on his keyboard. I go on to tell him all about the new little Sampson baby anyway. I am already thinking of her as *our* new little baby—the four of ours. Lucius is glad to hear about her, I guess, but he is too much into his new computer to get really excited. Also, he smells like a bowl of potpourri. I am suspicious.

"What's that I smell?" I ask him. My nose is tickled by his odd aroma, something like ashes, smoke, and red pepper.

"Maybe it's the cologne Ifa gave me. It's called Mojo. It's good stuff. Listen, Zena, I have learned a great deal about this religion of Ifa's. It has a lot of power."

"The baby is underweight, but if she gains half a pound, they may let her go home," I say.

"Their adepts really can transform themselves into animals, especially reptiles. At least there are witnesses who say so."

"Vy had to have a C-section, and they tied knots in her tubes. She gave them permission to do it. She figures if she has another baby, it might have worse problems. So we all have to pray for this one to make it. —You mean, I really saw that thing?"

"Yes."

This is scary news.

"And listen to this: 'The juju man's main function is to protect his village from evil. He does this by dispensing evil to its enemies. Curses, insanity, illness, and death can all be accomplished at a distance through juju.' "

He finally swivels to face me, weirdly excited about juju instead of our godchild. "Zena, I think I've found out what's wrong with Oloris, why they have so many problems and can't make progress. Their religion focuses totally on evil. It does nothing but keep them in fear."

Some Christian preachers do the same thing with all their talk of hellfire and damnation, I am thinking, but I don't say so. I believe in God, and Jesus is my main man, but damn if I am going to sit up in church every Sunday and listen to that preacher try to scare me and call me a miserable sinner.

If I ever find a preacher who makes me feel better after I visit his church than I felt before, I will be up in there to hear him every week. Meantime, I will continue to spend three out of every four Sunday mornings in bed, and keep my hard-earned dollars. But I will pray every day for little A'Zena.

"Ifa doesn't live here anymore," I remind him. "Why are you so interested in her religion?"

"When you struggle against the Devil, it helps to know his tricks." My husband laughs and swings around again in his swivel chair to face me. "Besides, if it can help her to get a Beamer, I'd like to know some juju too."

"She has a BMW now?"

"Bright red. Brand new. She rolled up in it today and came in here to get some of her things. Singing. Happy as a mocking-bird." His face turns very serious. "You asked why I was reading up on juju. Zena, did I ever tell you why I refused to run for of-fice again? When women volunteer to work on a campaign, they expect a piece of the candidate. I didn't want to go along with that sort of thing."

I don't get the connection. Later, I will realize I should have paid closer attention. But my mind is still back at the hospital.

"Zena," he says intensely, "I'm a *Christian* man."

I should be listening to this. But I always tune out when peo-ple brag that they are Christians. It usually means that they have been sinning, but since this is information about the past, or so I think, it does not interest me, and I let it slip by me without snagging it for closer inspection.

I am, however, thinking about Ifa's new car. "Maybe her em-ployer loaned her a car," I say. But the BMW convertible parked in front of the Macintyre mansion was black, not red.

"Maybe. She said it was hers, though."

I am uneasy. I remember that outfit she had on and its proba-ble four-figure price tag.

"Do we know anybody named Cecil?" my husband asks then.

"No. Why?"

"He keeps calling here, along with somebody named Rodney. They have foreign accents."

That nasty taxi driver, that Magic man, was parked at the end of our block when I drove up. His name was Joseph, though, not Cecil or Rodney. I never told Lucius about him. I do so now.

Lucius goes to the front door. I hear him open it, then a pause before he slams it shut. Finally he comes back. "I didn't see any taxi. He must be gone. Why didn't you tell me about him when it happened, Zena?"

"You weren't home, as I remember. Besides, I didn't want you to feel you had to fight somebody." I am a little troubled, because my answer is only half the story. I think that maybe I didn't tell Lucius because I enjoyed that cab driver's attentions—up until the time he went berserk on me.

"I think Ifa may be mixed up with some bad company," my husband says, stirring up waves of expensive scent when he moves. He smells like Two Thousand Pound Sterling. Like money.

"I don't care who she's mixed up with," I tell my fragrant husband. "Vy's new little baby is named for us, and she is struggling to live. I have to go back to the hospital and see how she and Vy are doing. It would be nice if you stopped in too, Lucius."

If he hears me, he doesn't react.

Ifa is a big girl—she can take care of herself. I do not want to think about her. I am only interested in how little A'Zena Lucia is doing. I roll her pretty name around on my tongue, getting used to it.

I used to laugh at the odd-sounding names African American mothers give their children, especially daughters. Names like Phontella, Moesha, Teraya, LaRissa, Rolonda, Roshumba, and, yes, Vyester, which my friend told me her mother invented by combining the names of Vashti and Esther from the Bible, because she wanted her to have a little bit of each woman's personality. Later on I realized the reason for creative naming. It is bad enough that our children will carry the slavemasters' surnames.

The phone rings. I pick it up. A heavy voice with a British accent asks, "May I speak to Ifa?"

"She doesn't live here anymore," I say.

"I do not believe you," the voice says. It is arrogant and faintly threatening, and sounds like that man who called himself Magic.

I hang up.

 THIRTY-FOUR

LUCIUS CAN TAKE CARE of himself, too. I have something more urgent on my mind—something that has ten fingers, ten toes, all of the other human equipment in miniature, and weighs only five pounds. Little A'Zena Lucia is struggling so hard to live, she has grabbed my heart.

I can hardly wait to run out and buy booties and bonnets and other small, dainty stuff, but at this point it would be bad luck, so instead I get a toothbrush, a robe, and two pairs of slippers—one pair apiece for Vyester and myself. If Fred minded, it would be different, but he has already asked me to stay. So, until I'm sure his baby girl is going to make it, I have no intention of leaving the hospital again.

I wish the waiting rooms were furnished with cots and mattresses, though, or at least comfy sofas instead of hard plastic chairs. After trying for six hours to sleep in one of the chairs, I give up. The hospital is very quiet now. It is past midnight, and one nurse is making rounds to wake people up and give them sleeping pills, while another sits at the nurses' station reading something with great concentration.

I yawn horribly. A female attendant who has passed by several times notices my misery, and comes in. "Zena?" she inquires.

And guess what? It is Fast Fanny Davenport, wearing green

scrubs instead of a G-string, her entwined braids and amber Fulani beads hidden by a matching cap.

"Fanny? I didn't know you worked here."

"Fifteen years," she says.

"But I thought you—"

"You thought I danced at the club for a living? I do. But after the last show, I grab a bite, then come here and work the four A.M. to twelve noon shift. One paycheck just don't cut it, especially when you're trying to buy a house. Whoops, I forgot. Excuse me."

I thought glamorous Fanny had all of her teeth, but she has to turn her back and slip in her plate. "Mmmff," she says. "I been back to the dentist three times, and these damn things still don't fit right. You here to see about Vyester and her baby?" I nod. "Don't worry, they'll be all right. I've seen babies a lot smaller than that one go home from here and do fine. The mother's strong, too. But you look like you could use some rest."

"I'm exhausted," I admit. "I can't sleep on these hard chairs."

"They could do better by the patients' families, put in a sofa or two, but these people just don't care. The stories I could tell you about this place—ooh!" Her eyes grow big. "I better not take the time, though. Listen, I got an idea. I think I know where you could get some sleep." She puts a finger to her lips. "Don't say anything. Just be quiet and follow me."

It is amazing, the way her setting has changed her. Usually her spine seems made of rubber, but there is no trace of the exotic dancer in Fanny's hospital walk—just a brisk, businesslike stride on thick crepe soles. I am glad Fanny has this job. It will last long after her shake-dancing equipment has worn out. She leads me through a pair of swinging double doors, down a long corridor, through another pair of doors, and down some steps. Like all city hospitals, this one is constantly growing in all directions, and the result is a maze. The area we are in now smells of paint and plaster, and feels deserted.

"This wing ain't finished," she whispers, "but the furniture is in. You could take a nap in any room you want. Help yourself. I'll keep an eye out for you."

Beds, blessed beds, made up and empty, furnish each room. After thanking Fanny, I pick the nearest one and fall deeply asleep in an instant. My dreams are a confused jumble of babies, bombs, and Africans. But I get some of the rest I need, and awaken at five a.m. It is still dark out. I tiptoe back down the corridor.

A different nurse is at the station, reading a tabloid news-paper with a headline about Hollywood Half-Wits. They're all half-wits out there, if you ask me, except for Denzel Washington, who is not only good-looking but seems to have good sense. I like him not just for his looks, though they are fine, but because he is married to a sister, and will not kiss white women in his movies. I slip past the nurses' station to the waiting room, trying not to make a sound. Fred is there, sitting straight up and sleep-ing, his head rocking forward with each snore. I shake him by the shoulder, and he opens his eyes.

I put my finger to my lips, lead him down the long corridor to the empty wing that is furnished like a hotel, and point out the rooms. "Your turn," I say. "Don't tell."

We work this game for two nights in a row, and no one ever notices. I figure we could both go into the new part of the hospi-tal and sleep at the same time, and still get away with it, but that would be taking more of a chance. Besides, one of us has to wait for news.

On the third morning, I arrive in Vy's room at the same time as her breakfast. She looks better now—rested and healthy, and with her natural ruddy-brown color in her cheeks. I know how fast they throw new mothers out of hospitals these days, and I am glad someone decided her case merited a little extra time. Her hair needs attention—it is wild, woolly and dirty—but I will take care of that the next time I come.

"How do you manage to get here so early?" she asks me.

"Oh, secret magic," I say, because I see a nurse hovering in the hall. "One of these days we'll have a good laugh about it."

She shifts her position and moves the edge of the sheet so that I can see the back of a very small, very curly head.

"She's eating," Vy says. "Good thing. She was losing weight."

Light streams in the window, enclosing Vy and the baby in a halo. I can barely breathe because of this miracle. "We can't have that, can we?" I say.

"Oh, they always lose weight at first, but she doesn't have any to spare, so it's good she's eating. She latched right onto me, the little piggy. She's got some hard little gums, too. Ouch! You better stop that, girl, fore I put you on the bottle." But Vy's proud, tender smile shows she is not about to do that. "She's off oxygen now. The doctor says she can breathe on her own.—How are things at the shop?"

For a moment my mind is blank. I almost say, "What shop?" I remember just in time that I have a business. "Oh, I canceled all of our appointments this week. We're closed for vacation."

"Was that a smart thing to do, Miss Zena?"

"It was the only thing to do. Something more important was going on." And then I bring up something that keeps bothering me. "Vyester, we work side by side, we go places together, I'm at your house all the time, and I practically birthed this baby along with you. When are you going to stop calling me Miss?"

She drops her eyes and mumbles softly, "I don't want to low-rate you."

"Well, I don't want to feel old," I say, though I know this issue is not about age. It's more about who owns the shop. That's not all of it, either, but selling her a share of the business might help. "Let's work on it, huh? I plan on spending a lot of time with you and your daughter."

"Okay," Vy says, not meaning she will change her habit, only meaning she will work on it. She is stubborn, all right, but I love her like a little sister.

I lean forward and begin making idiotic cooing noises that I didn't know I knew how to make. I don't even know where they come from.

And then Vy passes me this tiny new person, who at last is breathing on her own, and who has the strength to grip my finger even as she falls asleep, and I do not want to stop holding her, ever. I am trembling a little with fear because she is so tiny, and a lot with happiness because she is so perfect. I say "Hello, A'Zena," and she opens her eyes and smiles as if she knows I am speaking to her, and my heart is utterly lost.

Finally I return the baby to Vy and go to wake her father, who thanks me. I remember at last that I have my own husband and home to look after.

If Vy noticed that I was wearing the same red print silk dress three days in a row, she didn't mention it. Nor did she mention the aroma I am carrying around with me after three days without a bath. But I know that my first order of business is a shower, followed by a change.

I NOTICE THE horrible stench as soon as I open my front door. That python is coiled on my couch again, grinning triumphantly.

"Later for you," I say, pretending courage I do not feel, and blink. It disappears, leaving its horrible odor behind.

I head for the shower to make sure that none of the bad smell in the house comes from me. I spend twenty minutes in there, scrubbing with a long-handled brush, and use up practically a bar of transparent soap and half a bottle of strawberry bath gel.

"Lucius!" I cry when I come out, wrapped in my jade green terry robe. "Lucius, are you home?"

He is, but he can't hear me. I soon find out why.

The unholy shrieks and yells coming from behind our bedroom door are unnerving. It sounds as if a woman is being beaten up in there. But that is not exactly what is going on.

All Oloris are loud, but Ifa would deafen even the yelling, bickering crowd in the Olori-Buruku marketplace.

I soon understand that the python was there as a challenge to me. An announcement that she is planning to take over.

I walk into our bedroom and throw myself into the squirming, heaving jumble of arms and legs I find there. First I scream my husband's name and whack him on the butt with the belt of my robe. "Get up from there, dog! Up!" I holler. He obeys. His face has a terrible expression, like a man undergoing torture. Then I go after the pythoness who was wriggling around under him. Soon two naked women are screaming and flailing at each other on the bed, while one nude man cringes against the wall.

"Stop it, Zena, before somebody gets hurt!"

I ignore him.

I am older than Ifa, but I am in pretty good shape after my workout at the Divas' luncheon, and I am inspired by my rage. For an old woman, as she calls me, I beat up on her pretty good. I whack every piece of bare skin I can reach. Scrambling to get out of bed, she turns her bare back to me. I reach around and find a yardstick I had put out to measure for new curtains, and break it cross her backside. She yelps and turns to face me, so I whack her in the tits, causing a scream, then bop her cross the mouth and nose. I work her arm around to her back with one of my hands and twist it upward, inflicting both pain and a handicap. Then I take the fingers of my other hand and go after her eyes. I am out to do serious harm.

She covers her face with her free hand and cringes.

"Mum, Mum, please stop. I am sorry. I did not mean any harm. It did not mean anything. We were wearing the masks."

On the floor are two of her hideous carvings, the scary ones with eyes that seem alive. I look briefly at them, then go back to the business of blinding her.

Lucius clears his throat and puts on his most pompous voice. "Zena, Ifa explained that if one wears the mask of a spirit, one becomes that spirit. By putting on those masks, we were no longer ourselves. We were not humans fornicating, we were deities in divine communion. We were—"

I cannot believe he accepts this bullshit, or that I am hearing it from him.

"I'll get to you later, Deacon," I tell him. "First, I have to kill this big snake that just crawled in our bed."

"Zena, you're right, she is a snake. When she turns into one, she has superhuman powers. I couldn't help myself."

Again, I ignore him and focus my attention on the snake goddess I called my daughter.

She is crying now, tears streaming down her face, pleading desperately. "Mum, Mum, please don't kill me. I was trying to help you both. Dod needs an heir. Since you are too old, I wanted to give him one."

"Dad has an heir," I inform her. "His name is Leon. He's a C.P.A. in San Diego." I like Leon. He has his own accounting firm, and he comes east once a year to help me with the business taxes. He understands that, should something happen to his dad, everything will be mine first, his later, and he wouldn't have it any other way. "Where did you get the idea of giving us an heir?"

"M-m-mum, Mum, Cecelia said I should try. She s-said I should do everything possible to try to stay here with you and Dod. She said it would be best to become Dod's second wife and have his child."

This is news. I thought Professor Ugmo had left the country. "When did she tell you this?"

"I call her every night in Olori," Ifa explains. "She said to get close to Dod, because the m-man is in charge of the household. If I pleased Dod, she said, I would be able to, to stay. Since I have not been able to become a citizen, she said, it would be best if I had a child. A child born here would be a citizen, and it could bring my whole family into the country."

So that is why pregnant Olori women are always rolling off of airplanes in New York and having octuplets in the airport. Each one of those babies can bring in eight more Oloris, all pregnant. Of course, I know that's not the way it happened. The way it really happened was worse. That mother got fertility treatments here, and I couldn't. She had eight babies, and I couldn't have one. It's not fair!

I try not to bawl, but a few angry tears escape. I turn my back to Ifa and Lucius, and sit down on my side of the bed. I have to sit because I am out of breath from pummeling her, and also because my bad feet have finally worn out my knees, and I cannot stand for very long. I keep a stool at work, of course, and another in the kitchen. It is another sign of age, like the flaps on my arms that mean no more short sleeves. That other Middle Passage was sho nuff rough, but so is this one that I am on—the passage from youth to old age.

"Bring your whole family here?" I ask incredulously. "So then we would have a whole houseful of Oloris? Was that the plan?" I ask Ifa.

"Only temporarily, Mum, till one of us got a job. Then we would be able to move out. P-please understand, Mum, I had to save my family. That was my mission here."

"And we are not your family?" She has played so many games on us and our feelings that I have to get this straight.

"No." She has the nerve to laugh, and it is a harsh laugh. "How could you be?" Ifa seems suddenly to have lost her beauty. She is downright ugly, with blemished skin, dull eyes, and a mouth drawn back in a sneer.

I have read a few things about conditions in Olori—the cruel military government, the corruption, the seizure of property, the punishment of rich families like Ifa's. Harsh conditions create tough people, I am thinking. But maybe Ifa was never nice. Maybe, under her sweet outer layer, this girl was always hard, like a Jordan almond. Well, she told me she was a trained actress.

My heart is a chunk of ice. My voice is a jagged piece of it. "And how many of you Olongos are there back home?"

"There is my mother, my aunt, my sister, her husband, her three children, my two brothers, and then all the other relatives in our village. I cannot count them all.—M-mum, please, my family needs to come here. We are not safe at home since my father died."

I cannot believe she still thinks we might take her relatives in.

Her eyes brighten. "We have plenty of money in Switzerland, Mum, and we will pay you well. "

This girl is hopeless. In just one sentence, she has managed to insult us and tried to con us.

"You have played with our feelings, Ifa. You have used us and deceived us. You have screwed us both."

Her only answer is a shamed grin.

"I don't want to hear any more. I can't even stand to look at you. Just go. Get dressed and go. I hope you still have that job to go to. I hope those people haven't gotten their phone bill yet."

"Mum, I was fired."

Stands to reason, I think, with her at Vyester's every minute she wasn't running her mouth at her employer's expense. Well, it isn't cold now. She can sleep on the street if she has to.

"That crooked Sonny Sampson is in jail," I say, "and that is where I suspect you belong, too. I think the police will agree with me. I will give you a head start of six hours before I call them. You have exactly ten minutes to pack up your stuff and get dressed and get out of my house."

I don't know how that girl manages to pull it off in the time I have allotted her, but she does.

"Don't let the door hit you on your way out!" I cry as she leaves, wearing a cashmere sweater I bought her.

I watch as Magic's taxi takes her out of my sight forever.

 THIRTY-FIVE

THE FIRST THING I do is purge the house, starting with Ifa's room. Out go Ifa's waist-length necklaces, her scary little snake, her baleful, evil masks. It takes all of my courage to pick up the python skin, but out it goes. I hesitate over the spooky Jesus picture, but finally it goes, too. After I air and scrub this room, I go on to the others.

Out go my mudcloth place mats, my lion and leopard wall hangings, my collections of kente hats and scarves, my piles of cowrie jewelry and wooden necklaces. Out with the painting of Shaka Zulu, the carving of the African mother and child, and the ebony Ivory Coast masks I thought were so elegant. Also, out with our Kwanzaa candlestick, our *Ipi Ntombi* video, and my recordings of djembe and bata drums.

I find the lovely round African piano Ifa ultimately gave to Lucius, a hollowed melon with iron keys on top that played fairy tunes on a five-note scale. Out! I don't want anything African in my house.

"Don't you think you're being a bit extreme?" Lucius asks as I haul his spear and his shield and his chieftain's stool from the Back Room to the trash.

"No," I say. It is the first word I have spoken to him in three weeks.

If I were extreme, I am thinking, I would put you out along with the rest of this stuff.

Her AIDS test came back negative, so I guess Lucius can stay, but he will never know how close he came to spending his last days on a leper farm.

I make him give our bed to charity and get a new one. I cannot sleep where that python lay. Nor can I sit where her coils rested, so he must also replace my beautiful red sofa. He is lucky that I am not replacing him.

For now, the new bed is mine, while I make Lucius sleep on that iron torture rack in the Back Room. He keeps apologizing and insisting that he was hypnotized by her juju, fascinated by her snake powers, unable to control himself. I refuse to believe any of it. He says he is praying very hard to be forgiven. I say he'd better.

Vy says I should give Lucius another chance. Everybody should be allowed one mistake, she says. He is a great guy, better than most men, she declares. According to her, we are a couple who were made for each other. She says it's enough that he begs the Lord to forgive him—he shouldn't have to beg me, too. Besides, she says, from now on he will be as meek and agreeable as a lamb. I don't know how she can be sure of that, and I don't ask.

I don't have much time off right now, and it is a good thing. Working hard keeps me from fretting about my home life. After I purge our house of African objects, I scrub it from top to bottom with lemon water and sweep and mop it front to back. Then I burn white candles in all the rooms.

At the shop, I have to catch up on all the appointments I canceled the week A'Zena was born, and continue to juggle Vy's appointments with mine while she recovers. Sometimes I find myself working on four heads at once: curling one partway, pressing another, and combing out a third while a fourth waits under the dryer.

I am the kind of person who works harder when she is upset, though, so the extra load is welcome. Some people deal with stress by drinking and taking drugs, some by going on trips or getting a lot of exercise. I work. It's cheaper than a vacation and healthier than drugs, and besides, I get paid.

When I have a little free time, I spend it at Vy's house, helping her and getting acquainted with my godchild. A'Zena still has wires attached to her that must be hooked up to a monitor at night, but she is showing signs that she intends to stay with us awhile. She is getting fatter, and has big milk cheeks, long eyelashes that sweep them, and deep dimples. She is a little Leo, which means she will demand and get lots of attention. She still laughs when I talk to her. She thinks I am the funniest person she has ever seen. Vy lets me hold A'Zena as much as I want, except when she is hungry.

I wish she were not hungry so often. This child eats, it seems, every half hour. The sun comes in the top of Vy's kitchen windows as it always does this time of afternoon, and puts a golden glow on mother and child. I admire them, and am envious.

On Thursday after work, I kick my shoes off, sigh with relief, rub my bunions together, and stir my coffee. "It's a shame to say it," I say to my best friend, "but, these days, I hate to go home."

"That is a shame," Vy agrees. "Nobody should like someone else's home better than her own. That is a sure way of losing it."

"I know," I say, "but after what that man did—"

"Did he do it all by himself, Zena?"

Sometimes Vy is so frank she makes me uncomfortable. At least I've gotten her to drop the 'Miss' in front of my name— some of the time. That's progress.

"No," I admit. "I left him alone too much."

There is a long pause before Vy says, "Ain't you still doing that?"

She is right. I shrug. "Other mistake I made was, being one of those fools who rush in. I was so anxious to have a daughter, I rushed in and let that girl make a fool of me. She never thought of me as her mother at all, Vy. She was just pretending."

"Don't be so hard on yourself, Zena," Vyester says. "We all do things like that." Vy slings A'Zena over one shoulder and pats her back to burp her. Even the baby thinks I'm foolish. She is laughing at me again. "I just had this baby, right? Fred and I are crazy about her. But I was crazy about the first one, and look how he turned out. Still, here I am, trying again. Doesn't that make me a fool?"

"No, I don't think so, Vy," I say.

"Neither do I," Vy says, "because this is a whole new baby, and a whole new ball game, and maybe we have learned a thing or two. I have to believe that. If I only thought about Sonny, I'd think having children was nothing but a bad trip."

"I wish you could convince me of that," I say sadly.

"I wouldn't try," my friend says. "But when you get to feeling blue over what you've missed, don't forget, you've also missed having a child like Sonny."

I never thought about it like that. "That must have been rough."

"It still is. The way he turned out almost killed me." Sonny is now serving out a two-year sentence for burglary and weapons violations. "Thinking about him still kills me a little bit, every day. But this new one is making up for it, ain't you, Boo-boo?" She nuzzles the tiny nose with her own, and the baby giggles.

"People are always thinking things will be different this time, or different for them than for other people. Once in a while, they're right. It's human nature. Hope springs maternally, isn't that what they say?"

"Something like that. Are you saying I should still consider adopting?"

"Hell, no," says Vyester. "I think you should consider being happy with what you already have.—Ooh, there she goes, spitting up again. Hand me a towel. No, wait."

She goes for the towel herself, first handing me the baby. She comes back, bends over, and wipes the milky little chin, not in time to keep it from spilling over onto my silk blouse. Mothers, I am learning, cannot have silk blouses or much of anything else that is delicate. An enormous toothless grin rewards us. Such a good-natured little girl. I think she was born laughing. Even when she had enough tubes and hoses in her to equip a fire engine, she was smiling.

Vy tickles her daughter. "Say, 'Silly Mommy and Auntie, I'm

gonna give you a whole lot more trouble before I'm through. Spittin' up ain't nothin'. You may think I'm a little angel, but I'm gonna do a whole lot worse. Just wait and see!' "

I hold A'Zena up and study her. That smile would have me under her spell all by itself, but with the dimple it brings out, I am her helpless slave.

"Still, I envy you, Vy," I say, burying my nose in the baby's incredibly soft and fragrant neck.

"Why, Zena? You have everything, don't you know that?"

"I do?"

"Of course. What I was about to say before Drool-face here interrupted me, was, 'Be grateful for all the good stuff you already have. Don't mess it up by getting greedy.' "

"What do you mean?" I ask her, though I know. I have been most ungrateful for my good life, and almost ruined it by trying to add an extra goodie to my plate, an extra bauble to my crown.

She sighs as if worn out by my stupidity. "You have me, for starters. Me and Fred. You have your godchild here, whenever you want her. She is like a rental car. We'll do the maintenance on her and let you have all the fun."

"Thanks," I say. I know it's not the same as having my own, but it's still better than I hoped for, and more, maybe, than I deserve.

"You also have your health, your business, some money in the bank, a home, a car, and a good husband."

"You call Lucius a good husband?"

"What else am I supposed to call him? So he made one mistake. So what? Do you throw away a sweet melon because it has one soft spot? Do you throw away a whole bunch of grapes because you see one bad one? No, you don't. You cut that one spot out, toss out that one rotten grape, and keep the rest."

At last, she is making me think. I have been so angry with Lucius I have hardly spoken to him in ages, and of course I haven't slept with him, but last night he looked so downcast, so worn, so doggone *old*, I caught myself feeling sorry for the man.

"You know what else I think? I think sometimes people can

have everything they need and most of what they want, but they still ain't satisfied. They start looking around for something else to want. If they ain't careful they can lose all they have, reaching out for that extra something. Like that little girl with a lap full of apples who thinks she sees a better apple on the top branch of the tree. She jumps up to get it, and spills all the apples she already got."

"Am I like that, Vy?"

"You was," Vy says. "Except, you luckier. You didn't lose it all, at least not yet. Nobody could tell you not to want that little extra something, though. You had it all right here at home, but you had to go looking for something special from overseas. It was a snake you took in, but nobody could tell you that till it bit you."

I look down at the baby. She laughs. I guess I deserve to be laughed at.

"Another thing some romantic-type people do," she adds, "is try and make a thing into something that it is not. That girl was not your daughter. She was your guest." She pauses for a moment to let this sink in. It is true. In Olori, I have learned, children call any older woman whom they like Mum. If they do not feel so close to her, they call her Auntie.

Vy adds, "I am not your daughter, either. I am your friend."

Boy, am I getting cold water splashed on my face today! It doesn't feel good, but I need it to wake me up. "Nobody could want a better friend, Vy," I say.

"I guess not," she agrees. "I am a good friend because I am not afraid to tell you the truth. Plus, I am willing to share everything I have with you."

We hear Fred come stomping in the front door. "I'm home!" he yells.

"Well," she amends, "almost everything."

Vy holds out her hands to take her baby, then changes her mind. "Keep her awhile," she says. "I am going to take me a nice slow bath and get changed."

Soon, the baby's long, silken lashes are sweeping her brown

velvet cheeks. She is asleep. I hold my breath at the sweetness and wonder of it—her peacefulness, her trust in me. My chest gets tight, but I am still afraid to breathe.

Maybe Vy is right. Maybe I was like Eve in the Garden of Eden—surrounded by all that good fruit, yet pining after the one fruit I couldn't have. I look down at the stain on my good blouse. It bothers me. The baby snorts and wakes up, kicking hard. She starts to cry. I get up and start to walk her back and forth. It only makes her cry louder. I jiggle her up and down. I make noises in her ears like I am blowing bubbles. None of it works. By the time Vy comes back and takes her, I am frantic.

Maybe, I think, that forbidden fruit was something I wasn't supposed to have, something I couldn't have handled.

And maybe I am luckier than Eve, because I haven't been kicked out yet.

 # THIRTY-SIX

I LET LUCIUS back into my bed tonight. We take our time. When we need to talk, we talk. When we need to sleep, we sleep. And in between, when we need to, we make love. I am so relieved, so happy, I cry.

Somewhere in our conversation, after I refuse to believe in Ifa's magical power over my husband, he admits, "For a little while, she made me feel young, Zena. I know I was only fooling myself, but it was wonderful while it lasted."

This hurts. The truth often does.

"Lucius," I ask timidly, "have I gotten so old?"

"I haven't noticed." He turns on the light. "Let me see." First, he takes my chin in his hands. "Your face hasn't changed." Next, he dives down to the region below my waist and starts counting what hairs are left there. He plucks and comes up with two gray ones. "This is very serious," he says. "I will have to order you some Geritol and some Rogaine in the morning."

"Idiot," I say, and hug him hard. "I guess I shouldn't have worried about getting bald down there."

"At least you have hair on your head. Nobody is supposed to look down there but me, and I am aging, too. I have wrinkles in places you can't imagine."

"Where?"

"My testicles."

"Really? Let me see!" I am playing with him, but my curiosity is excited.

My husband clutches the blankets to himself in fierce protection of his privacy, and I fall back on my pillows, laughing.

"Baby, I understand," I say. "If someone came along and made me feel young again, I might like it, too." I am remembering how that taxi driver, Magic, made me feel young for a little while. I don't mention him, though.

Lucius growls. "You aren't thinking of getting even, are you, Zena? Because if I catch any young studs hanging around here—"

"I don't want any young studs," I tell him. "I like my comfortable old shoe." And I really do. After all the coldness and estrangement, I am happy with the warm, familiar feel of his big old body. I can't imagine how I thought I could do without it. I love it all, even the belly he has begun to grow. I am reassured by his broad shoulders, his hairy chest, his big arms that I can't get my fingers around. I like the bear noises he makes when he is asleep, and the jealous noises he makes when he is awake. Maybe I will mention Magic, just to get him jealous again— some other time. "You are good for a few more go-arounds, I guess," I say.

"Damn right I am, woman," he says. "Come here."

Much later, I say, "It was not all your fault, Lucius. I should not have left you alone with her so much."

"You mean I can't be trusted by myself?"

"Well," I say, "I did not need to spend all that time at the hospital looking after Vyester's family. I should have been at home, taking care of my own."

I was blind to what was going on at home because I didn't want to see it. It's always easier to take care of other people's problems.

I was also blinded, for a long time, by my longing for a daughter. Ifa called me Mum, and called herself my daughter, and it was what I wanted to hear, so I believed it. I believed it right up until I heard her talking to her real mother over in

Africa. That was when I knew Ifa would never be my daughter. And that was when I was through with her and ready to put her out—not when she started to come on to my husband. I think back and realize that she had started that stuff long before. So, no, I can't blame him totally.

I still don't go to church more than once a month, but for Lucius's sake I talked him out of resigning from his Deacon Board. I said, "Honey, if you had done half the things the preacher and the other deacons have done, you might have good reason to resign. But you've just begun to sin."

Lucius said, maybe so, but he didn't intend to finish.

"However," I said, "it might not be a bad idea to get off that Missionary Board, unless you can convince them to stop trying to convert Africans. That is a hopeless assignment."

Suddenly, I have an idea. "Lucius, let me go in front of your Missionary Board, at least for one meeting. I have a lot of things to say to them."

"I'm listening," he says.

"I would say, 'Stop lying! Somebody is telling Africans that if they just get here, everything will be easy. Stop convincing Africans that the streets here are paved with gold. Tell them the truth! Tell them we are lucky when the streets in our neighborhoods are paved at all.'

"Say, 'Everybody here has to work to live, so they had better come here trained to do something! We are not like Father Divine or Sun Myung Moon. We are barely making it! We do not have enough money to feed foreign people forever or buy businesses for them, or enough house room to take them all in as nonpaying guests. We do not even have enough jobs! So if they are not willing to work and are not qualified to do something special, they should stay home.' "

"Say on," Lucius says, and begins humming loudly like an old buzz saw, the way he does in church.

"I would say to your missionaries, 'Do not encourage those people in Africa to think they are better than we are. Too many of them think that already. And too many of us think we owe them something. We did not sell anyone—so, if anything, they owe us! Stop treating them like special people. They are just people. And stop bowing down to their kings and queens! We do not bow down to royalty over here. This is a democracy. We broke with the King of England a long time ago.' "

"All right, now," Lucius intones. "Preach it, Honey."

"Tell them that if they want favors from us, they should appreciate us, instead of the other way around. Tell them, 'Maybe we were slaves once, but we African Americans have come a long way since then. We started out way behind everybody else in this country, but we are catching up, and soon we will be even. We deserve everybody's respect! We are not rich, but we are achieving and surviving. So do not be so arrogant, you Africans. You do not know it all. You have a lot to learn.' "

"That's all right," Lucius chants.

"Learn the ways of this country, and do not be so quick to condemn and criticize. We do not have to adjust to you. You are the guests. You have to adjust to us!"

"Yes ma'am, mm-hmm."

"Another thing I thought of saying is, 'Those of us who used to be slaves do not respect ourselves enough. If we did love and respect ourselves, maybe we would not go chasing after other folks all the time. So let us start every morning with a little reminder of self-respect. Let every church service and radio program include a call for self-respect. Let us have songs about self-respect, poems about self-respect, school lessons about self-respect, and sermons about loving ourselves!' "

My husband socks his fist into his palm. "All right, now!" he hollers.

"And finally, I would say to your Missionary Board, 'Are you sure, really sure, that missionaries are not needed more here at home than abroad? Why do you not try converting some crack addicts and the drug dealers who supply them? Sonny Sampson could wear out three missionaries all by himself. Why don't you send them to him? Why don't you feed some hungry black American children and teach them to sing "Jesus Loves Me"?

They might believe it before the Africans do. Africans are not really going to change, you know. They may put Jesus on their list, but they will still keep their snake god and pray to him, too.' "

"Amen!" my husband shouts. "They won't like it, Zena, but it needs to be said! I will arrange for you to speak to the Board at our next meeting."

I have to admit that Vy was right about Lucius. After we kissed and made up, my husband became so sweet, he was unreal. It spooked me sometimes, he was so considerate. He kept fresh flowers in the house. He bought me a new emerald bracelet, though not in the shape of a snake. He did the dishes every night and took me out to dinner one night a week.

One night, though, when I tried out a new recipe for meat loaf with ground chicken instead of beef or turkey, he complained like the old Lucius I used to know.

"What is in this mess you served me, Zena!" he yelled. "It tastes like dog food! Cheap dog food, at that!" I apologized, and I kissed him. He did not understand why. But I was so happy to have my real husband back, a Lucius who is sometimes cheerful and loving, sometimes angry and grumpy, I was flooded with joy.

My husband has grown as fond of A'Zena as I am, and that is saying something, because I am crazy about that child. Lucius even baby-sits when Fred has to work late and Vy and I are still at the shop. I know now that I don't need to be like white folks and look overseas for someone to adopt. There are diamonds and needy people in each of our backyards. Like I told that Board, plenty of work for missionaries right here!

I think I shocked those old deacons, but from the reports Lucius brings me, they are considering what I said. Trouble is, he says, they are as in love with Africa as I was—even though none of them has been there. I may have to get on the Board myself, just to give them the benefit of my experiences and try to help them fall out of love.

I didn't call the police on Ifa as I threatened, but they came around anyway and asked us questions. They wondered about

Ifa's expensive new clothes and her car, which the neighbors had noticed. Did we know how she had acquired them? Of course we said that we had no idea. Nor did we know where she might have gone. And that, at least, was the truth.

For a while, I was afraid of all foreigners. But then I hurt my shoulder and was treated by a divine doctor from Zaire, whose manners were so angelic they made me almost swoon. A Chinese puncture doctor cured the migraine headaches that began after I caught Lucius and Ifa together, and relieved some of the pain in my right shoulder that comes from jiggling too many curling irons. And I met a couple from Ghana who were so warm they seemed like cousins. I did not invite them to my house, however. Maybe I will sometime, but I am still afraid that all Third World people are looking for places to put up their relatives.

I finally bought a new record of African drumming, because dancing is good exercise. I also rescued the African mother and child statue from the trash at the last minute, though I did not take it out of my closet until yesterday. I think the mother looks like Vy.

I still avoid Oloris. I don't want to have bad feelings about a whole group of people, but I don't want to suffer all that I've been through again, either.

My next birthday will be the Big Five-Oh. I am admitting my age these days, though I am still not letting my gray hair show.

A lot of the time, as I sit on Vy's porch rocking A'Zena Lucia, I am plotting how I can get to spend more time with her and less time at the shop. Vyester is all healed up now and back at work, and the baby is weaned. I figure I will turn more of the business over to her mother, a little bit at a time, and hope she does not catch on that she is making a trade.

No one asks where Sonny is these days, and no one better ask me about Ifa, either. Wherever she is, she is trouble. Fred was right—she was running drugs and money to and from their house for Sonny—only, some of the money trickled through her fingers. That girl claimed to be spiritual, but she was too much in love with things. Clothes. Jewels. Cars.

I guess Ifa had some good traits—she could be sweet and helpful when she wanted to be—but they were outweighed by the bad. In many ways, she was nothing but a great, big, confused, spoiled child, but I had no business trying to raise someone over twenty. Some of the things she did that were "bad" in our culture, like worshipping snakes and planning to give us a baby, may have been "good" in her village—but we live here, not there. I am sure that we did not understand her any better than she understood us, but I did not have time to go out and get a degree in foreign relations.

That girl—no, that woman—had no understanding of our way of life, and she was not willing to learn anyway. But not everything that went wrong was her fault, or Lucius's, either.

I had no business fooling myself that Ifa could be my daughter. Maybe I was her Mum, but I am not her mom—never have been, never will be—any more than Lucius was her dad. Those people in that faraway place are her real family. Lucius and I were just conveniences to be used for their benefit.

I am still angry and hurt because Ifa deceived me into feeling like her mother, when the only mother she loved was far away in Africa. Mostly, though, I deceived myself, because I was in love with Africa, and in love with the idea of having an African daughter, and that is causing me the most pain. I think discovering Ifa's attachment to her own mother hurt me worse than catching her with Lucius, though it was silly of me to think she could forget about her real mother, and stupid of me to leave her alone with my husband so much. He is only human, after all.

I have decided to forgive Lucius, because half of what went wrong was my fault. But it is taking me longer to forgive Oloris. I mean, maybe they aren't all like Ifa and Magic, but who has the time to check each one of them out? To me, they are like that family that once lived next door to us in the projects—after one of them broke in and took our TV, and another one stole my radio, I didn't feel like getting to know a third.

Seems to me like, every time I see Oloris in the news, it is because they are giving black American folk a hard time. I am sure that there are some good Olori people, but there are millions of

Oloris, and life is too short to go hunting through the crowd to find one. Not long ago, a big old loudmouth Olori tried to cause trouble for Labor Secretary Alexis Herman. I bet his problem was that girlfriend wouldn't give him none.

Another thing I am sure of now is, if you want to adopt a child, whether a large one or a small one, you'd better know who its parents are and what its home life was like. I think that may be more important than its age.

What's the matter now, A'Zena? Hungry again? So soon? You eat an awful lot, you know that? Come on, then, let me make you another bottle. What—you're wet again, too? Sometimes I think you require more attention than my beauty shop.

I guess we'll both be glad when your mother gets home.

THIRTY-SEVEN
EPILOGUE

IT WAS A STEAMY DAY in July when nothing seemed to be going right in the shop, and everybody was cranky. It was the hottest summer on record, and nobody seemed to have a clear head or a nimble set of fingers. It was one of those days when everybody should have just stayed home under a fan, with a tall glass of iced tea or Kool-Aid.

Vy left the relaxer on a woman's head too long, and burned her scalp. Florine burned a customer's ear with a hot comb. I pulled a comb through Latasha's hair too hard, and she began crying.

To top it off, A'Zena had just learned to walk and was wobbling all over the place like a drunk doll, slipping between customers' legs, falling on her fat bottom with a shriek, then laughing and using the handiest pair of legs to pull herself up with. She is adorably cute, but even cuteness wears thin after a while.

It is the third day in a row that Vyester has brought her to the shop, because her baby-sitter is sick.

I want to send Vy home with A'Zena, but she has four customers waiting. They have been enjoying the baby's antics, but by now their smiles are beginning to look pasted on.

To make matters worse, my godchild gets tired and begins to cry. She is loud, too. I pick her up, planning to hold her in my lap, and she is sopping wet. I quickly put her down again. My patience has just run out.

"Take her home!" I yell to Vy.

"Do you see all these women I have waiting? You take her home."

"Whose baby is this, anyway?"

"Ours."

I have been saying that since she was born, having adopted this child in my heart, but in that moment, I instantly de-dopt her.

"No, she's yours. All yours."

Maybe Vy didn't hear me. I hope not. She is whispering something to Latasha, my lovely teenage protégée who helps us out around the shop after school, sweeping up hair, checking supplies, combing out braids, stuff like that. Latasha has just turned fourteen, and is still getting her Corkscrew Curly Girl at a student discount because she is so helpful. Latasha nods and scoops up A'Zena.

"Did you work something out with Latasha?" I ask Vy.

"She'll keep the baby for me at her house till I'm done here. Later on tonight, I'll stop by and do her hair for free."

Thank God, I think, and breathe a sigh of deep relief, and sit down. The shop suddenly feels cooler, as if a breeze has blown through it and swept out all the steam. In that moment I realize that if I had really wanted a baby, I would have had one somehow by now, probably before Lucius came into my life.

As Latasha carries the child past me, I recognize her yell as a cry of hunger. I dig a bottle out of the diaper bag that weighs down Latasha's shoulder and hand it to her, and realize that I never really wanted to deal with any of that. Motherhood was probably something I was not cut out for, for all my talk about wanting a child. But I did not want to spend the rest of my life alone, so I found a man who would not insist on our having kids, because he already had a couple of his own.

When I get home, Lucius is not there yet. He has been putting in long hours lately at party headquarters, working for Booker Brown's election. I turn up our central air, drink some iced tea, and get an extra burst of energy.

I am not supposed to clean the Back Room, but it has not seen a broom or a mop in months, and the dust and the cobwebs in there are really getting to me.

Before preparing dinner, I go back there and start picking up things in order to dust tabletops. I am trying to put everything back in its exact same place, so my husband will not notice that I have cleaned, when a letter flutters out of an old copy of *Black Enterprise*. It is headed, "#3866544, Women's State Farm and Correctional Institution," in a small town upstate, and is dated a few months back. Of course I read it:

Dear Dad,

They make us work twelve hours a day here. I have just come in from picking string beans all day. If we do not pick enough beans, we get punished with starvation and solitary confinement, and sometimes with beatings, too. I have been waiting a month for my turn to use this pen, and now I am so tired I can hardly hold it. But I have a few minutes before supper, so I will try to write to you about my situation. If I am caught trying to mail a letter, I will be put in the hole, but I have a friend, a guard, who will sneak this letter out for me. Please, do not show it to Mum.

What happened is this. The police caught me a few weeks after I left your house. I had no other way to support myself when I left you, so I had to go on working for Magic, doing things I will not describe except to say that they were against the law. Because they say I am an illegal immigrant, I had no hearing or trial. I was given a choice between farm labor and

(The guard interrupted me. It was time for supper, so I had to stop writing for a while. The food here is terrible. We never get to eat the fresh things we pick. They make mashed potatoes and scrambled eggs out of powder, and everything else comes from cans. I do miss Mum's cooking. I would even be happy to have some of those big chicken pieces with black bones she once brought home. Smile.)

I am back from supper. We have a few minutes before Lights Out, so I will attempt to finish writing to you.

I think now that I can understand what slavery was like. Given the choice between coming to this place and being deported, I chose this, because Olori-Buruku is dangerous for me. But I did not know it would be so hard here. We work all day for no pay, and no one cares if we are tired or hungry or sick. If this is my fate, I will accept it, but I am afraid it will soon kill me. I will not get a hearing for seven years, and they tell me there is even a new law that will require me to pay rent for my cell!

Dad, I did not get in touch with you when I was arrested because I knew Mum would not be sympathetic. I do not blame her. I did something very wrong. I was wrong about so many things, including the lives of black people in America. I am sorry about all of that. I wish I could make it up to Mum and to you, too. But I cannot, and now I must beg you to help me once more. I am in slavery here, with no chance of parole unless someone helps me. Please do what you can to help your poor daughter,

Ifa

Well of course. She was a crook; where else could she end up but jail? My righteous indignation lasts about five minutes. Then I begin to feel sad about Ifa's fate, and deeply sorry for her.

"I couldn't help reading this," I tell Lucius when he gets home.

He looks down at the piece of paper, then at me, searching my face for clues to my feelings.

"She's out," he says finally. "I called Congressman Miller, and he arranged it."

"Did it cost us anything?"

"A little," he admits. "Double the usual campaign contribution. But mainly I owe the party a lot of work. You know the deal."

I do know. There will be meetings and speeches and parades, fund-raising parties and dances and coffee clutches. I will do my part. It will tire me out, but it will bring the two of us closer together. "Where is she now?"

My husband hesitates, then says, "The last I heard, she was in Boston, working in a nursing home. She only called once. I told her not to call here anymore. I hope she stays out of trouble."

I go outside and walk around, trying to decide how I feel about this news. I am steamed about my husband's secrecy, but at the same time, I am calm and relieved. For all of her faults, Ifa was once part of our family, and I care about her. I have often wondered what became of her.

Like most immigrants, Ifa thought life was easy in America.

Sheltered and spoiled, she was not really prepared to survive in our world. I hope prison has humbled her, though I wouldn't wish it on anyone.

Lucius is still sitting in the kitchen with his head down, awaiting my reaction like a defendant expecting to hear the worst from the judge.

To my surprise, I find I am angry, but not with him or Ifa. "They still have slavery in this country, don't they, Lucius?" I say.

"Yes," he says with infinite sadness. "They didn't abolish it. They just moved it to other locations, like prisons." He sighs. "Sometimes I think Americans can't survive without slavery, that they are addicted to it."

I pause to absorb this depressing information.

"Well, I'm glad you got her out," I say finally. "We're having turkey meat loaf tonight. No more ground chicken. Do you want string beans with it, or salad?"

"Salad," he says. "Somehow I don't have an appetite for string beans right now."

Neither do I.

It will probably be a long time before I want to eat string beans again.

APR 0 4 2000